School For Jamie

by

Angela Rigley

Dedication

To my granddaughter, Jessica, for helping to publicise my books in her school and local library.

Chapter 1

Biting his lip, Jamie Dalton turned away from the sight of the rain-sodden garden. His little sister, Alice, took her thumb out of her mouth and surprised him by saying, "Bella."

"No, darling, Bella isn't…she can't…" How could he explain that her twin sister was dead? Today of all days. Even though Annabella had died a few months before, Alice still didn't understand. She didn't know what dead meant. She just wanted her twin. Her birthday must have reminded her.

"I know what we can do, Alice. Let's play raindrop races. It's not the same as having a picnic like we were going to, but we can't do that now, can we?"

She nodded, her blue eyes, framed by dark lashes, looking bleak as she replaced her thumb. She probably didn't understand what a picnic was, either, being only two. He pointed to one of the raindrops cascading down the window. "That's yours. See if it beats mine—that one up there—to the bottom."

"You win." He clapped, but she didn't seem interested in the race.

Picking up her rag doll and clutching it tightly, she toddled over to the tallboy on the other side of the nursery. Looking back at Jamie, she frowned.

"What's the matter?" he asked.

"Dolly." She pointed to the empty space where her twin's doll usually sat.

His eyes opened wide. Where was it? It always sat there. "Oh, golly gosh," he muttered, peeping up at the ceiling, scared that, somehow, Annabella might have returned as a ghost and reclaimed her toy. Everything looked normal up there. No hazy patches or blurry shapes. What did a ghost look like, anyway?

His fears unfounded, he hurried across to Alice and hugged her, taking one more peek upwards, just to make sure. Then he looked down both sides of the cupboard, pulled out the drawers, opened the door and searched inside. No doll.

"Did you take it to bed with you last night?" She'd never done that before, but like his mama often said, 'There's a first time for everything.' When she shook her head, he rushed over to the bed, pulled the covers off and checked underneath. Still no doll.

"Maybe Nanny's moved it," he tried to console her as her eyes filled with tears.

The door opened and Nanny appeared, as if by mentioning her name he'd conjured up the real person. She descended on him like a giant in a grey dress and apron. Her dark eyes bore into him whenever she looked his way, making him shy away from her, feeling guilty, even though he knew he hadn't done anything wrong. She looked Chinese, like a person he'd once seen in a book in the library, or maybe her black hair, pulled tightly back off her face into a bun, just gave her that appearance.

When nobody could see, she sometimes pinched his earlobe between her nails. When he'd warned her he would tell his mama, she'd said he would go to hell if he did so. He'd never seen her do it to Alice, thank goodness. If he had, he would have told the whole world, even if it meant he'd be damned forever.

Why couldn't Auntie Ruby come back? He missed her so much. She often came to call, but she and Uncle Sam lived in a cottage down the lane. The last time she'd called, she'd smiled all the time, much more joyful than her usual self.

Nanny picked up Alice. "What's the matter, my little pumpkin?" She turned to Jamie. "What have you done to her?"

"I ain't done nothing."

"You ain't done nothing," she mimicked. "Speak properly, boy."

He drew in his breath. Why did he always revert to his old way of speaking when she looked at him like that?

"So why is the little darling crying?" She stroked Alice's head, cuddling her to her massive bosom. "'Cos Bella's doll's gone missing. Have you taken…um…seen it?"

"Bella? Oh, you mean, Annabella?"

The nanny had never known his other twin, so didn't need to be so particular in calling her by her proper name. "Yes," he answered through gritted teeth. "*Bella*. We can't find her doll that usually sits there."

"Oh, I threw it out. The child's gone, dead and buried, so there didn't seem any point in keeping it."

Jamie gasped. "But Alice still plays with it. She loves it nearly as much as her own." How could she be so cruel?

Alice struggled to be set down, crying, "Bella, Bella." Nanny let her go and Jamie ran to pick her up.

"Don't cry, darling." He'd been about to say he would ask Mama to buy her another one, but it wouldn't be the same. She wanted her sister's. He turned to the nanny. "Where've you put it? I'll go and rescue it."

Nanny turned her back and started making Alice's bed. His little sister had only just started sleeping in it. Nanny had said she had outgrown the cot she had shared with Annabella. She had cried and cried the first night, he felt sure because she'd missed her twin's presence. Presence and ghost had a separate meaning. He couldn't quite explain the difference. He'd tried to persuade his mama to let her back into her crib, but she'd said, "Nanny knows best", though he thought he'd seen a tear in her eye on her way out.

She still hadn't replied, so he repeated, "Nanny,

where is Bella's doll?"

Without turning, she said, "I do not have to answer to you, boy. It is not your concern."

Anger began to boil up in his throat. He looked out for his little sister. Of course it concerned him. He wanted to yank the woman's collar, look her in the eye, and tell her what he thought of her, but he knew he couldn't. She had threatened him with a cane once when he'd been just a little bit cheeky, so what punishment would she dole out if he actually touched her? "Spare the rod and spoil the child," she often said to his mama if she tried to defend him.

Opening the door, he said to Alice, "Let's go and find Mama." He knew she would be busy. Now the rain had spoiled the picnic, she had been trying to organise a party instead, but he couldn't just let the matter drop. He heard Nanny calling, "Leave the child here. It's time for her nap," but he ignored her.

On the stairs, they stepped aside for Betsy, the new parlour maid, who had replaced Martha, when she had mysteriously disappeared on his birthday. When he'd asked Nellie where she'd gone she'd looked at him with such an angry face and snapped, "Don't talk to me about that girl", that he hadn't been any the wiser.

Betsy, however…how had he heard Freda describing her? A different fish kettle, or something like that. Almost as short as Bobby's mother, she smiled all the time.

"Hello, you two," she squeaked in her high voice. "I mean…good day to you, Master Jamie and Miss Alice." The youngest—a year older than Jamie—and the only girl in a family of seven brothers, one of them the stable boy, Fred, she lived in one of the neighbouring villages. She received many a scolding for forgetting how to address them.

"Good day, Betsy. Have you seen Mama?"

"Um…no, sir…I mean…Master, I didn't see her

upstairs."

"Thank you." His arms ached from carrying Alice, so after Betsy had squeezed past—she seemed in a hurry—he put her down and held her hand as they carried on downstairs. Talking to Betsy had put him in a better mood, but he still fumed inside at Nanny's actions.

Crossing the hall to look for his mother in the lounge, when he could not find her in the morning room or the drawing room, they met Betsy again, struggling with a hod full of ashes.

"They look heavy," he said. "Can I carry them for you?"

"Oo, no, you mustn't do that. I'd be in real trouble."

Alice put up her arms as if she wanted to help as well. "No, Alice, you wouldn't be able to lift it," smiled Jamie. "You're much too small."

Betsy scuttled off towards the kitchen.

She'll never make it, thought Jamie, but knew she had to if she wanted to keep her job.

The front door opened and his father hobbled in. Leaning on one crutch for support, while trying to take off his cloak with his other hand, rainwater splashed over the floor. Purvis appeared, took his cloak and hat, and then disappeared in the same direction as Betsy, calling, "I'll fetch a towel, sir."

His papa bent down to Alice, showering Jamie with droplets from his hair. "And how's my gorgeous little girl today? Are you enjoying your birthday?"

She beamed up at him, raising her hands to be picked up.

Jamie quickly intervened. "Papa can't lift you, Alice, not 'til he's sat down." He wondered whether to bother his father with the problem of the doll, but decided against it. He didn't like to hassle him with trivial matters. He had enough problems of his own with his leg, and the estate and everything.

"It is raining cats and dogs out there." His father stretched.

"Cats and dogs? That's a funny expression, isn't it?" The image of hundreds of animals falling from the sky and landing on their lawn always made him laugh.

His papa smiled. "It is probably derived from the olden days when the gutters of the big towns would be awash with dead animals whenever it rained hard. Anyway, where's John? I need this wet boot off."

"Ugh, I'm glad we don't live in a big town. But I'll help you, Father." He followed him into the lounge, waited until he'd sat down, and pulled off his boot. Alice sat next to him, still clutching her doll.

"Anyway, my darling," his father said to her, "what are we going to do today now the picnic has been abandoned?" Purvis came in and handed him a towel, and he dried his face and hands.

"I think Mama's organising a party." Jamie could see a drop of rain clinging to his father's moustache and itched to wipe it off, but put his hands in his pockets instead, knowing that being fussed over made him cross. He studied the fuzzy hair that had only been growing for a few weeks. It made him look very different, sort of older somehow. Leaning forward, he examined it closer. Yes, even a grey hair, among the gingerish streaks.

"What's the matter? Do I have spinach in my teeth?" His father reached into his mouth and scraped his nail down his front tooth.

Jamie stepped back, becoming aware of his bad manners. "No, no, Papa, I mean…Father. I'm sorry. I didn't mean to…"

"Ah, here's your mother."

Jamie turned, grimacing.

"It's still raining then?" she asked, kissing his father, then picking up Alice. She looked at Jamie. "What's the birthday girl doing down here? Why isn't she having her nap?"

He looked from her, then to his father, remembering he hadn't wanted to trouble him. "Um…" He would have to tell a little fib. "We were looking for her…um…" But would it upset his mama if he mentioned his dead sister's name? Best not to. "We were wondering about her party."

"Well, Freda's making lots of jellies and cakes, and she's even made some ice cream."

"Oo, lovely. I adore ice cream."

"One or two neighbours will be coming and, of course, Auntie Ruby, and Uncle Sam will pop in for a short while." She turned to his father. "Matty and Jessie can't come, unfortunately. It would have been nice to see them and the children, but Lily's very poorly and they're quite worried about her."

"Oh dear, I hope it's nothing serious."

"Me too, we've had enough sadness in the family this year. We don't want any more." She cuddled Alice, who had nodded off on her shoulder. "Anyway, I'd better get this little one upstairs." Passing Jamie, she asked, "Where's Nanny? Why isn't she looking after your sister?"

Jamie waited until they were out in the hall before answering, "I didn't want to bother Father but…"

"Why, Jamie, what's the matter?"

He quickly answered to remove the anxious look on her face, "Oh, nothing really, Mama. Please don't concern yourself. It's just that…" How could he tell her without mentioning Annabella's name?

"Come on, out with it."

"Well, you know the doll that sits on the tallboy in the nursery?"

"Annabella's?"

He held his breath, expecting her to start crying, but she just looked concerned. "Yes."

"What about it?"

"Nanny's thrown it away."

"She's what?"

He explained what had happened.

Grabbing his arm, Tillie marched up the stairs. "We'll see about that," she retorted.

Oo, dear, I hope it won't mean she'll pinch me even more. Perhaps I shouldn't have said anything.

Reaching the nursery, she laid Alice in her bed without saying a word. Jamie had thought she would start shouting at Nanny straightaway.

He stood in the doorway, ready for a quick getaway, if necessary, praying the nanny wouldn't burn a hole in his favourite grey shirt she stood ironing. He could see her eyes narrowing as she watched his mother and he narrowed his own in imitation. Putting the iron on the stand, the nanny stood with her shoulders back, hands on her hips. "Good day, ma'am. Is everything to your satisfaction?"

His mother looked at the empty space on top of the tallboy. "I hope so, Cecelia." She walked across and ran her finger over it, as if checking for dust. "Annabella's dolly seems to be missing."

"Ah, yes, ma'am, I meant to tell you. I took it to my room to mend a little hole in its foot."

Jamie gasped. "But you said…"

She merely raised her eyebrows at him, challenging him to continue.

"Oh, that's good." His mother turned to him. "You must have misheard Nanny, my darling."

He knew perfectly well he hadn't, but kept his lips clamped shut to stop himself making a rude retort. Over his mama's shoulder, Nanny glared at him with such an evil eye, he backed out and ran downstairs. Now what punishment would she set him? If only he dared stand up to her. Through the open study door he could see his father rustling through papers. Better not disturb him.

He went into the kitchen. He felt safe in there. Maisie looked up from chopping onions. Her eyes looked watery, but they lit up when she saw him. In fact, her whole face seemed to light up.

"Oh, Ja...I mean, Master Jamie. These onions don't half sting yer eyes." She looked around, then bent forward towards him, whispering, "I heard a servant in the village say she sucks a piece of bread to stop it, but..." she looked around again, as if she thought someone might be lurking in the shadows, "but Freda says it's an old wives' story, and that it doesn't work."

"Well, can't you pinch a crumb while she's not looking? If you kept your mouth closed, she wouldn't know."

"No, I dares'n't. She seems to know everything, even when she's not..." She straightened up as the cook came out of the pantry.

"Haven't you finished those onions yet, young lady?" Freda snapped, adding, with an aside to Jamie, "I hope you haven't been hindering her, young man. She has a lot to do today, with the party and everything."

"No, I just..." Trying to think of an excuse for being there, he pulled a face at Maisie behind Freda's back. "I...um...just wanted a drink of your gorgeous lemonade." Maybe that would pacify the cook. That was one of his new words—'pacify'. His mama had used it for Alice. Would it still work on a cook?

Freda gave him an odd look from under her eyebrows, but went back into the pantry and brought out a jug of cold juice. "Pass me one of those glasses," she said, pointing to the shelf.

Jamie did so, watching the bubbles fizzing up as she poured. He drank the tangy liquid in one swig. "Is Maisie allowed some?" he asked, holding out the glass.

Shaking her head, the maid's mouth turned down,

and she looked at him as if he'd suggested something dreadful, but surprisingly, Freda poured another glassful and handed it to her. To top it all she added, "I'll have one myself as well, if it's so good." They both watched in amazement as she sipped her drink slowly, seeming to enjoy it as much as they had.

"I think there's going to be a storm later, it's so sultry." She put the glasses on the side and wiped her brow. "Now, chop, chop, young Maisie, we don't have all day. There's a party to organise."

"Can I do anything?" asked Jamie.

"Well…"

"Please. I'm bored. There's nothing to do and if you have so much…" He watched Maisie begin to chop again. "Not onions, though."

Freda smiled. "No, we wouldn't ask you to do anything like that." She looked around the kitchen. Jamie could see her brain working from the expressions on her face—her lips stuck out, and a frown on her forehead. She looked like a frog he'd once examined down by the lake. It had hopped away when he'd tried to touch it. He didn't think Freda would if he touched her. Imagining her hopping with both legs, he had to hold back a grin.

"You could…" she began. "But no, better not."

"I'll be ever so careful."

"I'll think of something. Give me a minute." Pulling the scales towards her, she weighed out some flour, took off one weight and replaced it with a larger one, then sifted it into a large brown bowl.

Jamie moved closer, fascinated by the scales. "Can I do some of that?"

"No, no, these measurements have to be exact. I usually just guess, but it has to be right today."

He lifted off the weight, and the metal dish she'd just replaced landed with a clang. She knocked his hand away. "Leave it alone. It isn't a plaything." Balancing the sieve on the side of the bowl, she wiped her hands down her apron. "Here, take this tray of cutlery into the dining room."

Pulling a face, he picked up the tray. He'd wanted to do something interesting. Surely they could find him a more exciting job? Maybe his mama would think of something. Giving Maisie a final smile, he left.

Neighbours began arriving during the afternoon. Crossing the hall, Jamie heard one of them say, as she shook her umbrella out of the door before giving it to Purvis, "There's going to be a storm any time soon."

Freda had said that earlier, but Jamie hadn't seen any evidence, no thunder or lightning, only the non-stop rain. He'd thought he'd heard a rumble an hour or so before and had become quite excited, but nothing had developed. He loved storms, and now Auntie Ruby had left, he'd be able to enjoy one. She hated them and would hide, telling him to come away from the window when he wanted to watch the streaks of lightning shooting from the heavens to light up the sky, and count the time between each bolt and the following thunder clap.

The doorbell rang and another guest came in. "It's so warm. I think there will be…"

Here we go again, someone else saying it.

He wandered into the dining room, and found Betsy arranging some trays of food on the large extended table—sandwiches, scones, red and green jellies, small cakes, sweetmeats, trays of ham and pork.

Grinning, she bobbed a curtsy. "Don't it look magnificent?" she squealed. "I never seen such a spread."

Nodding, Jamie reached out and picked up a funny-looking pastry thing. "What's this?" he asked before popping it into his mouth.

Grinning, the maid moved the rest of the pastries to cover the gap. "I think I heard Freda saying they were horses' hooves."

"Horses' hooves? They don't look like them."

"I know. That's what I thought, but I didn't like to argue with her. Quick, someone's coming." She hurried to the door as Jamie quickly finished chewing. He could taste cheese. Horses didn't eat cheese, so how could…? Betsy must have misheard and, anyway, wouldn't they be hard and crunchy?

He spent the next half hour helping Purvis take the guests' umbrellas and wet coats.

"Oh, Jamie, you're such a good boy." His mama came downstairs carrying Alice, looking pretty in a red dress. She hugged him. "But you're soaked."

"I know, and I haven't even been outside."

She laughed. "I hope our guests haven't been waiting too long. I thought this little one would be awake earlier, but she's had a really long sleep."

Jamie stroked his little sister's face. "I better not pick her up. We don't want her wet as well."

"No." His mother peeped through the doorway into the lounge, where the guests sat or stood around, talking and laughing. "I shouldn't think they've missed me. Your father seems to be holding court."

"I heard him telling people Alice was having a nap."

"I hope he didn't tell them I dropped off as well, waiting for her," she whispered.

"No, Mama, he wouldn't do that." He looked into her eyes. "Did you really?"

Grimacing, she nodded. "Well, I suppose I'd better go in. Ah, Ruby…"

Jamie turned as his aunt emerged from the kitchen, and ran to her. "Good day, Auntie Ruby."

"Good day, Jamie." She hugged him and then took Alice. "Hello, my beautiful birthday girl. Don't we look pretty?"

"Is Uncle Sam coming?"

"Yes, in a moment. He's just…"

"Are you coming in?" he heard his father call from the lounge. "Your guests await you."

"Yes, dear," his mama called back. "We're coming." She took Alice. Jamie and his aunt followed.

Later that evening, Jamie sat with Alice. The birthday girl had been dressed for bed in her white nightgown, her fair hair tied up in rags. He read one of her new books to her, seeing how many animals she recognised.

"What's that?" he asked.

"Mooooo," she lowed.

"That's right, a moo cow." He turned the page. "And that?"

"Meow." Alice pretended to wash her whiskers.

"Yes, and this one?"

"Line." She put her little fists up to her face and roared. "Grrr."

"Oo, please don't eat me, Mister Lion." He pretended to be scared so she repeated it. "Grrr."

Thank goodness she hadn't had the magic lantern show. He'd wanted to ask all day if she would, but thought he'd better not bring it up, in case they thought he wanted her to have it. She would have been more terrified than he'd been on his birthday. He still trembled at the memory of seeing the lion on the wall, thinking it had eaten his parents.

Blowing out his breath, he turned the page again.

"That's enough," Nanny called. "You're exciting her." She put down the sock she'd been darning and picked her up. "Time for beddy byes, little girl."

So engrossed in the book, Jamie had almost forgotten about the witch. He stood up. "I'll go and tell Mama, so she can give her a goodnight kiss."

She ignored him, crooning to his sister as she tucked

her up in bed, but he heard her saying something about, "That nasty brother of yours."

Not as nasty as you, you horrible... What was the worst thing you could call somebody? *...slimy, stinky toad.*

Chapter 2

"I didn't hear that storm everybody kept saying we'd have," moaned Jamie the following day. "I stayed awake for ages so I could hide under the sheets and pretend to be scared like Auntie Ruby, then run to the window to watch it, but I fell asleep."

Tillie tied Alice's bonnet and, giving her a kiss, set her down on the carpet. "Well, I'm glad the sun's shining today. We wouldn't have had a very enjoyable time with rain pelting down on us as we visited Pemberton House, would we?"

"Have I been there before?"

"No, and neither have I. Your father says it's really grand."

"Is he coming with us?"

"No. He would have liked to, but he has estate matters to attend to. It's Nanny's day off, so Auntie Ruby's coming."

"Hooray."

Tillie looked at Jamie closely. "You don't like Nanny much, do you?"

Turning away with a slight shrug, he began fiddling with the rocking horse's tail. Alice toddled over and tried to climb onto it, so he lifted her up and rocked her.

"Jamie?"

"Pardon?" He seemed to be deliberately avoiding eye contact, but she knew he'd heard her by the expression on his face when she'd first spoken.

"Gee up, horsey, gee up." He pushed Alice harder.

"Horthey," she squealed. "Horthey."

"Be careful. We don't want any more accidents." She reached out, screaming when he pushed again, "Slower, Jamie, for goodness sake." Visions of Alice being catapulted into the air ran through her head.

He looked at her then, as if coming round from a dream, stopped the horse and lifted Alice off. "Sorry, Mama."

"What's got into you today?"

Alice began to wail, "Horthey, horthey."

"No more now, darling, we're going out."

Her thumb went back into her mouth, and she lifted up her arms to be picked up.

"Shall I fetch my jacket?" Jamie asked, opening the door.

Tillie still hadn't received a reply about Nanny. "Yes, dear, the brown one fits you best." Fast outgrowing his clothes, he had been measured by the tailor for new clothes to take to school, although they would need a trip to Leeds for his uniform. She shuddered, clutching Alice close to her bosom. How would she bear the wrench of his leaving?

They found Ruby in the kitchen talking to Freda. From the symptoms she described, their babies would be only a couple of months apart. Tillie hugged Ruby, thrilled for her younger sister.

"Sam's preparing the carriage. He won't be a moment." Ruby took Alice and gave her a cuddle. "Thank goodness that horrible storm's passed, eh, little one?"

Jamie came in, pulling on his cap. "What storm? *We* didn't have one."

"Didn't you? Well, we did."

"Aw, that's not fair. Your cottage is only a mile down the lane. How come it stormed where you live, and not here?"

Tillie patted his shoulder. "We did have one, Jamie, during the night. You must have been sleeping too deeply to hear it." At the mixed look of disappointment and fury on his face, she tried to placate him. "Never mind, my darling, I'm sure there'll be plenty more storms to witness, but right now we have a stately home to visit."

Blowing out his cheeks, he opened the door, looking out as if he hoped he might see the tail end of the lightning or hear a faint rumble of thunder in the distance. She hoped not, and it didn't seem likely from the clear blue sky.

Sam brought the carriage forward, and she climbed in after Ruby, passing Alice to her as Goldie ran around the corner. Jamie tried to stop her jumping in as well.

"Can…?" He looked up hopefully, but Tillie shook her head. "No, Goldie." He pulled her back. "You can't come with us. You'll have to stand guard and look after the house."

On the way, Jamie's usual spirit seemed subdued. She had expected him to be looking around and pointing things out, with the carriage top being down. "Are you feeling well, darling?" she asked.

"Yes, thank you, Mama. I…" He smiled but it didn't quite reach his eyes. "I just wondered what we'll see at Pemberton House."

"Yes," said Ruby. "I wondered that, too. Is it very large? I have never been inside a bigger house than The Grange."

"Well, actually," admitted Tillie, "I'm not sure. This will be my first visit."

"So how will we know what to do?" Ruby cried.

Jamie nodded as if he'd been thinking that as well.

"I've been assured the housekeeper will show us around, so there's no fear of becoming lost or anything like that. But you mustn't touch anything, Jamie. There will probably be expensive antiques and ornaments that have been handed down through the generations. It's a very old house."

Alice had fallen asleep in Ruby's arms. "Do you want me to take her?" asked Tillie.

"No, no, it's really lovely to cuddle her again. I've

missed her."

"I've missed you, Auntie Ruby," cut in Jamie. "It's not the same since you went."

As Tillie began to ask him about Nanny again, he pointed skywards, exclaiming, "Oo, look, there's my buzzard."

She and Ruby looked up and saw three birds circling around and around.

"Which one? And how do you know it's *your* buzzard?" asked Ruby, smiling.

"Well, I don't really. I just like to think it is." The expression on his animated face looked so different to how he had looked earlier. "Do you remember, Mama, when we seed…sawed…it kill the crow and eat it? That was amazing."

"Ugh, it sounds horrible," said Ruby.

"Yes, highly nauseating," agreed Tillie. "I wouldn't want to see it again."

"Did Papa ever buy those binoclars, whatever they're called?"

"I think they're called 'binoculars'. Anyway, yes, he's ordered them, and they should be delivered very soon."

"Before I go to school?"

"I think so."

"Oh, I do hope so. Just imagine seeing my buzzard up close."

"What's them then, these binoculars?" asked Ruby.

"They're like extra strong glasses, Papa said. You can see all the details on things far away."

Ruby shook her head, clearly unimpressed.

"I'll be able to tell the boys at school about it."

"Yes, but let's not think about school for now." Tillie could think of nothing worse to talk about. "We should be there soon, I think. Your father said it would take about half an hour. Ah, is that it? Can you see through the trees?" She pointed to her right, calling out,

School for Jamie

"Is that Pemberton House, Sam?"

Facing the rear, Jamie had to crane his neck. "That big house? Gosh, it's huge, much bigger than The Grange."

Sam half turned, replying, "Yes, ma'am."

"Do they know we're coming?" asked Ruby, looking nervous.

"No, but I'm reliably informed we don't need an invitation."

"Well, I hope the maids have all completed their chores before we arrive. I shall be checking for dust," Ruby added.

Tillie giggled. "You'd better not. Don't let me catch you doing so, I should be mortally embarrassed."

"Shall I do it as well, Auntie Ruby?" Jamie grinned. "Shall we run our fingers along the shelves and say—" His voice rose to a higher pitch "—Oh, my goodness, luck at all this dast!' like Nanny did once?"

Ruby chuckled at his pronounced accent, but Tillie couldn't bear the thought of them doing anything so impolite. "Oh, no, you won't. You'll both be on your best behaviour."

"Yes, ma'am," said Ruby cheekily as the carriage circled the drive and pulled to a halt.

Sam jumped down, gave Ruby a wink and opened the door. Tillie descended first and Ruby handed a sleeping Alice to her. The front door opened, and a butler came out and greeted them.

"I hope it is not inconvenient—" Tillie bowed her head "—for us to arrive unannounced."

"No, no, ma'am, of course not."

"We wondered if it would be possible to take a tour of the house, if it is not too much trouble?"

"I shall fetch the housekeeper, ma'am."

They entered the large hall, and Tillie heard Ruby gasp behind her, "Look at that massive chandelier."

"Yes, ma'am." A tall lady, who Tillie assumed to be the housekeeper, appeared. "We have it on good authority that it was made by the same firm who supplies Her Royal Highness, Queen Victoria."

Jamie stood with his mouth open, pointing to the paintings of previous owners covering the walls and up the wide staircase in front of them. "It seems like they're all looking at me," he whispered.

Ruby smiled, whispering back, "They're keeping their eyes on you."

Alice awoke as they advanced into the drawing room so Tillie put her down, for she had grown heavy, and walked over to a magnificent cabinet. She saw Ruby reach out a finger and glared at her. Her sister merely grinned.

The housekeeper described the decorations adorning it. "That is mother-of-pearl, and that part is tortoiseshell." She pointed to the beautiful inlays on the furniture.

"Tortoiseshell?" asked Jamie. "Off a real tortoise?"

"Um…I'm not sure." The flustered housekeeper hurried over to the next cabinet, pointing to the contents.

"Jamie, don't ask awkward questions," Tillie hissed at him.

"But, Mama…"

"If you have seen enough in here, shall we proceed into the next room?" asked the hapless servant.

Turning to follow, Tillie put out her hand for her daughter. "Where's Alice?" she cried. Ruby didn't have her. She could see her sister examining an article of furniture across the room.

"Where's Alice?" she repeated, grabbing Jamie's arm.

"She…" Jamie twizzled around, his eyes wide. "I saw her a minute ago."

"Do you mean the little girl?" asked the housekeeper.

"Yes, my daughter, where's she gone?" Tillie ran to

the door and looked out. "Oh, God, please don't let her be lost."

A faint humming came from behind a large sofa in the corner. "Alice," she yelled, running over to it. There sat her daughter, happily playing with her rag doll, clearly oblivious to her mother's panic. Tillie grabbed her, unsure whether to scold or cuddle her. "Thank God you're safe," she gushed, clinging to the child, as Ruby and Jamie ran across.

Jamie stroked her head. "She wasn't really lost, was she, Mama?"

"No, not lost at all." She turned to the housekeeper, her enthusiasm for looking around the house disappearing. "I think we've taken up enough of your time. Thank you so much for showing us around."

"But, ma'am, what about the rest of the house?"

"Perhaps another time."

"Of course." She bobbed a curtsy and led them out.

Sam stood leaning against the side of the carriage, smoking a cigarette. He looked surprised to see them as he quickly stubbed it out and opened the door for them to climb in, saying aside to Ruby, "I didn't expect you to be finished so soon. Surely you can't have seen it all in such a brief time?"

"We had to cut our visit short," she replied. "Alice…"

"Alice decided to play hide and seek," piped up Jamie. "Didn't you, you little imp?" He tickled her, making her giggle. "Fancy scaring us all like that."

Tillie still hadn't recovered from the shock. Taking deep breaths, she tried to calm down. The child hadn't even been missing. But the memories of Annabella's disappearance had come flooding back, and she'd been so frightened.

Ruby reached over and took her hand. "Are you all right, sis?"

She tried to nod, but could barely move, couldn't even open her eyes. Although she desperately wanted to cling on to her daughter, her muscles refused to obey the command to prevent Ruby from taking her, as she felt the carriage move.

Count to ten, she thought, but that didn't help.

Jamie's anxious voice penetrated her brain. "Mama, what's the matter? Please talk to me. Mama?"

"Just…a minute."

Her breathing gradually returned to normal, and her eyes opened to see Ruby's face directly in front of her. "Do you want me to ask Sam to stop?"

Startled to see her sister so close, she shook her head and gasped, "No, take me…home."

Jamie reached over and took her hand. "Are you better now, Mama?"

Nodding, she took another deep breath and murmured, "Yes, darling, I'm fine." Although far from it, she patted his hand, and leaned back, trying to control herself. The baby inside her needed calm. She couldn't lose another one.

The breeze fanned her hot cheeks, and she felt much more composed by the time they arrived home.

David stood near the front door, talking to one of the farmer tenants when they pulled up. He turned towards them as the farmer walked away.

Tillie sat up, surprised at the angry expression on his face.

Sam opened the door and Jamie jumped down.

"Should you not wait for your mother to alight first, Jamie?" David asked brusquely.

"Mama's not well."

"I'm fine, honestly," Tillie replied as she stepped down.

"What is the matter? You were not gone very long. I did not expect you for a couple of hours."

"We lost Alice…" Jamie began as Goldie came bounding across to him.

"No, we didn't." Tillie put out a hand at David's aghast face. "She was just… Shall we go in? You look very tottery."

Jamie laughed. "Tottery? That's a funny word."

Alice started to run down the drive, and Goldie chased her, almost knocking her over. Ruby ran and caught her, calling, "It's a lovely word, isn't it, Jamie? One more for your collection."

"Never mind all that, I'm going inside." Tillie turned to David. "What did Farmer Askew want? You didn't seem very pleased with him."

"He…" His crutch slipped off the step and Tillie grasped hold of his arm to stop him falling.

"That was close, Father." Jamie grabbed his other arm, and they manoeuvred him into the lounge.

"All right, all right, you can let go now." David shrugged them off. "I can manage."

Jamie gave Tillie a rueful grimace. She patted his shoulder. "Why don't you take Goldie and Lady for a run down by the lake? I'm sure they'd like that."

Nodding, he went out as Ruby took Alice to the kitchen for a drink.

"I do not know why you want to go gallivanting around the county when we are still in mourning, anyway." David plonked down onto the sofa.

"You know it was to please Jamie. I thought it would be something nice for him before…you know…"

"Well, do not forget he has that rowing trip next week."

"Are you sure that's a good idea?"

"Tillie, we have discussed this over and over again. He is really looking forward to it."

She sat down next to him. "Anyway, you were telling me about Farmer Askew."

"Oh, something and nothing. Shall I pull the bell for some tea?"

"David! Oh, all right, then." She knew she wouldn't receive a sensible answer if he felt disinclined to tell her.

* * * *

A few days later, Jamie jumped out of bed excitedly. The rowing trip, the most thrilling thing he'd ever done. Should he wear his best trousers? They fitted perfectly and didn't scratch. But his mother had said he might get wet, and he didn't want them spoiled. His old ones would do, being only slightly too short.

Pulling on his clothes, he grabbed his cap and ran downstairs. He considered popping into the nursery to say hello to Alice, but didn't want to face Nanny. She would only ruin everything. She'd already tried to persuade his mama not to let him go, all because she'd caught him pulling faces at her behind her back. He hadn't realised she could see him in the mirror. His mama had made him apologise, and had said it could be forgotten, but he knew Nanny wouldn't see it like that. He rubbed his head, still sore from when she'd pulled his hair so hard it had brought tears to his eyes after the incident with the doll.

Seeing his father going into the study, he called, "What time are we going, Father?"

"When Mister Hodges arrives, probably about ten o'clock."

"Are just you and me going? Why isn't Mama coming with us?"

"Because she thinks it is too dangerous. Run along and have your breakfast. I will let you know when it is time." His father went into the study and closed the door.

Jamie went into the kitchen. Maisie seemed to be grating something into a bowl. "What're you doing?" he asked.

The maid looked up and smiled. "Grating suet for the plum duff. Freda's going to show me how to make one today."

"Oh, I love plum duff."

"Me, too. I hope there's some left for us."

Freda came through the back door carrying a basket full of carrots and cabbages from the garden.

"Have you eaten yet, young Master Jamie?" When he shook his head, she continued, "Although you're not so young, now, are you?"

"No, I'm not. I'm so grown up Papa's taking me rowing today."

"Rowing?" Maisie looked surprised.

"Yes, with Mister Hodges."

"You'll need a good breakfast inside you, then." Freda turned to the range and put the heavy frying pan onto the heat. "Sausages and bacon?"

"Yes, please." Taking off his cap, he sat down at the table, watching Maisie. "Do you want me to ask Father if you can come?" he asked her.

Her violet eyes looked up sadly, and she shook her head.

"Now don't go putting ideas like that into her head." Freda turned the sausages. "The zoo was a special treat because of your birthday. It won't happen again." She turned to the little maid. "Have you finished that suet yet?" When Maisie showed her the bowl, she took it, saying, "See, she has too many chores to do here."

He ate his breakfast in silence. It had never struck him before how different his life would have been if his mama hadn't married his father. He would probably be working as a servant, like Maisie, or a farm hand. Bringing in the harvest had exhausted him. He couldn't contemplate doing it all day and every day. And his mama? It didn't bear thinking about.

Two hours later, Jamie sat in the carriage next to his father. "Will there be lots of folk there or just us?" he asked, craning his neck to see ahead.

"There should be quite a few others." Mister Hodges smiled indulgently.

"I can see the river." He gazed at the water gently flowing over stones and tree roots. It looked more like a brook, deep enough to stand in. "But it don't look wide enough for boats."

"It broadens out farther up, you'll see."

"Oh, good."

His father sat back with his eyes closed, the wind ruffling his hair. "Are you well, Papa?" he asked, worried that the trip would be too much for him. "Is it too windy with the top down?" He turned to Mister Hodges. "We could…"

"I am fine, Jamie." His father put on his hat. "Thank you for your concern."

Rounding a bend in the road, Jamie pointed to a large gathering of people. "You're right, Mister Hodges, the river is a lot wider here."

"Thank you, Master Jamie, I usually am."

They pulled up behind a row of carriages. Sam jumped down and opened the door.

Standing on the step, Jamie could see rows of boats lined up. People sat inside some, checking out their oars. "I'n't this exciting? I can't wait."

He began to run towards them, but heard Sam calling him. "Master Jamie, wait." Looking back, he saw his father stumbling out of the carriage, so hurried back to help him.

"Stop fussing." His father made it to the ground. "I am not an invalid."

"Would you like me to unbuckle the wheelchair?" asked Sam, holding his arm.

"No, I shall try to manage with the crutches. The

path is not very smooth. It might be too bumpy for the chair."

"Maybe there'll be a seat further along."

"Yes, yes."

Jamie watched his father struggling on the stony path, feeling guilty that he'd agreed to the trip. He hadn't realised what the ground would be like, how difficult it would be. Subdued, he followed behind. "Shall we go home, Father?" he called but, with so much noise from people shouting, and dogs barking, he carried on without replying.

They eventually found a seat. "I shall be as right as rain watching from here," his father said.

Someone walked past with a hot drink and Jamie noticed a large tent nearby. He pulled at the groom's sleeve. "What's in there, Sam?"

"Ah, that'll be the tea room. Would you like me to fetch you some, master?"

"A cup of tea would be very welcome, thank you," his father replied, tucking a blanket around his legs.

Jamie hopped from one foot to the other, wishing the groom would hurry back. It seemed an age before he saw him returning.

"David, I'll take the boy to look at the boats." Mister Hodges took Jamie's hand, and they began to walk towards the water.

He heard his father calling, "Be careful, Jamie, do not do anything stupid."

Jamie waved, calling back, "I'll be good, Father."

Approaching the water's edge, Jamie's enthusiasm turned to unease. "Is it really safe?" he asked, remembering his mother's warning.

"Aye, lad, as long as you do as I say."

"Will I be able to hold one of those long oar things?"

"No, not on your first outing."

How disappointing. They looked good fun.

Climbing into the boat proved more difficult than he'd imagined. It kept moving about. Eventually, he settled into his seat, and they moved off. The choppy water beneath them churned his stomach and, for a moment, he thought his breakfast would come back up.

"Is it as exciting as you thought it would be?" asked Mister Hodges, leaning forward as he pulled on the oars. He had a smile on his face, so must have been enjoying it.

Taking a deep breath, Jamie nodded. *Actually,* he thought, *it's brilliant.* With his stomach now settled, he watched the riverbank zoom by. A heron flew in and stood near the water's edge, its long legs keeping its body clear of the water. It stood peering intently into the shallows and reached forward, grabbing a fish in its beak. When it tilted its head back, Jamie could see the bulge as the fish went down the bird's gullet.

"Oo, look at that," he exclaimed. "It's nearly as wonderful as a buzzard."

"There's another one over there." Mister Hodges indicated with his head to the other bank, and slowed down. "This stretch is renowned for them." They drew to a halt as he held the oars out of the water. Another boat passed them, the occupants calling out greetings, and waving. Jamie waved back until the wash from the other boat stirred up the water and he grabbed hold of the side.

The heron flew off, and they started moving again. Feeling braver, Jamie trailed his hand in the cold water. A family of ducks approached and he called to them, "I'm a duck today, quack, quack."

Maybe if I reach out far enough I could touch one.

He leant out, but yelped as he felt the boat heel to one side.

"Sit back," yelled Mister Hodges but, try as he may, he found himself sliding as the boat capsized, and they both plunged into the freezing river. Flailing and

School for Jamie

struggling to keep his head above the water, he sank down into the murky weeds spotting the duck's feet, paddling madly, trying to escape from him.

He couldn't breathe. The bubbles around him sounded like his dead cousin, George, whispering in his ear, 'Now you know what it's like,' reminding him of the time his cousin had fallen into the lake some four years earlier.

"No!" he wanted to shout, but opening his mouth brought in more water and weeds. Just as he thought he couldn't hold out any longer, he felt strong arms pulling him upwards. Who could it be? It could be the man in the moon for all he cared. His head popped out of the water, and he took a huge breath. A stranger hauled him to the bank where he lay spluttering.

Voices shouted all around him. Someone yelled, "Where's the oarsman?"

Someone else replied, "I can't see him."

Realising they were talking about Mister Hodges, he tried to sit up.

"Stay where you are, boy," his rescuer ordered, wrapping a blanket around his shoulders. Eager to obey, Jamie sat down, searching the surface of the river. A man took off his jacket and dived beneath the water, followed by another. Mister Hodges's hat bobbed up and down on the water, the only sign Jamie could see of him. He realised he'd lost his own cap. *Better not let Nanny find out.*

They'd travelled too far down the river to see his father, and he wondered if he ought to run back and tell him. Or should he jump in himself and look for his friend. After all, he knew himself to be at fault for the incident. Stepping to the water's edge, he heard someone shout, "You, boy, what are you doing?"

Shrugging off the blanket, he replied, "I have to find him. He's my father's best friend."

The man pulled him back. "Don't be stupid, boy.

The current's really strong here. You'd be pulled under in no time."

"But…"

A shout from behind made him turn. "They've found him." Everyone ran downstream. Jamie scrambled up the bank and overtook them. He reached the scene as two burly men hauled out his friend.

"Is he dead?" he asked, pulling the sleeve of the man pressing Mister Hodges's back. "What're you doing?"

Water gushed out of the huntsman's mouth and he began to cough.

"Thank God," exclaimed the stranger, turning to Jamie. "That's what I was doing, clearing his lungs."

The relieved murmuring around him increased as Jamie began to shiver, wishing he'd brought the blanket.

"Take off your sodden jacket, boy." A woman came across and helped him. "You'll dry off quicker without it. What's your name?"

"Jamie," he replied. "Is he going to be all right?"

"Yes, look, he's sitting up."

He wanted to move closer to speak to Mister Hodges, but thought he'd probably receive a scolding for causing the accident, so he hid behind the lady, peeping through her skirts.

Mister Hodges sat up. "Where's Jamie? Is he still in the water? I have to save him." He tried to stand.

The man put his hand on his shoulder. "Don't fret, sir. The boy's safe. He's around somewhere."

"He's over here," the lady called, pulling him out from behind her, "looking somewhat bedraggled, but perfectly well."

He had no option but to show himself. "I'm really sorry, Mister Hodges. I didn't mean to do it."

"Don't blame yourself. I should have made you more aware of the dangers." Coughing once more, the huntsman stood up, pulling a small fish out of his pocket.

"Well, at least we'll have something for dinner," he joked, making everybody laugh.

He looked towards the water with a concerned expression. "Did anyone manage to save the boat?"

"Yes, sir, don't worry about that," someone replied, with the deepest voice Jamie had ever heard. He stared at the man, the tallest he'd ever seen. Would he start saying, 'Fee-fi-fo-fum', like the giant in the Jack and the beanstalk story?

He dragged his gaze from the man when Mister Hodges took his hand. "We'd better go and find your father."

"Shouldn't we wait here a while longer to make sure you're better?"

"I've recovered enough. He might have heard about the mishap and could be worried."

"Do we have to tell him?"

"I think he'd probably guess something had occurred by the state of our attire, don't you?"

"Um, s'pose so." Jamie's shoulders slumped. He would be lucky to escape without retribution.

"I shan't tell him how it happened, if that's what you're worried about."

"Really?" He perked up. "You'd do that for me?"

"I think your father has enough troubles on his plate without adding to them."

"Aw, fanks."

Jamie's shoes squelched as they walked back towards the start. His shirt had almost dried in the warm sun, but his thick trousers chaffed his legs. He shivered. Mister Hodges put his arm around his shoulder, shaking also.

Chapter 3

A few days later, Jamie dragged himself out of bed. He'd been coughing for half the night. Another spasm overtook him, and he sat down on the rug. Several moments passed before he could pull on a clean shirt. He wondered why his chest looked red. His eyes hurt and he could barely look at the light streaming in through the window.

"I'm supposed to be going into Leeds to be fitted for my school uniform today," he muttered. Perhaps if he explained to his mama that he felt unwell, she'd postpone the trip. He couldn't even summon his usual enthusiasm for school. What would happen if he became poorly there? He remembered they had a special room called an infamy, or something like that. They'd been told about it on their visit but hadn't actually seen it, in case it contained somebody infic…

"Oh, I can't remember the word." He didn't have the energy to rack his brain. Lacing up his boots, he wondered if his wet, comfortable ones had dried out with the newspaper stuffed inside them. Nellie had said they might have shrunk. He hoped not. She had given him a look from under her eyebrows as if she knew the accident had been his fault but, as Mister Hodges had covered for him, he hadn't been chastised.

Instead of going to the kitchen for his breakfast, he wandered into the dining room, and lifted the lid off a food dish. Normally, he would have grabbed one of the remaining sausages, even if he'd already eaten, but that day he didn't fancy them at all.

A piece of cold toast sat at the side. He took a bite, but his throat hurt so much he put it down, took the cosy off the teapot, and poured some out. The cool drink soothed his throat.

School for Jamie

Betsy came in to clear the dishes. "Have you had enough?" she asked.

Jamie tried to answer, but found he could only croak. He began coughing again.

She backed away, her usual smile disappearing. "Oh dear, looks like you're poorly. I'd better not come too close, it's me afternoon off, and I don't want to catch anything."

Jamie slouched out. Opening the door to the lounge, looking for his mama, he peeped in. The sofa looked inviting. Maybe he could sit there for a while, and find her later. Resting his head on the soft cushion, he closed his gritty eyes.

"Ah, there you are."

He forced his eyes open. He must have been asleep, for he'd been dreaming of frogs and newts appearing in his pockets each time he put his hands in them. "Are you unwell?" asked his mother, feeling his brow. "It isn't like you to be lying down in the middle of the day."

Her hand felt cool.

"Oh, my goodness," she exclaimed, "you're burning up, and look at that rash." Lights flashed before him, hurting his eyes as her hands flapped up and down. "Please, God, don't let him be coming down with that awful…" She touched him again. "Stay there while I fetch your father."

He didn't have any problem doing as she'd bid. He couldn't have moved if he'd wanted to.

Closing his eyes once more, he heard his father's worried voice. "We had better call the doctor, and do not let Alice in here. We do not want her catching anything, or you, Tillie, for that matter, not in your condition."

Jamie would have loved a big hug from his mama, but he couldn't risk her becoming poorly. Through half-open eyes, he watched her go out after turning back to give him a watery smile.

The doctor arrived soon afterwards and diagnosed the measles. Vaguely aware of being carried upstairs to his bedroom, he remained in bed for several days, sleeping most of the time, Nellie his only companion. She kept the bedroom curtains closed because any light hurt his eyes, but he wouldn't have been able to read or draw, anyway.

He awoke one morning, unsure how many days later, in a cheerful mood. The red rash had disappeared, and his eyes no longer smarted. Wondering if he'd be allowed out of bed, he sat up, half expecting his head to hurt.

"I'm better," he declared, gingerly putting his feet to the floor. So far, so good. He took the few steps to the window and, pulling back the curtains, shading his eyes from the sunshine, he squinted at some birds flying past. "Are they starlings? What's the word for a group of starlings?" he tried to remember. "A murmur…"

A hand on his shoulder made him jump.

"What are you doing out of bed?" Nellie cried.

"When did you come in?" he asked. "I didn't hear you."

"Never mind that, back into bed."

He didn't want to admit it, but his wobbly legs had almost given way. He gripped her hand as she helped him cross the room.

"Why are you whispering, Nellie?" he asked.

"I'm not." She looked at him with a worried expression. "Your ears are probably blocked after the illness." She tucked the covers around him and offered him a drink of water. He drank it gratefully.

"Do you think you could manage some warm soup?"

He nodded. "And a cup of tea, please, Nellie."

He wiggled his fingers in his ears.

"No, Master Jamie, please don't do that." She pulled

his hands down.

"But I want to clear them. I can't hear you proper."

"Just give it time. You've had a nasty illness, and you can't expect everything to clear up straightaway."

"Will I be better enough to go to school?"

"I should think so, but you must stay in bed now." Her voice still sounded blurry.

"I don't have me uniform yet. I was s'posed to go to Leeds for a fitting, wasn't I, before I come down with me illness?"

"Don't fret about that." Nellie went across to the window and drew the curtains closed. She turned back to face him. "So that will be better, won't it?"

"What?"

"Didn't you hear…?" She looked concerned once more, but fussed with his blanket—it already seemed straight—and, murmuring something about soup, went out, leaving him in semi-darkness again.

He stuck a finger in his ear again. *All I need to do is clear the fuzziness inside.*

* * * *

Betsy put some clean cutlery onto a tray. "I had measles once. Me and my brothers all caught it, Fred first, then one by one the rest of us. Me ma said she had the curtains drawn permanent like for weeks."

"And did any of you end up deaf?" asked Maisie, pouring some vinegar onto a cloth.

"Stop your nattering, you two, and carry on with your work." Nellie hadn't realised the maids had heard her apprising Freda of her worries about Jamie's hearing. She didn't want to worry the master and mistress unduly though, so decided she would wait another day or two, and see if his situation improved before telling them.

Taking the warmed-up soup from Freda, she went

back upstairs.

Jamie sat up. "I think I've cleared them."

"What?"

"Me ears. I've wiggled me fingers in them and they seem all right now."

"I told you not to put your fingers in your ears. You'll do more damage than good."

He didn't appear to be listening, his head bent, concentrating on the soup she'd placed in front of him.

"Mm, this is good." He took another spoonful. "Do you remember when I first come? You gave me soup like this then, didn't you?"

"Yes, you were a poor scrap of a boy then. Just look at you now."

He looked up. "I beg your pardon?"

"It doesn't matter."

* * * *

Several days later, Tillie helped Jamie into his new school uniform.

"Are you sure it'll fit?" he asked.

"The seamstress rushed it through, so I hope so."

"Yes, there's only two days left, isn't there?" He tried the buttons. "They're easier than the ones on me funeral suit." He looked up with a grin. "I never told nobody, but I couldn't fasten one of them and went to Annabella's funeral with…" Not finishing his sentence, he walked sadly over to the window.

"You still miss her, don't you?" Tillie followed him and put her hands on his waist.

He didn't answer.

"Jamie?"

He turned then. "Yes, Mama?"

"Did you hear what I said?"

"Um…" Screwing up his face, he looked at her with

a frown. "I'm not sure. Sometimes I think I hear things, but then other times..." He shrugged.

"Well, don't worry about it. I'm sure it will right itself once you're fully recovered."

Freda had intimated something earlier about his hearing not being as acute as usual, confirming Tillie's own fears. She hadn't mentioned it to David, but Jamie would be going away to school the following Sunday, and she hoped it would have recovered by then.

"Take it off and hang it in the wardrobe." Thankfully his uniform seemed to fit. "Are you coming downstairs?" She noticed that he seemed to hear if he looked at her when she spoke. He nodded.

"I'll see you in the lounge." She sighed, but her attention was diverted by a hammering on the front door, and she hurried downstairs, arriving as Purvis tried to restrain a dishevelled man.

"Who...? Oh, my goodness, it's the Major."

"Madam." The Major held out his hand. "I am so sorry to intrude on you in this fashion."

Shocked at the man's appearance, she gasped, "Have they let you out?" and then realised how ill-mannered she sounded. "I mean..."

"Out? Out of where?"

"The..." Should she use the word 'asylum'?

"What on earth is going on?" Tillie turned to see David hobbling towards her. "My God, man, whatever has happened to you?" He looked enquiringly at her. "Has he been released?" he whispered.

She shrugged. "I don't know."

The Major put his arms out to David and began to cry. "My dear friend, you are the only sane person in this godforsaken world. You will help me, won't you?"

David's crutch was nearly knocked from under his arm as he tried to extricate himself from the man's grasp. "Of course, Major, I shall do everything in my power to help. Come into the lounge and sit down." He raised his eyebrows at Tillie above his friend's shoulder and grimaced.

Purvis steered the Major into the lounge and Tillie and David followed.

Nellie hurried in.

"Please bring some strong coffee for the Major," David ordered.

The housekeeper looked enquiringly at Tillie who merely hunched her shoulders and shook her head.

The Major sat in the armchair, biting the ends of his fingers. His unkempt hair stuck up at all angles and his ripped jacket sported a host of unsightly stains.

"Surely they look after him better than this?" Tillie whispered to David.

"Well, maybe he has been released, although I was not aware of it." He turned to his friend. "Major, where are you living now?"

The Major's eyes opened wide, and a wild look came into them. "Eh?"

"Are you living back in your own home?"

The man shook his head frantically from side to side.

Nellie came in with the tray of coffee, and the Major leaned forward before she had chance to put it down, grabbed one of the cups and lifted it to his mouth. Taken aback, the housekeeper almost dropped the tray. She set it down on a table near David, who had sat down on one of the hard chairs. Leaning forward on his crutch, he asked, "Nellie, have you heard whether the Major's house has been renovated? I have not been in that direction for a while, so have not seen it for myself."

"I honestly don't know, sir. Do you think he's been living there? I hadn't heard he'd left the asylum."

David shrugged. "Nor had we. Could you make enquiries, please?"

School for Jamie

The Major sat back, stretched his arms above his head and yawned.

Tillie poured out the coffee and handed it to him. "Ah, tea." He brought his arms down, took the cup and sat staring at it cupped in his hands. "Delicious."

"Aren't you going to drink it?" she asked.

"What?"

David shook his head at her so she sipped her own drink, wondering what to do. "Shouldn't we call someone?" she whispered. "Doctor Abrahams? He should know whether the poor old duffer is back in his own home, or still in the asylum, shouldn't he?" At David's nod, she pulled the bell ring. When Betsy came in, she asked her to send for the doctor.

Jamie came wandering in, stroking a small fluffy, black kitten. "Look what I found, Mama. May I keep it?"

He jumped back, startled, as the Major leapt out of his chair and grabbed the kitten, stuffing it inside his jacket.

Jamie ran to Tillie with a look of amazement. "Mama?"

"Stand back, Jamie, the Major…the Major is not well."

"But my kitten?"

David stood up and hobbled across to his friend, who had sat down and leaned his head back on the cushions, seemingly forgetting about the animal in his jacket.

"Major, please give Jamie his kitten."

"Of course, old chap." He closed his eyes.

Jamie moved towards him, but changed his mind and backed towards Tillie. "Shall I try and snatch it?"

"No, darling, you'd better not go near him. We're not sure of his state of mind."

He had evidently not heard her, for he pounced on the Major, ripped his jacket open and grabbed the kitten.

"I have her," he pronounced, walking away.

Roaring, the Major rose up. Jamie turned and ran out of the room, clutching the animal. The Major began to follow him, but David stuck out his crutch and tripped him up. He toppled to the floor, lying blubbering like a baby.

Tillie gasped at her husband.

"I had to do something," he protested. "I could not let him catch Jamie. Heaven knows what he would have done."

"I know but…" She bent down. "Are you hurt, Major?"

He jumped up. "Hurt? Of course not, what do you take me for, a milksop?" He staggered back to the armchair and slumped into it, panting and gasping for breath.

"I'd better go and see how Jamie is." Tillie walked towards David. "Do you think you'll be safe?"

"Yes, he seems quieter now. I shall make sure I stay on this side of the room."

"I'll send John in, just to make sure. Would you like a fresh pot of coffee?"

"Something stronger would be better, to calm my nerves."

Tillie went to the sideboard, poured out a generous measure of brandy and handed it to him. "What about the Major?" she pointed her head at the crazed man, who seemed to be asleep. "Should I pour one for him?"

David shook his head. "No, wait and see what the doctor says when he arrives." He took out his pocket watch. "Hopefully, he will be here soon."

She kissed the top of his head and went out. Where would Jamie most likely be? She tried the kitchen first. "Did Jamie come through here?" she asked Freda, who seemed to be peeling the potatoes with more haste than usual.

"I didn't see him, but then I've been attending to young Maisie. She's unwell, so I took her up to bed."

"Why, what's the matter with her?"

"A fever."

"Do you think she's caught the measles from Jamie?"

"Could be, but there's no sign of a rash." The cook dropped the potatoes into the boiling water and placed the lid on the pan.

"Poor Maisie, she's usually so healthy."

"Yes, it's the first time she's been ill since she came here." Freda wiped her wet brow with the corner of her apron. "It's unusually hot in here, don't you think?"

Tillie couldn't say that she did. Obviously, the kitchen would be warmer than the rest of the house, with the range burning all day long, but it didn't seem to be any hotter than usual. "I hope you're not coming down with something as well, Freda. We can't manage without you."

Realising that sounded rather callous, she tried to make up for it by adding, "I mean...I hope, for your sake...Oh!" She jumped back as the cook fell to the floor in a faint. "Oh, my goodness! Freda?" She bent down to touch her brow. It felt hot and clammy. "Oh, my goodness," she repeated. "What should I do? Somebody help!"

Nellie came rushing in. "What's the matter?"

"She said she felt hot and then...oh, thank God."

As Freda tried to sit up, the Major ran in, pushed Nellie out of the way, and shouted, "Did someone call 'help'? Major Duncan Ambrose Wallace at your service." Saluting, he pushed Freda back down onto the floor, listening to her chest.

Tillie tried to pull him away. "Major, please leave her alone." She and Nellie pulled at the veteran's coat, yelling at him to come away.

"No, I need to check her pulse." Shrugging them off, he grabbed the cook's hand.

Freda jumped up, knocking him over. "I'm fine, thank you, just leave me alone." Wiping her brow, she sat on a chair, trying to catch her breath.

David came hobbling in. "I could not stop him."

What a farce! Tillie looked at the tableau before her—David shouting at the Major to be quiet, prodding him as he lay curled up on the floor, muttering obscenities, Freda leaning her head on the table, moaning and clearly still unwell, and Nellie muttering to herself, trying to adjust her bonnet that had fallen off in the mêlée.

Then Jamie ran in, screaming.

"What now?" she yelled.

"I took the kitten outside to escape from the Major, and it scratched my arm." He lifted his shirt sleeve to show her a red weal.

"Is that all? I thought you were, at the very least, being murdered."

He then appeared to notice the situation before him. "Father, what're you doing to the Major?"

"Nothing for you to worry about, Jamie," his father answered. He turned to Tillie. "Isn't the doctor here yet?"

"Shall I go and see?" asked Jamie.

"Yes, thank you. That would be useful." *Anything to have him out of the way,* thought Tillie. She turned to her husband. "Stop poking the Major, he's quiet now."

David sat down. "Yes, he appears to be, for the time being, anyway. I think I could do with that cup of tea now."

Nellie hurried over and picked up the kettle. "Certainly, sir." She made the tea and put the pot on the table. "How are you feeling, Freda? You gave us all a shock."

Freda stood up. "A lot better, thank you. I don't

know what came over me."

"Well, take the rest of the day off." Tillie patted her arm. "It seems ages since you had a break."

"Thank you, ma'am, I'll do that."

Jamie returned. "Doctor Abrahams is here."

"At last. Show him in." Tillie turned to the cook. "Perhaps he should examine you as well."

"Oh, no, no, please, I'm fine. There's no need."

Chapter 4

Jamie lay tossing and turning, sleep eluding him. The following day he would be off into a new, unknown world and, now the time had come, he began to think maybe the reality would not live up to the dream. His mama had seemed tearful as she'd wished him good night after his bath. He sensed she still didn't want him to go. But it had been his decision, so he would have to go through with it. Pulling the sheet over his head, he prayed again that Nanny would be kind to Alice while he could not watch over her.

He awoke to his favourite of all birdsongs, the melodic voice of a blackbird singing outside his window. Pushing back the covers, he jumped out of bed and began to dress in his new clothes, ready for church. He hesitated. Maybe he ought to put on his old jacket, though, because he wanted to go out and say goodbye to all the animals and birds first and, also, Alice might put her sticky fingers on him. Keeping on the new trousers but taking off the shirt, he found an old one with a missing button.

"I expect Nellie will throw this away when I've gone," he muttered, pulling down the frayed cuffs. "I wonder if she'll miss me. She won't have so much washing to do." He grinned, remembering the muddy trousers he'd tried to hide once, when he'd fallen into a deep puddle and soaked his clothes.

Recognising Nanny's voice out on the landing, he hung back, waiting until she'd gone. He really couldn't face her, and hoped he wouldn't have to speak to her the rest of the day.

After her voice had faded away, he peeped out of the door to make sure the coast was clear, and made his way downstairs.

Maisie had caught the measles, leaving Freda to cope alone in the kitchen. "Sausages for your last breakfast before you go, Master Jamie?"

"Yes, please, Freda." He sat at the table. "Are you feeling better?"

The cook's round face looked redder than usual, but otherwise she seemed normal. She nodded. "It was just a funny turn, nothing to worry about."

"Did the Major scare you?"

"No, dear, although he didn't help." Placing a plate of sausages in front of him, she grimaced, rubbing her stomach.

Maybe she's pregnant, he thought. *Mama does that.* Tucking into his breakfast, he asked, "Can old ladies have babies?" It would be improper to ask her outright.

"Not usually, it depends how 'old' you mean. Why do you ask?"

Trying hard not to look at her belly, he mumbled, "Um…nothing."

He thought she said something else but didn't catch it. To change the subject, he said, "Poor old Major, he didn't want to go, did he? Do you think the doctor's arm's broken?"

"Probably."

"Those men what came were a bit rough with him." He looked up. "Mama says he'll have to stay in that place for the rest of his life, locked up for his own good."

Freda nodded, turning away, rubbing her belly again. *Yes, she most definitely is pregnant.*

Finishing his meal, he told Freda he intended going outside. As he stepped out the back door his cap nearly blew off. Pulling at his jacket, he hurried down past the lake, and into the woods, to his tree house standing there, as solid as ever. "S'pose I'll be too grown up to play in you again," he murmured as he climbed up the ladder. "But Alice can, when she's older." The blue tit hovered nearby, but instead of landing on the rail as it usually did, it flew off. "Bye-bye, Bluey," he called after it. He hoped he might catch sight of his squirrel but, after waiting several minutes, he gave up and picked up the cushion, ready to go back down. A piece of paper fluttered out from beneath it, drifting to the ground. Puzzled, he leaned over the rail to see what it could be. He didn't remember leaving a picture there. It looked like a portrait. After one last glance around the tree house, he climbed down. As he bent to pick up the paper, the wind caught it, and it blew behind some trees. Running after it, he thought he heard voices.

"Please, God, don't let it be Jake," he prayed, afraid he might have been released from gaol. Rounding a large oak, his mouth opened and his breath caught in his throat. Beth stood looking at the picture.

Her brother, Bobby, grabbed it from her. "This looks like you, our Beth."

Realisation dawned. Her portrait he'd drawn a while before. He'd been wondering where it had disappeared to. Snatching the paper, he turned and ran before they could see his red face.

Arriving home, he met his mama, coming downstairs. "What are you doing in those old clothes?" she asked. "It's time to go to church."

Too breathless to give an intelligible reply, he mumbled and ran upstairs to his bedroom. The creased portrait had ripped down one side. Trying to smooth it out, he changed his mind and screwed it up.

"What's the point in keeping it? I'll never see her again, anyway."

* * * *

After lunch the family assembled in the lounge. Time to say goodbye to Alice. He took her from Nanny without looking at his enemy, and hugged her, trying to be brave. "Bye-bye, my little sweetheart. Be a good girl."

She took her thumb out of her mouth. "Bye-bye, Jamie."

"She can say my name proper now, can't she, Mama?"

"Yes, darling." Even though his mother would be coming in the carriage, he could see her sniffing already.

He turned to his aunt, who had also come to see him off. "I wish you was looking after Alice, Auntie Ruby," he whispered into her hair as she hugged him. She didn't reply, merely hugged him even harder, and when he pulled away, he saw tears in her eyes, too.

"Come on, then, time to go." His father went out first. All the servants had assembled in the drive and, feeling grown up, Jamie shook hands with each one.

"Say goodbye to Maisie for me." He turned to Freda, looking up at her attic window with the curtains drawn. "I hope she'll be better soon."

Stroking Lady and Goldie once more, he gave Nanny the fiercest glare he could summon up, hoping it would warn her not to hurt his sister. He then climbed into the carriage after his parents, leaned out of the window as they pulled away, and waved madly until the house could no longer be seen.

Sitting back, he tried not to look at his mama, sniffing and dabbing her nose with her handkerchief. He felt guilty. She'd tried so hard to persuade his father not to send him to boarding school, but once he'd seen it, he'd become excited at the prospect of learning new things, and meeting lots of new friends. Now they were on their way, more doubts began to creep in.

"What about my clothes?" he asked. "We've forgot them."

His father sat opposite him. "Did you not notice the trunks strapped to the back of the carriage?"

He hadn't. He'd been too intent on etching everybody's faces into his memory, so he wouldn't forget them.

* * * *

A rough hand shook him awake. Jamie rubbed his eyes. "Come on, Dalton, time to arise."

Sitting bolt upright, he remembered. "Yes, sir."

"I'm not sir, and it's just as well, or you'd receive the birch for being late."

He jumped out of bed. Some of the other boys in the dormitory sat up, also rubbing their eyes, and stretching. Why hadn't he told them to hurry up?

He dressed quickly, just in case the older boy had been serious, and stood beside his bed, not knowing what to do next. A photograph of his parents and Alice stood on his bedside cabinet. He wished he was back home. Why had he thought this place would be exciting? He sighed, the memory of his mother, sobbing as she said farewell the previous evening, clear in his mind. Even his father had seemed reluctant to leave him, but maybe that had been his imagination giving him the wrong message. It had been his father's idea in the first place, so he shouldn't have had any regrets.

"Your bed…" hissed the boy next to him. "Make your bed, quickly."

Copying the other boys, he straightened the white cotton sheet, and covered it with the rough brown blanket.

The housemaster came in. "All line up beside your beds for inspection, and then you will go down to breakfast in an orderly fashion."

They lined up. "What's your name?" Jamie asked the boy at the next bed.

"Silence," roared the housemaster. "You have not

been given permission to speak."

Opening his eyes wide and grimacing, he followed the other boys downstairs into the refectory.

After saying grace—the same as they said at home—so he was able to recite it confidently, they all sat down.

"I hope we aren't fed gruel like Oliver Twist," his new friend said.

Jamie hadn't a clue what the boy meant. "Pardon?" Perhaps he'd not heard him correctly.

"Haven't you read it?"

"What?"

"'Oliver Twist' by Charles Dickens."

"Um, no, but I've heard of him. This porridge is good, isn't it?" Feeling rather ignorant, Jamie kept his head down, scooping the oats into his mouth. When he looked up, he saw several boys watching him. *Oh no, am I doing sommat wrong?* He sat up straight and put down his spoon.

One of the boys across from him muttered to his neighbour, and they both sniggered. Jamie wondered why, hoping they hadn't been talking about him. They still looked his way, though. Trying to ignore them, he turned to the boy beside him, but he had struck up a conversation about Charles Dickens with another boy, and Jamie didn't feel knowledgeable enough to join in. The boy on his left had his back to him, talking to the one across the table, so he sat with his hands in his lap, hoping the meal would soon end.

After breakfast they assembled in the hall, hundreds of boys, jostling and pushing each other, until the headmaster, Mister Trout, called them to order. Prayers said, they sang the school anthem, which, of course, Jamie didn't know but, not being the only one, he didn't feel too bothered. He spent the time examining the headmaster's face, trying to work out if his long, hooked nose made him look like his name, but decided that, because he had hardly any hair, he bore more resemblance to a bald eagle.

Mr Trout told the new ones to stay behind as the others filed out to their classrooms, and divided them into 'houses', Jamie being separated from his friend. He didn't even know his name, but thought he'd call him 'Dickens' until he did. He found himself being jostled again as they arranged themselves into their respective groups, raising their hands as their housemaster called out each name. How they could hear their names above the rabble, Jamie couldn't fathom. Feeling that his head would burst, just like when Sarah had been hurt in the park the first time he'd gone to Harrogate, when all the people had been shouting at him, he covered his ears, wishing the noise would stop.

He wondered why everyone had turned to look at him, until Mister Sumpton, the teacher who'd introduced himself earlier as head of year one, marched towards him, shouting, "Dalton?"

"Yes, sir, sorry, sir." Cringing as the other boys started laughing, he tried to run out of the hall but the master grabbed his arm.

"You are Dalton, aren't you?"

"Yes, sir," he repeated.

"Then why did you not answer when I called your name?"

"I…I didn't hear you, sir, because of all the noise. It hurt my ears." That brought a fresh burst of laughter.

"Silence!" Mister Sumpton yelled. The racket gradually faded. Giving Jamie a peculiar look, he kept hold of his arm, but more gently. He called over the tops of the boys' heads, "Please make a single file now everyone knows their house—silently, if you please—and make your way to the classrooms."

Letting go of Jamie's arm, he nudged him towards the back of the second line when he'd been about to join the first. He followed the other boys, not knowing to which classroom he should go. He must have missed that as well.

"Classroom three," the master whispered in his ear.

"Three?" he repeated.

The master nodded.

He tried to smile his thanks, but his mouth wouldn't move. Entering the rowdy classroom, it seemed full to bursting. The teacher pointed to the end of the long desk at the front, so he squeezed in as the other boys shuffled along. The din deafened him once more, until Mister Sumpton shouted for quiet.

The first lesson passed uneventfully, much to Jamie's relief. The new exercise books smelled divine as he opened them, and he inhaled deeply of each one as they were given out, until he saw the boy next to him give him a funny look. *I don't care!* he thought. *I'll sniff them if I want.*

The following day they had a science lesson. Jamie thought it would have been very interesting if he'd been able to understand it, although knowing about atoms helped. He sat looking out the window, trying to work out the answer to a question the master had just given them. A jackdaw, its grey neck and black plumage glinting in the sun, strutted up and down on the grass outside, pecking at the ground, then it looked up, right at him.

Pain seared through him when he felt his knuckles being whacked by a cane. "Ouch", he yelled, jumping up as a red mark appeared on the back of his hand.

"That's for not paying attention, boy," sneered the master whose name he couldn't remember. "Sit down and write your answer."

Obeying, he heard giggling behind him, but he rubbed his hand, trying to ignore it. The boy next to him gave him a sympathetic glance, and then carried on with his work. Jamie racked his brain for the answer and tried to look at his companion's book, but he pulled it away and shielded it with his arm so, although not confident, he wrote down what he hoped would be the correct one. The rest of the lesson consisted of copying work the master wrote on the blackboard so, even though his hand stung, he could do that.

He wondered why he hadn't seen Sebastian, the boy who lived near him. He'd been to his house to a few times, and he had said he would be coming back to school but, being older, he wouldn't be in the same class, probably in a different house as well, so they wouldn't mix. It would have been nice to have a friend, though.

Lying in bed that night, exhausted but unable to sleep, he wondered what the rest of his family would be doing at home. He offered up a prayer for each member, putting extra emphasis on Alice—that Nanny wouldn't hurt her. Not there to protect her, he imagined all sorts of horrible tricks the witch might play on his little sister, and fell asleep dreaming of large blackbirds with Nanny's face, flying around, plucking hairs from her little golden head.

"Amo, amas, amat," he joined in with the chanting in the one lesson he enjoyed that did not involve sport.

"What does that mean?" asked the Latin master.

Jamie's hand shot up. At last, something he knew. His father had been teaching him the basics of the language over the past few weeks. Disappointed when the master chose another boy to give the answer, he whispered to his neighbour, "I knew that."

"You, boy, what's your name?"

Dismayed to see the master pointing at him, he turned to see if anybody else would reply.

"Yes, you." The teacher strode over and jabbed his cane in Jamie's chest.

"Jamie," he croaked. Titters behind him made him look up. "I mean…Dalton, sir."

"And do you have something you wish to share with us?"

"No, sir."

"Then what were you whispering about just then?"

"I was just saying that I knew the answer...sir."

"Then you had better come out to the front of the class and recite the whole conjugation."

Warily, he stood up as the class went quiet. *I bet they think I'll say it wrong,* he thought, but he recited it perfectly.

"Sit down," ordered the master, looking as if he would have preferred Jamie to have made a mistake.

Going back to his seat, he grinned at the boy next to him, who smiled back. Maybe he would have a friend, after all.

* * * *

Playing marbles a few days later—rain meant they could not go outside—he became aware of an older boy with bright ginger hair watching him. The attention put him off, and he cursed under his breath when he missed his opponent's marble, a magnificent green and yellow one, much more splendid than any of his. He would have loved to own it. The older boy murmured something, but Jamie couldn't quite catch what he said above the din, so he turned to face him.

"I need another fag," said the other boy.

His father had warned him about fagging. He tried to look uninterested as the older boy pulled his ear forward, looking behind it, just like Auntie Ruby used to, before pulling down his chin and looking in his mouth. "What's your name?"

"Jamie Dalton, shir." He found it rather difficult to speak with his mouth open and head tilted back.

"You don't have to call me 'sir' but you may do. My name is Hugh Fenner. Do you have any fag masters?"

Jamie shook his head.

"Good. Come to my room later, and you can start

by blacking my shoes."

His shoes looked black enough already.

"In fact, you may as well come with me now, so I can show you where it is," Fenner continued, his bulging, green eyes staring like a frog's.

Jamie wanted to finish his game first, but thought better of it, and bent down to pick up his marble. His opponent knocked his hand away, saying, "You can't have it back."

"It's mine."

"Well, I've just…"

Jamie couldn't hear the end of the sentence.

"You've what?"

"Are you deaf? I've WON IT."

"But…" He only had two others, and if he lost them, he wouldn't be able to play again. The boy pushed him away, so he had no option but to leave it and follow Fenner, still seething from losing his favourite marble. It might not have been as bright as the one he'd been trying to win, but it had been next best.

Fenner stopped to open a door, and Jamie almost ran into him. He realised they had reached a part of the building he hadn't entered before. The bell rang for the first afternoon lesson. Hugh turned. "Come back this evening. Go to your classroom now."

Jamie hadn't been paying attention to his route. He hadn't the faintest idea how to find his way back, but Fenner had disappeared into the room and closed the door behind him. *It shouldn't be too hard*, he told himself, walking back along the corridor until, arriving at a junction, he began to worry. Right or left? Looking both ways, drumming his fingernails against his teeth, he scanned the pictures on the walls to see if any looked familiar. One showed a man with a ginger beard and moustache, just like the Major.

"That must be a sign," he muttered, so went right.

Fortunately, the corridor led to an area he recognised, and he soon found his classroom.

"Thank you, Major," he whispered. "I'll know which way to go in future." Hoping he wouldn't be too late—the corridors looked deserted, so he assumed the other boys must already be inside—he opened the door.

He'd never seen the master before and, for a moment, thought he'd gone into the wrong classroom, but then he recognised the boy he'd sat next to earlier. He walked in and closed the door behind him.

"Who are you, boy?"

"Dalton, sir." He remembered to say it right.

"Why are you late?"

"I couldn't find my way." The other boys laughed. Jamie felt like putting out his tongue at them but knew it would only cause trouble.

"Sit down."

He squeezed in again, noticing that all the others had a new exercise book. He put up his hand, but the master had his back to the class, writing sums on the board.

"Please, sir?"

The master turned, his face full of fury. "Who dares interrupt me?"

"Sorry, sir, but I don't have a book," Jamie squeaked.

"You should have been on time." The master reached across to his desk, picked up a book and threw it at Jamie. It landed on the floor a few feet short, so he had to leave his seat to pick it up. Trying not to look at the sniggering classmates behind him, he sat down and tried to smooth out one of the corners that had curled up.

He found the sums easy enough, similar to the ones he'd been learning from Miss Hetherington and wished he could be back at home with her as his teacher. Chewing the end of his pencil, he looked out of the window, imagining himself running around the lawn with

Lady and Goldie, instead of being cooped up in the classroom.

* * * *

Tillie sat watching the dogs playing outside. She could tell they also missed Jamie. Earlier on, she and Alice had taken them for a walk down to the lake, to give them some exercise. They'd been rather neglected since Jamie had left.

She put down her sewing, not feeling in the mood for it. In fact, she didn't feel like doing much at all lately since Jamie had gone. She counted the weeks until he would be back home. Too many. Part of her felt missing, like David must have felt when he lost the lower half of his leg.

Sighing, she stood up and walked over to the piano. David had been teaching her how to play. Lifting the lid, she sat down on the stool and put her fingers on the keys. Maybe she could make something up instead of doing the usual scales and boring things. She plinked and plonked for a while, enjoying herself, finding it soothing.

Nellie came in, looking surprised. "I wondered who was playing. The master has just gone out, so I knew it couldn't be him."

"It's only me making a racket."

The housekeeper came further into the room. "No, no, it made a beautiful sound. Where did you learn it?"

Tillie put her hands in her lap. "I just made it up."

"Oh, my goodness, I didn't know you were so talented."

"Well, I wouldn't call it that." With a smile, she stood up. "But I found it very pleasurable."

"It's good to see you smile for a change." Nellie put her hand on her mistress's arm. "I know you miss him. We all do."

School for Jamie

Tillie shrugged, rubbing her belly. "But I have to accustom myself to it."

* * * *

Jamie tied the laces on his football boots, eagerly anticipating his favourite lesson—sport. He pulled down his red shirt, so much softer than the grey ones they wore for classes.

The captain threw him the ball to carry, and he marched out, his head high. He still didn't understand the rules completely, but he hadn't been the only one who had to be reminded to move to a different spot when he'd run into the wrong area.

He looked up at the overcast sky as it began to drizzle. "I hope it won't be cancelled," he said to the boy running beside him.

"Me, too," the boy answered.

"Is football your favourite?"

The boy nodded.

Towards the end of the game, Jamie had possession of the ball and, as he lifted his foot to kick it towards the goal, someone tripped him. Jumping up, he turned to see who had fouled him—a boy who always picked on him for no reason, rarely being reprimanded. Seething inside, he looked at the referee, who shook his finger at him.

"He was the one in the wrong," he wanted to shout, but the game had restarted. *I'll let it go this time, but try again and you won't escape so lightly.*

On their way back, rain dripped off his hair and down his face, so he could hardly see his way. Someone pushed him in the back and he almost fell. Swivelling round, he saw the bully from earlier. He wiped the rain from his eyes and squared up to the taller boy. "What did you do that for?"

"I must have lost my footing."

Unsure whether to believe him or not, Jamie walked on. Everyone slipped and slid on the muddy field, so it might have been true. Receiving another nudge in the shoulder, he decided this one must be deliberate. He elbowed the boy, causing him to fall flat on his face in the mud.

"Oh, sorry," he called, hurrying away. "I must have lost my footing."

Once inside, he washed off as much mud as possible and changed into his uniform. The bell rang and he made his escape.

He didn't see the bully again until supper. His cronies surrounded him, so he took no notice of Jamie.

On the last morning of term, after prayers, the whole school sat in the hall, facing the headmaster and the other teachers up on the stage.

A hush descended on the hall as Mister Trout stood up to call out their marks, class by class. "Year one: third place goes to…" Jamie knew he wouldn't be awarded any prizes and couldn't care less who had done well in what. Then he heard, "And first prize goes to Silas Brown." *Oh no, it would be him, wouldn't it?* His arch enemy on the football field. Everyone else clapped as Silas went up onto the stage for his prize. Being on the end of the row, Jamie could have put out his leg and tripped him up on his way back, but thought better of it. The bully didn't give him a second glance as he strode back to his seat, his head in the air. His cronies congratulated him as he sat down.

Jamie just wanted the morning to finish so he could return home. Alice would be waiting for him, and Maisie. He knew she'd recovered. His mama had told him in the second letter he'd received.

At last, time to sing the school song. They had been taught the words, so Jamie sang out with confidence.

Filing out of the hall, he could feel eyes boring into his back, and sensed Silas behind him. He would not acknowledge the bully. It would only spoil his pleasure at going home. He thought he heard something about 'the little runt'. They couldn't be talking about him. Admittedly, he might have been one of the smallest in the class, but Anthony Robins had a calliper on his leg, making him at least an inch shorter. The word 'runt' caused gooseflesh to tingle up his arms. George had used to call him that. He hurried away. He didn't want to think about his dead cousin either.

Finally, he climbed into the train carriage that would take him home, along with Sebastian and two older boys. He didn't have to worry about his trunk, for it had been sent separately. Looking out of the window, wishing away the miles, he couldn't wait to reach home.

Chapter 5

The train pulled into the station. "Oo, I can't wait," Jamie squealed, jumping up and down as Sebastian reached out of the window and opened the door.

Jamie scanned the platform to see if either of his parents had come to meet him, but didn't recognise any of the people craning their necks for glimpses of their loved ones.

"Come on, Jamie, what are you waiting for?" called Sebastian. "You're coming in our carriage."

"I know, I just hoped…" He'd been told in his last letter from home that Sebastian's groom would pick him up, but hoped there might have been a change of plan. Clearly not. He dragged his feet out of the station, still searching the faces of all those around him, just in case.

It didn't take long to travel the few miles, and he soon overcame his disappointment. With renewed excitement, he gazed at the familiar green fields and the purple heather-covered hills, the doors of the scattered cottages where people often sat outside closed because of the cold. He pictured the occupants sitting round their warm fires in their cosy rooms.

Looking up, he gasped. "Look, Sebastian, up there. It's my buzzard." The carriage rocked as he forced his upper body out of the window.

"Sit still, or we'll be thrown out." His friend half-heartedly looked out the other side, but just muttered, "Oh."

"Don't you think they're magnificent?"

Sebastian shrugged.

"Aren't you glad to be going home, to leave that horrible school?"

"S'pose so."

Jamie frowned at him. How could he not be happy?

"But..."

"It looks like Papa and Mama have been fighting again. That's why I ran away from school last time. I wanted to go home, to make them see sense."

Jamie didn't know what to say. Once, when he'd asked Nellie about his parents having 'words', as she called it, she'd told him all parents argued at times. They all had their own opinions and couldn't agree all the time. He wondered whether to say that to his friend, but they were pulling into the drive. He craned his neck to see who would be waiting to greet him. Nobody.

They pulled up outside the front door. Jamie waited, expecting someone to come out.

"Aren't you alighting?" asked Sebastian.

"Do they know I'm coming home today?" Jamie stood up slowly.

"Of course." Jamie thought he heard him call him 'little man' but he had his back to him. It seemed an odd thing to say, but then Sebastian would be fourteen, nearly fifteen, so perhaps...

The front door opened as he stepped down, and Purvis, good old Purvis, hurried out to help him.

"Master Jamie," he exclaimed, reaching forward to shake his hand. Jamie looked for anybody else coming out. Nanny appeared at the door, looking more like a witch than ever, holding Alice, so pretty in a new blue dress he hadn't seen her wearing before. His little sister wriggled to be put down, then ran to him, squealing, "Jamie, Jamie."

"Are you pleased to see me?" He picked her up, inhaling the fresh babyish smell of her clothes and hair. Then he checked her earlobes to make sure they didn't look sore. They seemed fine, soft and pink. Kissing her cheek, he noticed the carriage turning and pulling away. He waved to Sebastian. "I hope you have a happy Christmas," he called, thinking that if his parents kept arguing, he probably wouldn't.

Once inside he asked Nanny, not bothering with niceties, for she didn't deserve any, "Where's Mama?"

"Bed," said Alice before she could reply. "Mama in bed."

"Oh, is she poorly?" He lowered his sister to the floor, his brow creasing.

"Yes, Mama poorly."

Nellie came hurrying into the hall. "Master Jamie, let me look at you." She held him at arm's length. "I do believe you've grown."

"Me grown." Alice took out her thumb, stretched out her arms to make herself look big, then put the thumb back in her mouth.

How good it felt to be back with his family, even if his mama lay in bed, too ill to meet him.

One important person hadn't appeared, though. "Where's Father?"

"He's out on business." Nellie straightened his cap. "He hoped he'd be back before you arrived, but it must have taken longer than he anticipated."

"And is Maisie really better?"

"Yes, come and see for yourself."

"I'll take Alice up to the nursery for her tea," said Nanny, as Jamie and Nellie went towards the kitchen.

"Bye-bye, Alice, see you later on," he called.

Maisie ran to him as soon as he entered. They both hesitated, their arms held out, unsure if they should hug each other. They looked at Freda. She nodded.

"What's it like at school? What do you have to do?" Maisie bombarded him with questions once they pulled apart.

"Let the lad catch his breath, my girl," said Freda, smiling.

Jamie looked at her belly. Did it look any rounder than when he'd left? Not really. Could she be pregnant?

School for Jamie

He knew Tom Briggs, the gamekeeper, came frequently for a cup of tea and some cake. He could be the father. She rubbed it, a look of pain crossing her face.

He heard a loud clanging as Maisie dropped a spoon on the floor, diverting his attention away from the cook. When he turned back, with a smile on her face once more, Freda declared, "We've cooked your favourite dinner tonight, Master Jamie."

"Oh, thanks." He didn't know he had a favourite and wondered what it could be. "Will Mama be coming down?"

Freda resumed chopping up some apples. "Why don't you go up and ask her? She's...never mind. She'd love to see you."

"Oh, may I?" Not waiting for a reply, he ran out, rushed up the stairs two at a time and knocked on her door.

"Come in," a faint voice called from inside. He didn't need any further bidding. He opened the door and hesitated, shocked at his mother's pale face.

"Oh, Jamie, come here. It's so good to see you." She reached out her arms and he flew into them. "I've missed you so much."

"I've missed you, too, Mama."

She began to cry.

"Please don't cry, Mama, I'm here now."

Reaching under her pillow, she pulled out a handkerchief and blew her nose. "I'm sorry, darling. I'm just so happy."

Relieved when she stopped, he thought it seemed odd that someone should weep when happy.

"Have you seen your father yet?" She dabbed her eyes with her handkerchief.

"No, he's out on business, but Nellie said he should be back soon." He wanted to ask what ailed her, but knew it would be impolite.

She hugged him again, sniffing in his ear. "You'll have to tell us all about school tomorrow, when I'm feeling a little better."

A knock on the door, and his father appeared, out of breath and red in the face.

"Papa!" Jamie rushed over to him, almost knocking him over.

"Let me look at you." His father tried to balance by holding Jamie's shoulder with his free hand. "You have grown."

"That's what Nellie said."

"Come and sit down, David, before you fall," his mama croaked. "We can't be doing with any more accidents."

She slumped back onto her pillows, her face as white as a ghost. Jamie helped his father into the armchair, and sat on the edge of her bed, stroking her hand.

"Don't look so worried, darling." Her lips smiled, but not her eyes. "I'll perk up no end, now you're home."

Is it my fault she's ill? Jamie studied her face. He could see more wrinkly lines at the side of her eyes than before. He would talk to his father later about not going back to school. He couldn't bear the thought of her being ill because he'd left her. He reached across and gave her another cuddle.

"Let us leave your mother to rest, Jamie," suggested his father, trying to climb out of the chair. "You can come back later."

Jamie stood up, kissed her hand and helped his father out of the room and across the landing. "She seems really poorly."

"It came on a few days ago, but as she said, she will feel better now you are home."

His father had become adept at resting one crutch on the stair below, hanging onto the banister rail with his free hand, and then almost hopping down to it. They went into the lounge and sat down. Betsy followed them in, her face beaming as usual. "Would you like some tea, sirs?" she asked, her voice seeming even higher than Jamie remembered.

"Jamie?" his father looked at him with raised eyebrows. "Do you drink tea now?"

"Yes, please, Betsy. I would *love* a cup of tea." How good it felt to be important again, instead of being the underling, kowtowing to everybody's wishes. He'd heard one of the older boys use his new word and had added it to his list.

* * * *

A few days later Tillie felt well enough to leave her bed. Looking at her swollen belly in the mirror, she wondered how David could even contemplate being around her, for she resembled a large whale or a sea lion.

She gave the bump a pat. "Surely I wasn't as big as this when I was expecting the twins. I do hope there's only one of you in there." She pulled on her new pink dress. David had told her they could dispense with mourning garb on the approach to Christmas. The seamstress had brought the frock the previous week, but Tillie had been too ill to wear it.

"I'd better not put on much more weight, or I won't be able to wear you very long." She fastened the lower buttons but, unable to reach the ones at the top, she twisted and swivelled, trying to reach them.

David walked in and kissed her. "Hello, darling, it's good to see you out of bed."

"Ah, just in time, could you please fasten my buttons?"

"Sit down, then. I can't do it one-handed."

She sat on the stool as he pulled a chair across and sat behind her. He looked up, and their eyes met in the mirror. Their gaze held for a moment, and he leaned forward to kiss her neck, his hands reaching round to caress her breasts. She leaned her head back, revelling in the pleasure of his touch. "Why didn't you come in before I put this wretched dress on?" she murmured.

"Take it off."

She laughed. "It's taken so long to put on, I don't think I'd have the energy."

Giving her one last kiss, he pulled away. "I keep telling you, you should have a lady's maid. Why do you insist on doing everything yourself?"

"Oh, I don't know." She shrugged. "Pride, I suppose."

"Well, put your damned pride away and let me find you one. You are doing yourself no favours remaining stubborn."

"Very well, then, after Christmas."

He shook his head indulgently as she picked up her brush.

"It's so good to have Jamie home, isn't it?" she asked.

Taking the brush from her, he ran it gently through her long curls. "Yes, I have to admit, I agree. I had not realised how much I missed him until he came home, if that makes any sense."

"Um, not really, I missed him every second." Closing her eyes, she leaned back, enjoying the rhythmic strokes, until he caught a tangle. "Ouch!"

"Sorry." He kissed her neck.

"What's Jamie doing?"

"He went to the woods with Tom and Sam to chop down a tree to decorate, and to find some greenery."

"Oh, good, he's been looking forward to that. We'll make this Christmas really special. After the year we've had, we deserve a little happiness, don't you think?"

He put down the brush. "Yes, we do." He kissed her

neck again and pushed himself up. "And I hope having Annie and Sarah here won't spoil it."

"Oh, yes, I'd forgotten they were coming. Well, Sarah's presence will be very welcome, especially to Jamie, but Annie's…"

Standing up, after putting up her auburn hair in a bun, she straightened her dress and added her pinafore. "Is it tomorrow they arrive?"

"No, the following day, and Victor will join them on Christmas Eve."

"Will I do?" she asked, holding out her hands to the sides. "It seems peculiar not wearing black."

"You look blooming, my darling, absolutely lovely."

"Why, thank you, fair sir." She blushed at the unusual compliment. "You don't look so bad yourself."

He smiled and kissed her hand, then reached across and kissed her lips as well. "Are you sure you do not want to take off that dress?" he moaned.

"Oh, David…I promise I'll…tonight. I'll come to bed early and be ready for you."

"I suppose that will have to suffice. Stay awake, though. Last time you promised that, you were snoring your head off by the time I came up, and I could not wake you."

"You poor dear. I shall take a nap this afternoon so I won't be tired tonight."

"Please do. You wouldn't want me looking elsewhere for my pleasures, would you?"

Stunned, she couldn't think of a reply. Would he really be that desperate?

The shock must have registered on her face for he took her hand. "I did not mean it. I jested. Of course, I would not do anything like that. I would never hurt you. You are my world." His eyebrows lifted. "Although I have heard tell that Christine Wilson has come back into the area."

"Who?" Still recoiling from his statement, even if he hadn't been serious, the expression 'There's no smoke without fire' came to mind.

"It does not matter, come on, let us go downstairs. I have a pile of work to do before lunch."

She followed him down, wondering whether she should have changed her mind, and offered to take off her dress after all, or even suggested they made love fully clothed. Her head in a whirl, she almost ran into the back of him when he stopped.

"Whoa, careful," he cried. "You almost knocked me down."

"I'm sorry." She shook herself. "Let me help you."

"No, it is easier if I do it myself."

"David?"

"Yes?"

"Did you really mean it when you said you were jesting before?"

"Of course I did." He looked back to reassure her and, missing his footing, fell down the last two steps, landing awkwardly at the bottom.

"David!" she shrieked as Purvis came hurrying into the hall. Her heart seemed to stop. Racing down the remaining stairs, she knelt beside him. "Are you hurt?" She felt sure she'd heard a cracking noise. He didn't reply for a moment, or move. "I'm so sorry, my darling, I shouldn't have distracted you. Please wake up."

"I am awake," he muttered, opening his eyes.

"Oh, thank God." She turned to the butler, bending over his master. "Please, Purvis, make sure he's all right."

David stirred and Tillie pressed her hand to his forehead. He pushed it away. "Stop fussing. I only fell two steps."

"I know, but…are you sure you're not hurt? What about your legs?"

Nellie came into the hall, carrying a pile of laundry.

She almost dropped it when she saw the trio at the base of the stairs. "Oh, my goodness!" She rushed over.

"Oh, Nellie, the master fell downstairs."

The housekeeper's usual austere face looked ashen as she dumped the sheets on a chair and helped David sit up.

"Please do not exaggerate, Tillie. I fell down *two* steps." He pulled his trouser leg down.

"I knew something like this would happen," Nellie retorted. "I warned you, but you wouldn't listen."

"Will you all please stop," he shouted, making Tillie jump away. "I am perfectly fine."

"I'll go and find John." Nellie hurried away, muttering, "I just knew it."

Flapping her hands didn't help, so Tillie put them behind her back, desperate to help but fearful her efforts would be rejected. Purvis made the master comfortable, as John ran in.

"Just help me up, John. I do not have the time to be sitting here idling." David tried to make light of the situation, but Tillie could tell by his pursed mouth and furrowed brow that he wasn't as unscathed as he tried to make out.

Pulling at her lips as the valet and the butler stood him up, she winced as a groan escaped him.

"You *are* hurt, aren't you? Is it your leg?" She couldn't keep quiet or stand back any longer. She put out her hand.

David ignored it, flexing his shoulder, and bringing his arm up and round. "No, my legs are fine, what is left of them. It is only a twinge, it will pass." He turned to John. "Please, assist me to my study. I'll be fine once I sit in my chair. Now, where are my crutches?"

Tillie could see one over by the far wall. She picked it up and looked around for the other. It lay behind David, almost broken in two. She let out her breath in relief as she realised that must have been the crack she had heard.

Thinking she could hear Jamie's voice in the kitchen, she passed the crutches to John and hurried to stop him from coming out. Hopefully, David had not sustained any injury, and she didn't want her son to worry needlessly.

From the state of his torn jacket and filthy trousers, Jamie would not be able to wear those clothes again, and had he lost his cap? His red face beamed with delight, though.

"Phwah, it's cold out there, Mama." He took off his grubby gloves and rubbed his hands together. "That was *bene*, collecting all that holly and stuff."

"*Bene?*"

"It means 'good' in Latin." He looked smug, his nose in the air.

"Oh, you're learning lots of new things, then?"

"Yes, do you want me to tell you about them?"

"Well, darling, not at the moment." At his look of disappointment, she added, "Maybe later. Now run along and change into some clean clothes." David should, by that time, be safely ensconced in his study, so Jamie wouldn't see him.

"When will we be able to put up the greenery?" he asked, going out of the door.

"Well, I thought we would wait until Sarah comes, and then she can help."

"Oh, yes, that's a good idea."

He seemed to have changed somehow since he'd been away. He wasn't her little boy any longer. She felt weak and sat down. Freda looked up from chopping carrots. *She doesn't look well either,* thought Tillie, studying her grey face. A spasm seemed to shoot through the cook, and she clutched her belly. "Are you well, Freda?" she asked, forgetting her own malady.

"Yes, thank you, it's just a bit of tummy trouble."

"I could call the doctor."

"Oh, no, ma'am, there's no need for that."

"Well, you take it easy, let Maisie do all the heavy work. We don't want a repeat of your fainting episode."

Freda set to once more. Worried about her, Tillie did not know what else she could do if the cook insisted.

"Did we discuss tonight's dinner menu? I really don't remember."

"Well, no, the master said you were too poorly, so I took it on myself. I thought chicken fricassee with carrots and runner beans?"

"That sounds lovely."

Maisie came in from the garden, carrying a basket full of vegetables. She curtsied, a look of surprise on her face at seeing her mistress. Some of the carrots dropped out. Tillie jumped up to pick them up but a wave of dizziness overcame her and she almost fell. The baby inside her woke up at that moment and decided to do his exercises, poking an elbow or a knee right into her ribs.

"Oo," she murmured, rubbing her belly, trying to move him as she sat back down. "Junior's very active today. Perhaps I'd better go and have a rest." It seemed as if she'd only just left her bed, but the thought of a lie-down sounded very welcome.

"Shall I send Betsy in with a cup of tea?" Freda asked.

Tillie nodded as she stood up again. "That would be very welcome, thank you."

"Lunch will be ready in an hour."

She hadn't even had any breakfast. Probably why she felt so peculiar. She went into the lounge and lay down on the sofa, falling asleep almost straight away.

* * * *

Jamie sorted through the greenery, eager to decorate

the walls. Tom had told him the glut of red berries on the holly meant they would be in for a cold winter, for Mother Nature made sure there would be enough food for the birds. There hadn't been any snow yet, but it seemed cold enough.

Wouldn't it be bene to look out of the window at the white landscape while I open my presents on Christmas Day? Maybe there will be so much snow I won't be able to go back to school. That would be even bene-er.

Wanting to make a start, he went in search of Nellie and found her in one of the side rooms, making a wreath.

"Please may I help?" he asked. She allowed him to put some sprigs of holly and a few pine cones into it, and when they'd finished, he hung it on the front door.

"Doesn't that look good?" he called to a blackbird watching him from a branch. "But not good enough to eat, I hope." He didn't want their efforts spoiled by the bird eating the berries. "You go and find some down there." He pointed down the garden to where several holly bushes grew. Of course, the blackbird didn't understand, but it flew away, anyway.

He wondered what time Sarah and her mother would arrive. He wandered around the garden for a while, but soon began to shiver. *Please, God, don't let it snow today*, he prayed, looking heavenwards to check there weren't any snow-filled clouds looming, *at least 'til they're here.*

He went back inside, his hands in his pockets. He should have put on his coat and scarf and even his gloves. *Shall I go and find them? No, I don't feel like going back out.*

The nanny came downstairs as he entered the hall. He'd managed to stay out of her way most of the time since he'd arrived. *She's seen me, damn, I should've hid.* Surprised at himself for swearing, even though only in his mind, he hurried across the hall, hoping she wouldn't be able to tell. Her beady brown eyes seemed to know everything. Trying not to look at her, he slipped into the first room he came to, the library. Good, he'd be able to spend lots of time hidden away in there. A rustling noise in the corner caught his attention. There didn't appear to be anybody in the room, so what could it be? Creeping over to investigate, he saw a little mouse scurrying along the skirting board. Before he could stop it, a black blur bounded out of nowhere and grabbed it, running over to the door.

"Drop it, Susie," he yelled. Finding the door closed, she crawled beneath the large armchair. Dropping to the floor to find her, he could see she had already killed it. "Naughty Susie," he moaned. "I don't love you anymore."

The kitten, now almost grown up, didn't seem to have suffered any lasting damage from being stuffed down the Major's jacket. "I'm going to tell Mama on you. She'll turn you outside and make you live in the barn with the other cats."

She seemed to understand, for she crawled out and dropped the remains of the mouse at his feet, looking up at him with sorry eyes. He picked her up and stroked her. She purred, wrapping herself around his neck, her soft fur tickling his cheek. "All right, then, I won't tell Mama, but you mustn't do it again."

Hearing a commotion in the hall, he dropped the cat and ran out. Sarah and Auntie Annie had arrived. Although annoyed that he hadn't been there to greet them, happiness flooded through him at seeing his cousin. He couldn't say the same about his aunt. He hesitated, unsure if he should hug Sarah, being grown up and attending boarding school, but she solved the problem by rushing across and hugging him.

"Have you had a good journey?" he asked, knowing questions like that should be used.

"It was not bad—" she began but her mother butted in.

"Not bad! It was atrocious. The service at the inn we stopped at was appalling and…" Jamie turned away so she wouldn't see him smiling at Sarah's raised eyebrows and pursed lips.

"Never mind, you're here now," interrupted his father, ushering her into the lounge.

"Did you see the wreath on the front door?" Jamie whispered to Sarah as they all followed.

He thought she said, "It's lovely," so continued, "I made it, well, I helped Nellie. She said we can make some more later, that is, if you want to?"

"Oh, yes, I'd love to."

He heard that all right. *Thank goodness, I've suggested something right for a change.* He hoped he hadn't spoken aloud, but she smiled, and not the sort of smile that would have followed if he had.

"And where is your delightful wife?" Aunt Annie asked as his father poured her a glass of brandy.

"She is resting. I'm sure she will be down very soon."

"Is she unwell?"

"She is having a few problems, you know…with the baby. Nothing serious."

"Well, I suppose if one allows oneself to become pregnant so often, problems will occur." She raised her glass to her lips. "I don't know why you couldn't have been content with the ones you already have, especially after losing the last one."

His father opened his mouth as if to speak and then closed it again.

"Mother, why do you have to be so rude?" Sarah intervened.

"Me, rude? I'm only saying what most people think."

"I'm sure they don't think that, Uncle David. Please excuse my mother."

His father seemed to have recovered. "It is fine,

Sarah. I ought to be used to my sister by now."

Jamie and Sarah spent the remainder of the afternoon decorating the Christmas tree with little presents, sweets, handmade baubles, and candles to light on Christmas Day, then they finished it off with a bright star on the top.

His mama appeared in time for dinner, looking very pale. Jamie thought about what Aunt Annie had said about babies. How could they control how many they had? He had a vague idea how they arrived in the mother's belly, having seen animals mating. But people? Surely not, his father wouldn't…? Animals bent over on all fours, so what about his leg? How would he balance?

He realised Sarah had spoken to him. "I beg your pardon?" He dragged his gaze from his mama's round figure to look at his cousin.

"I asked how you enjoyed school."

He pulled a face but, noticing his parents had stopped their conversation to hear his reply, he answered, "It's…" How could he describe it without revealing that he hated it? "It's rather noisy."

"What else would you expect with hundreds of boys?" said Aunt Annie. He never had any problem hearing her. It dawned on him that he did have a problem. He hadn't really considered it as such until then, but perhaps he ought to mention it to…whom? Not his mama in her poorly state. He couldn't bother his father. Nanny? No, she would only find some way of using it against him.

"But you are happy there, Jamie, aren't you?" He strained his ears to hear his mama. She looked so sad and wan he couldn't tell her the truth.

"I'm becoming used to it." He tried to smile to show he meant it. "We play football and learn Latin."

"Amo, amas, amat," his father recited. "I loved

Latin, all that conjugating."

Jamie tried to picture his father sitting in a classroom full of boys, reciting their verbs. He couldn't quite do it.

"But what good has it done you, David? Tell me that." Aunt Annie shovelled another spoonful of apricot charlotte into her mouth. Jamie watched her jaw moving up and down as she ate. She picked up another spoonful and some dropped into the low neckline of her yellow dress. Covering his mouth with his serviette, Jamie tried not to titter. He could feel Sarah shaking beside him.

"Mother!" she retorted.

Reaching into her bosom, Aunt Annie pulled out the pudding and stuffed it into her mouth. "We can't let it go to waste."

Jamie could not stop giggling, even though he could see his father shaking his head and glaring at him. Each time he tried, he pictured his aunt's hand delving into her bodice, and laughed all the more. Sarah kept digging him in the side and kicking him, but she chuckled just as much.

His father put down his serviette and tried to stand. "Enough!" he bawled, clinging onto the edge of the table.

Jamie made a concerted effort. He had to stop. He couldn't risk his father falling over. Covering his mouth with his hand, he pulled his chin down and squeezed his lips together. He daren't look at Sarah or his aunt. Out of the corner of his eye he could see her still eating as Betsy came in to take away the dirty plates. Everyone apart from his aunt sat with their hands in their laps, waiting for her to finish.

"Is there any more? That was delicious," she asked the maid. Jamie could feel hysteria bubbling up inside him once more, and had to bite his lip hard to stop himself bursting out laughing again.

"Um…" Betsy looked up, clearly at a loss. Nobody ever asked for more.

"No, Annie," snapped his father, "unless you expect Freda to cook another one."

"Oh, no, no." She dabbed her mouth and put down her serviette. "I wouldn't want to put anybody to any trouble."

His father's eyebrows raised a fraction. "Thank goodness for that. We would have been here all night."

"Now, now, David, there's no need to be like that."

Still gritting his teeth, Jamie watched his aunt eyeing up a morsel of dessert that Sarah had left. Her spoon snaked out and picked it up, putting it into her mouth with one fluent movement, reminding him of an adder he'd once seen. Her eyes narrowed into slits when she saw him looking at her, and she glared, defying him to say anything.

His mama stood up, creating a diversion. "If it isn't too impolite of me, I think I'll retire for the night. I'm sorry." Her face squeezed as if in pain, and she clutched her belly.

"I shall just have to read my book then, if you are too ill to grace us with your presence." Aunt Annie's mouth turned down. She looked very hard done by.

"I'm sorry," his mama repeated, walking out of the room, her head bowed. Seeing his father watching her with concern, Jamie, now fully composed, wanted to go after her and give her a cuddle, but decided he'd better stay put.

"Would Sarah play the piano for us?" his father suggested. "I always love to hear her."

"What a splendid idea." Her mother seemed to perk up. "Come on, we could do with some entertainment. This house is like a morgue."

"I am really sorry if you are put out by my wife being poorly, Annie, but you will just have to bear it. In fact, while you adjourn to the music room, and Sarah finds her music, I shall go and check that she is settled."

He stormed out, the clonk of his crutches echoing around the room. Pulling a face, she followed him.

"Do you really want to play?" Jamie asked Sarah. Nobody had actually asked her.

"Oh, yes. I've learnt a new piece. I'll go and fetch it from my bag."

Jamie jumped up as Betsy almost dropped a pile of plates. "Let me help."

"No, Master Jamie, you can't. I'd be in trouble." Her usually smiling face looked sad. She didn't seem nearly as cheerful as when she'd first come to The Grange. Sarah returned before he could ask her about it, so the moment passed.

* * * *

Tillie went up to her bedroom, feeling very unwell, sure the sensations in her belly weren't just the baby moving about. Undressing, she sat on the bed as another wave swept over her.

Please, God, don't let me be losing it, she prayed. *It's much too early for labour pangs.*

Not wanting to disturb the rest of the family, she lay down and covered herself with the blankets, hoping the pains would subside.

A knock on the door announced David's arrival. "How are you, my darling?"

"Just a little tired."

"Are you sure?" He reached over and kissed her forehead.

She nodded and closed her eyes. "I'll be fine in the morning." *I hope,* she added, silently.

"Sarah is going to entertain us on the piano."

"That's nice," she murmured.

"I shall come back up in a little while, but will not disturb you if you are asleep." He kissed her again and left.

    She curled up in a ball and tried to sleep, realising the pains seemed to have abated.

Chapter 6

Christmas morning arrived with no hint of snow. Disappointed, Jamie closed the curtains and jumped back into bed. It felt cold enough, why hadn't it snowed? He pulled his nightcap further onto his head and snuggled down under the blankets, hoping that Sarah would like the book he'd made her, a scrapbook he'd filled with pictures of birds. Would she find it too childish? She didn't very often talk about birds any more. They hadn't even been down to the lake to see any since she'd arrived.

He looked forward to seeing Auntie Ruby and Uncle Sam, who would be coming for dinner after they had all been to church. He loved singing carols. He'd been trying to teach Alice 'O Little Town of Bethlehem', so hoped they would sing that one.

Walking back to the carriage after the service, feeling uplifted from singing all his favourites, he held onto his mama. She still seemed poorly but had insisted on going.

"If you do not feel up to it, I am sure God will forgive you," Jamie had heard his father trying to persuade her not to.

Aunt Annie had made it clear she didn't agree. "Christmas Day is the one time of year that everybody should attend, no matter how they feel. It isn't as if you are ill. You are only pregnant."

"I will ask Sam to bring the carriage round," his father had said. "We will be taking the money and presents to the poor of the parish afterwards, so will need it for that."

Aunt Annie had grabbed Uncle Victor's arm and stalked off, her nose in the air, the fox head on her fur coat flapping up and down as if still alive.

I hope it jumps up and bites her. Jamie had had to bite his tongue to stop himself speaking aloud.

Once they arrived home, they took off their coats and scarves, and the children opened one present each, the rest being saved for after dinner. Sarah chose his, and he breathed a sigh of relief when she clapped her hands in delight. "Oh, thank you, Jamie. It's lovely."

He wondered what she had given him. Twisting the long, thin, oblong parcel in his hands, he guessed it to be a tool of some sort.

"Open it," she cried, a look of expectancy on her face.

Ripping off the paper, he took a beautiful white quill pen out of its box. "Oh, gosh, it's magnificent!"

"It's made from a goose feather," she explained. "Do you like it?"

"I love it, thank you." He smiled into her blue, sparkling eyes. He loved her, too, always had.

"Show me, my dear," his mother called from the sofa. He took it across. "What a lovely present. Thank you, Sarah."

They entered the dining room and sat down at the table the maids had decorated with red-berried holly arrangements and pretty candles. Ivy and mistletoe adorned the walls and pictures.

"Doesn't this look welcoming?" Auntie Ruby exclaimed. "Look at the Yule log crackling in the grate." She turned to Jamie. "That should burn for twelve days to bring us luck."

"I hope Betsy doesn't forget it, then," he replied, not wanting any more ill-fortune to befall them.

Jamie looked at his favourite aunt, sitting next to Uncle Sam, wondering why they kept smiling at each other all the time, much more than usual, even when they didn't speak. She looked fatter. Could she be having a baby as well? The whole house would be full of them!

Alice sat with them, instead of having her meal up in the nursery. "Don't you look pretty in your red dress?"

He stroked the ribbons in her ringlets. "It matches the decorations."

His father said grace, and they tucked into the first course of roast goose. Once the following three courses had been cleared away, the smell of spices wafted towards them as Betsy carried in the Christmas pudding in the shape of a tower, adorned with a sprig of holly, and set it at the centre of the table. They all clapped with delight as she poured brandy over it and set it alight, creating a purple halo.

Alice didn't like rich fruit, so she had jelly that Freda had made especially for her, but Jamie loved it and, savouring a mouthful, he bit into something hard. Reaching into his mouth to take it out, he remembered helping to stir the pudding the previous Sunday. He'd been told it had to be stirred with a wooden spoon—wooden to represent the baby Jesus's crib—in a clockwise direction, and Freda had put in some silver coins while he'd made a wish. He could have wished for so many things, one of them being that it would snow.

"It's a sixpence!" he exclaimed, holding up his trophy after licking off the remnants of pudding still stuck to it.

"I've found one, too," said Sarah.

"May we keep them?" Jamie had never owned a whole sixpence before.

"Yes, you may," his father grinned. Jamie couldn't recall seeing him look as happy for a long time. His mama seemed to have perked up as well. Her face looked red, maybe from the brandy, as did Aunt Annie's. She had drunk even more than his mama but, thank goodness, hadn't disgraced herself, probably because of Uncle Victor's presence, although he barely spoke a word.

After dinner, they pulled their crackers. Scared by the bangs, Alice began to cry but, to appease her, Jamie gave her the small toy that had dropped out of his, and a paper hat to cover her ringlets.

Once they had finished, everyone, including the servants, trooped into the music room and Sarah played the piano, while they either stood around it or sat on the sofas, singing carols.

* * * *

Two days later, Tillie felt like a great weight had been lifted from her shoulders when Annie, Victor and Sarah went home. Even though she'd had little to do, their presence, especially Annie's, had left her exhausted.

The pains in her belly had abated, but every now and again she had twinges. She couldn't recall having them when pregnant with Jamie or the twins. They did not seem the same as heartburn, which she experienced from time to time. She tolerated that, for it meant the baby would have a thick, luxurious head of hair.

Ruby once remarked that she had been told that reaching her arms above her head could make the umbilical cord become wrapped around the baby's neck and strangle it but, despite all her carefulness in not doing that, or any other of the old wives' tales she had heard, she still felt uneasy. She didn't voice her concerns to David. What could she say, with no physical symptoms, just a kind of sixth sense? He would only call her a worry-pot. She tried to appear hearty, and to enjoy his lovemaking, but, deep inside, she feared that could be the cause, that being poked would have a detrimental effect. But she knew he would never agree with her, so often pretended to be asleep if he came into her bed.

She dreaded having to part with Jamie once more. She had thought it would be easier this time, but the very idea of him going away again sent shivers through her, and that didn't help her mood.

Filled with dread at the thought of returning to school, Jamie had hinted to his father that he would much rather stay at home but, "You will soon become accustomed to it, son. It just takes time," had been his reply.

But I don't want to become accustomed to it. I want to stay here, he'd been tempted to shout, but had merely slouched off to the library to find a book.

Helping Alice with a new jigsaw she had received for Christmas, he showed her where the final piece fitted, and sat back. "I might as well make the most of my last day of freedom. Do you want to come for a walk with me?"

"No, she does not." He thought he'd said it quietly enough for the witch not to hear, but Nanny had crept up behind him. He felt his ear being tugged and tried to break free. "I told you earlier she has a nasty cold, so don't go putting ideas into her head about going out."

"Walk." Alice jumped up and ran over to the wardrobe, clearly hoping to overrule her.

"She seems fine to me." *Why should the witch have her own way all the time?* He followed his sister and took out her coat, but the nanny snatched it from his hand, and he saw her arm rise as if to strike him. Ducking, he dodged out of her way.

"She is not going out," she yelled, making Alice cringe and run to hide behind Jamie.

"Now see what you've done, you horrible cow," he yelled back. "You've scared my little sister." He picked up Alice and tried to reach the door, but the nanny barred his way with her arms across it. "Let me out," he hissed through gritted teeth.

"You may go with pleasure, but you are not taking your sister."

"I'll tell Mama." He glared into her dark brown crow-like eyes. Her drawn-back hair pulled them upwards, making her look even more Chinese than usual.

They glared at each other for a moment until Alice wriggled to be put down. She ran across the room and broke up the jigsaw.

"See, she doesn't want you anymore." The nanny picked her up, stroking her head as if she loved her. The little girl put her thumb in her mouth and rested her head on the nanny's shoulder.

Acknowledging defeat, Jamie stormed out. "I'll have my revenge one day," he declared on his way downstairs. "Just you wait and see."

He hadn't seen Nellie in the alcove and jumped when she asked, "Who are you talking to, Master Jamie?"

"Oh, nobody, I just…" Should he tell her? Although he'd threatened to tell his mama, he knew he couldn't bother her, but the housekeeper… "It's Nanny, she won't let me take Alice for a walk on my last day at home."

"Well, dear, your sister does have rather a bad cold, so it wouldn't be advisable for her to go out on such a frosty day." Seeing the look of disappointment on his face, she suggested, "Why don't you play with her indoors?"

"'Cos Nanny…" He clenched his lips, sucking in air.

"What? What's Nanny done?"

How could he say, 'Nanny pulled my ear and shouted at me?' It sounded so trivial. "Nothing, it doesn't matter. I'll fetch my coat and go for a walk on my own."

"That's a good boy. Make sure you wrap up warm. It's really cold out there."

Stepping outside into the freezing air a short while later, his breath caught in his throat. Maybe it would snow, then he wouldn't be able to go back to school. Looking up at the clear blue sky, he doubted it. Not a snow cloud in sight. Pulling his coat tighter, and wrapping his scarf around his neck, he set off in the direction of the lake. The white trees, covered in frost, resembled skeletons, and the surface of the lake looked tempting enough to stand on, but he thought better of it. Falling into the river in the summer had been bad enough. How much worse would it be frozen? Just the thought brought out goose bumps all over his body.

Blowing out his breath, he watched the white mist disappear into the air. He'd seen Uncle Sam blow cigarette smoke into rings and tried to do the same, but without success.

He found himself in the woods. Should he go further in and see if Bobby and…Beth…? Maybe not, he didn't know if their cousin, Jake, had been released from prison. He definitely didn't want to run into that bully. Those at school almost paled into insignificance beside him.

Turning to go, he heard voices—high, giggly voices. It had to be the girls. He didn't want to see Jake's sister. But maybe he could snatch just one quick look at Beth. One glimpse of her beautiful green eyes would set him up for the term ahead. Hiding behind a tree as the voices came closer, he felt his jacket being tugged. Turning around, he saw Bobby smiling up at him.

"'Ello, Jamie." He grinned. "What you hiding from?"

"I, um…I'm not. I just needed a rest."

"In this cold?"

Standing up straight and rubbing his hands together, Jamie grinned, trying to look casual. Relief flooded through him when Bobby declared, "Me cousin, Jake, won't be bothering you for a while. He'll be in prison for a whole year."

"Oh, good."

The girls came closer.

"Good?" shouted the horrible one. "You think it's good me brother's gone to gaol?"

Jamie closed his eyes. Why had she heard? "I didn't mean…" He turned to his friend. "Weren't you arrested as well?"

"Aye, but they let me go."

About to ask why, he noticed Beth staring at him with her oval, hypnotic, green eyes. Once he looked into them, speech or action deserted him. He stared back until Jake's sister—he still didn't know her name, but didn't really want to—pulled her cousin away.

"I'd better go home," he muttered, tearing his eyes away. Wringing his hands, he turned and began walking.

"Bye," called Bobby.

"Bye," he called back, waving his hand above his head, not daring to look back. He didn't hear if Beth called a farewell, and knew her cousin wouldn't.

His heart fluttered all the way home, Beth's face etched into his memory. She had become even more beautiful than before, and even more than Sarah, he realised. He had always idolized his cousin, but in a different way, more like an extra special big sister.

Maisie stood chopping onions as he entered the kitchen.

"Are you doing that again?" he asked.

She nodded, wiping her face with the back of her hand.

"It's a wonder your eyes don't drop out," he added.

Scraping them into the pot, she grinned. As he made to go out through the other door, she called him back. "Ja...I mean Master Jamie." He turned back. "I've made something for you to take to school." Quickly washing her hands, she dried them on her apron, reached up to a shelf and took out a package wrapped in brown paper from behind some jars.

Jamie looked at Freda to see if she would give any indication of what it could be, but the cook didn't appear to be listening. Bent over the range, she stirred a saucepan with one hand, clutching her belly with the other.

Maisie gave him the package.

"What is it?" he asked.

"That would be telling. I want it to be a surprise, so don't open it 'til you feel lonely."

That'll be as soon as I leave here, he wanted to tell her, but couldn't let her know that. "Thank you," he muttered, feeling choked that the little maid should be so thoughtful. Her violet eyes looked sad, so perhaps she did know. "I'll save it as long as I can, so each time I see it I can think of you and home."

* * * *

The rain fell in bucket loads the following day, so Jamie couldn't go out for a last tour before leaving. The servants lined up in the hall as he hugged his mama and Alice. Fortunately, the witch had caught a chill or something, so had stayed upstairs. Jamie hoped she had typheria—or whatever they called that awful disease that killed people—then he wouldn't have to ever see or speak to her again.

Shaking hands with his father, he tried to be brave.

"Now, remember what I told you," his father said, "and you will be fine. You are picking Sebastian up on the way to the station. He is a good lad. You would do well to emulate him."

Climbing into the carriage, he tried to work out what 'emulate' meant. Whatever it meant, it was another nice word to add to his list. Still saying it over and over, they pulled up at Sebastian's house. He'd expected him to be waiting at the door. *He's probably waiting inside because of the rain*, he mused.

When nobody came out, Sam jumped down from his seat and pulled the door bell. Not receiving a reply, he waited a few moments and then pulled it again. It opened and Sebastian ran out and climbed into the carriage without saying a word. Jamie could tell he'd been crying, and remembered what he'd told him on the way home.

Things must be bad for a grown boy to cry. They arrived at the station without a word passing between them, but once settled in their compartment on the train, Sebastian broke down. "It's Mama, she says she's leaving."

"Leaving?" He must have misheard. "Did you say 'leaving'?"

His friend nodded, took out a handkerchief and loudly blew his nose.

"Where's she going?"

"She's...she's going to live with her lover."

Jamie couldn't have been more surprised if his friend had knocked him over the head with a hammer. He sat forward, his arms on his knees so he could hear better. "What do you mean?"

"Apparently, she's been having a liaison with some fellow in the village."

"A liaison?"

Sebastian continued as if Jamie hadn't spoken, "She's going to write to me with the address, so I can go and live with them when I come home." He looked at Jamie with tears in his eyes. "But Father says he won't let me. I'm his heir, and I need to be with him in the house that will one day be mine."

Jamie didn't know what to say. How would he react if his parents split up? Sitting back, he studied his friend's face. Sebastian had calmed down and also sat back, his eyes closed. Jamie wanted to offer some words of sympathy but just didn't know which ones to use. He'd never experienced a situation like that. Better to say nothing.

As they approached their station, Sebastian pulled his jacket straight and adjusted his cap. "Please don't say anything to anyone at school," he begged. "You know what a roasting I'll receive. They'll say it's my fault."

Jamie stopped in his tracks. "How can it be your

fault?"

"Well, *I* thought it was, that I'd done something to drive Mama away, so the other boys are bound to. She tried to assure me it was nothing of the sort, but…" Reaching through the window as the train stopped, he opened the door. Turning to face Jamie as he stepped onto the platform, he added, "I still wonder if it is, though."

Jamie didn't have a chance to reply as they were swept up in the tide of passengers emerging from the train.

* * * *

Proud to be playing for his house, Jamie ran onto the football pitch in his red kit. The opposing team in their blue kit looked threatening, but his house captain had told them they could easily win if they played their best.

His side lost the toss, so the other team chose their goal, and his team captain took the first kick. Jamie ran towards the ball, nudging an opponent out of the way, and bent to pick up the ball, but remembered the rules. An opponent kicked the ball up the other end and, running after it, he soon caught up. Controlling it with the side of his foot, he won possession and ran back towards the goal. Looking up to check his position, he kicked as hard as he could and the ball sailed under the bar. His team cheered. He could hardly contain his excitement. He had scored a goal! What an achievement to write about in his next letter home. How proud his father would be.

Invigorated, he attacked every ball that came near, but couldn't score another one, although, on one occasion, the ball hit the post. The game finally ended in a draw, but he didn't mind. He'd played his part. Several

School for Jamie

boys, including Silas Brown, whom he had managed to stay clear of, clapped him on the back as they made their way in.

Hugh Fenner grabbed Jamie as soon as the evening study period finished. "You can black my shoes and brush my clothes, Dalton. You made such a poor show of it last time, they need brushing again."

Jamie had found his way around the corridors and knew where to go. "I'll be along in a minute."

"You will not. You will come now."

"But I…"

"Now."

He had no option but to follow. He didn't mind doing the chores, they had become part of his life, but he'd wanted to catch one of the other boys and show him some pictures he'd drawn. *Will Fenner be interested in them? Probably not.*

He followed his fag master to his room. Another boy whom he didn't know sat toasting bread with a toasting fork in front of the fire. Jamie's nostrils twitched. He loved the whiff of charred bread. "That smells good," he said, his mouth watering.

"Well, don't think you'll be having any." Fenner took off his hat and sat down in the armchair, his gown spread out around him.

"Will that be enough?" asked the other boy, putting down the knife, after spreading butter and jam onto the bread.

"Yes, Chivers, you may go now."

The boy hesitated, looking down at the toast as if he'd been hoping for some himself, but turned and walked out, his head bent.

"My shoes, Dalton." Bending down to pick up the shoes, Jamie could hear him crunching in his ear. With a sigh, he set to, to bring them up as shiny as they had ever been in their lives. He wouldn't be chastised again for not doing a good job. Brushing away, he began to hum.

"I didn't know…" Fenner said something, but Jamie didn't hear the end of it.

"I beg your pardon?"

"I said I didn't know you could sing," he repeated.

"Oh, I love singing. I sing to my baby sister all the time at home."

"You should join the choir. Quite a few of my friends are members. I'll have a word with the choirmaster, Mister Ewart."

"Aw, fanks…I mean, thank you." Jamie showed him the boots. "Are they black enough?"

"I suppose they'll do."

"May I go now?"

Fenner took his time giving his answer, looking Jamie up and down with an odd expression on his face. Eventually, he nodded, so Jamie made his exit.

Humming as he made his way down the corridor, he imagined what it would be like to sing in the choir.

* * * *

Tillie read Jamie's letter for the third time. He seemed to be enjoying himself at that awful place. Fancy scoring a goal. David had been so proud of him.

The baby inside her moved awkwardly. "Oo," she squealed, making David look up from his newspaper.

"Is anything the matter?" he asked, putting it down.

"This baby seems to move much more than the twins did." It kicked again, just to prove the point.

"Well, I suppose it has more room to do so, which probably means it will not be twins this time."

"Well, yes." She felt sure that did not explain her fears, but knew David wouldn't understand. She'd tried a few times to express them, but he usually fobbed her off, so she looked up in surprise when he suggested calling the doctor.

"No, there's no need to drag him out. I'll be fine."

David stood up and hobbled over to her. "Well, if you are sure. I am off to bed. Are you coming?"

"Not yet, I want to finish my novel. It's the one Sarah lent me ages ago, and I am still not halfway through it."

He gave her a kiss. "Be careful not to strain your eyes." He pulled the bell and Betsy appeared. "Please ask John to assist me upstairs."

Another twinge made Tillie gasp as he reached the door. He turned and hesitated, then said, "Goodnight. Do not stay up too long."

"No, darling, I won't." *Just long enough to make sure you're asleep.* Rubbing her belly, she tried to concentrate on the shenanigans of Elizabeth Bennet and Mister Darcy, but the discomfort grew stronger. It couldn't be labour pangs. The baby should not be making an appearance for a few more weeks. Putting her book down, she paced up and down the floor until, still trying to decide if she should be concerned about the regularity of the pains, she cursed as the candle fizzled and went out, leaving her in semi-darkness.

"Oh, just what I need," she muttered. Bending down to take a new one out of the cupboard, she doubled over with pain as water gushed down her legs. "Oh, no," she gasped. "This must be it." Once the pain had subsided, she shuffled across to the bell pull and yanked it.

Betsy came in, took one look at her mistress and ran back out, yelling, "Nellie, Nellie, come quick."

The housekeeper came hurrying in. "What's the commotion? Anyone would think…" She ran across to Tillie, who was in the throes of another spasm. "Oh, my goodness, it's much too early, isn't it?"

"Tell him that. He doesn't seem to realise."

Nellie took hold of her arm and steered her towards

the door. "Betsy, send Sam into the village for the midwife and make sure there's plenty of hot water and clean towels. I'll take the mistress up to her bedchamber."

"But Freda's gone to bed. She felt poorly."

"Surely you and Maisie can perform a simple task like that between you."

The maid ran out, her arms flapping like a chicken.

"If only Ruby could be here," moaned Tillie. "She proved a great help when I had the twins."

"When Sam returns, I'll see if he'll fetch her, but he might not think it advisable at her stage in her own pregnancy."

Halfway up the stairs another spasm stopped her.

"Has the master already retired?" Nellie asked as she made her mistress comfortable in bed.

"Yes, he came up a while ago."

"Do you wish me to let him know?"

The joining door opened and David called, "What is going on? Are you unwell, my dear?"

"She's in labour, sir. The baby's on its way."

"But, surely not…"

"Ahhhhhh!" As he shuffled into the room, Tillie grabbed his hand and squeezed it, trying to transfer some of her pain. His blue eyes filled with terror, his black hair fell forward, and his dressing gown came untied. "Go back to bed, David. I don't want you passing out on top of me, making matters worse," she told him.

He didn't need telling twice. He almost shot out of the room. She hadn't seen him move as fast since his accident.

Chapter 7

Jamie listened intently to the teacher, trying to take in his words. He didn't like Greek. He thought it sounded like gibberish. The teacher, a stickler for silence, turned and glared at him.

What have I done now?

The boy next to him nudged him in the ribs. "You were mumbling to yourself."

"Sorry, sir," he murmured, trying to write the last word into his copy book. A splotch of ink dropped from his nib, obliterating the word. "Oh, darn it," he uttered, patting it with some blotting paper. Concentrating on clearing it up, he didn't notice the master come towards him, until he felt a cane whack his fingers. "Ouch!" he shouted. *He looks as if he enjoyed hitting me. I'll have to be more careful,* he vowed, rubbing his hand.

"Which letter comes after alpha?" the teacher bellowed.

"There's no need to shout, I'm not deaf," Jamie retorted, adding, "sir" as an afterthought. A gasp went up from the rest of the class, who usually began to whisper amongst themselves whenever a teacher reprimanded anybody.

"Enough of your impertinence, boy!" Pulled out of his seat and shoved into the corner, he had a cone-shaped hat bearing the word 'DUNCE' shoved onto the top of his head. "You can stand there facing the wall for half an hour for being so insolent." Jamie had seen it happen to another boy a few days earlier and had thought it funny. He didn't think so this time.

"But, sir, how will I learn?"

"Silence!" the master roared. Jamie had no option but to remain in the corner, tight-lipped. Not daring to turn his head, he could only hear snippets of what the master taught behind him. He would never catch up. How could he be expected to learn anything when he couldn't even see what he wrote?

At last the bell rang for the end of the lesson. *Am I allowed to turn around, or take off the dunce's cap?* He hadn't noticed what had happened to the other boy. He'd been intent on hurrying out of the classroom to go and play. He decided he might as well just do it, anyway. Yanking off the cap, he threw it onto the teacher's desk, and ran out with the others before the master could shout him back. Thinking him deaf, he would know Jamie wouldn't hear him above all the hullabaloo.

Running outside into the playground, he wondered whether to join the group of boys playing marbles, but he only had one left, and didn't want to risk losing it, so decided against that, especially as he could see the boy who had won his favourite one.

"Do you want to play hide and seek, Dalton?" a boy he didn't know came up and asked him, as he stood hesitating.

"Oh, yes, that would be spiffing." He followed the boy, pleased he'd been able to use his word for the week.

The boy hid behind a wall, but Jamie wanted to hide somewhere more secret, so ran round the back of the building, and hid behind a tree. Sitting curled up, and pulling his jacket tighter to stop himself shivering, he peeped out. Not a soul in sight. The bell rang. "Oh, yikes," he squealed, and dashed back to the playground, just making to the door as it closed.

"Phew, that was close," he remarked to the boy he'd followed in, the one who had invited him to play. "Nobody found me," he said proudly.

"Me neither."

An older boy sniggered. "That's because nobody looked for you, you numbskulls."

"What do you mean?" Jamie asked.

"No talking," yelled one of the prefects lining the corridors. Jamie recognised him as Bullimore, his house captain.

"What do you think he meant?" Jamie continued in a quieter voice to the boy beside him, who shrugged.

"You, boy, remind me of your name." The prefect pulled Jamie out from the group, tugging on his ears.

"Dalton," he said, his head held high.

"Well, Dalton, when I say 'no talking', that's exactly what I mean."

"I wasn't talking, I was whispering."

The prefect glared at him, his blue eyes blazing. "You wish to defy me?"

"No, I was just explaining."

"Well, as your house captain, I shall listen to your explanation this evening after study time. Off you go to your classroom."

The rest of the pupils had gone, so he ran to catch up.

"No running in the corridors," Bullimore called.

"Grrr," moaned Jamie under his breath, walking as fast as he could without breaking into a trot.

All afternoon he tried not to look out of the window, wondering what the prefect intended. He'd heard that house captains had the power to thrash unruly boys, but he didn't consider talking as being very naughty, especially not in the classroom. Perhaps he would just make him do some jobs. He hoped so.

During the quiet study period that evening, he finished the homework set for the day, and decided to catch up on his letter writing. He hadn't written to his parents for over a week. Chewing the tip of his pen, he wondered what to put.

'Dear Mama and Father. I hope you are well and happy.'

He began every letter to them in that way.

'I might be joining the choir.'

That would please them.

'Fenner is going to put in a good word for me. He is not such a bad stick. I quite like him. Some of the fag masters are real bullies but he ain't.'

He wondered whether he ought to change 'ain't' to 'is not', but thought it would make a mess, so left it.

'How are Alice and Maisie and Nellie and Auntie Ruby and everyone else?'

He couldn't think of anything else to say. His stomach churned just thinking about going to the housemaster's room later. He decided not to mention that. He didn't want them to know he'd been in trouble.

He usually finished with *'love from'* but decided to use a longer word for a change, so signed off,

'Your afectiontate son, Jamie.'

It didn't look right, but it would have to remain. One more splodge would be too messy. Patting the letter with blotting paper, he folded it and put it in his pocket to hand in later, to be read by one of the masters before it was sent off, to make sure he hadn't written anything bad or offensive.

I'll write to Sarah tomorrow, he thought. He'd received a letter from her the previous day telling him about her private singing lessons. He couldn't think why she would need them. In his opinion, she already had a beautiful voice. Maybe, next time she came to visit they could sing a duet, if he was accepted into the choir and his voice improved. That would please the parents, something to look forward to.

Study time finished. Could he say he forgot to go to Bullimore's room? Not worth the risk. Dragging his heels, he made his way down the corridor and knocked on his door. At first, he didn't hear a reply. Maybe the prefect had forgotten. Then he heard a yell, "Come!" Opening the door an inch, he closed his eyes and took a deep breath.

"Come in, Dalton. I trust you've repented of your bad behaviour."

He went inside and closed the door behind him. "Um, yes, sir, I think so. Cor, you must like reading," he blurted out, looking around the room, covered in shelves full of books, just like a library.

Bullimore seemed taken aback. His flaxen hair fell forward onto his face, almost hiding his eyes. "Well, yes, I do," he replied. "But never mind that, you're not here to discuss books."

Jamie craned his neck to look up at Bullimore when he stood up. "But I love books, 'specially ones with pictures of birds. Do you have any of them?" He walked across to the side wall, peering at the titles on the spines on the shelf.

"Well, yes, but…"

"Oh, please can I…may I…borrow it?"

"Now, listen here, Dalton…"

"Which one is it, or do you have more than one? That would be…"

"Oh, very well." Bullimore walked over to the other side of the room and took down a battered book with a brown cover. Jamie rushed over to look at it but his housemaster held it out of his reach.

"This belonged to my father and his father before him, so I can't let you borrow it. It's falling apart in places." The prefect placed it carefully on the table and opened one of the yellowed pages showing faded pictures.

"Is there a buzzard? They're my favourites." Jamie tried to reach over to turn a page.

"Yes, there is, but please do not touch the book. Let me find it."

"What does 'raptor' mean?"

"It's another word for bird of prey, although, strictly speaking, only falcons are considered to be true birds of prey."

Jamie leaned over the prefect's shoulder, wishing he would hurry up and find the one he most wanted to see.

"Ah, here it is." Bullimore smoothed the page and stood aside for Jamie to look.

"But it's only a black and white sketch of its head. I was hoping to see its full body."

"Don't forget, this book is very old."

"Don't you have one with coloured pictures?"

The housemaster stroked his chin. Jamie could see a few bristly whiskers, not black like his father's, but fair, in fact, hardly noticeable unless you looked hard, and wondered whether he had to shave.

He realised he had been staring and quickly looked away.

It is bad manners to stare, he could hear Nellie saying.

"I do have one somewhere. I'm not sure where, though." Bullimore's eyes scanned the shelves. Then he looked back at Jamie. "Anyway, that's not what you're here for. Remind me why that is."

Jamie had hoped he'd forgotten. Maybe he had, if he needed reminding. Bullimore sat down in his armchair and leaned back, making a bridge with his fingers.

In his mind, Jamie played back the event in the corridor. Could he make up a different story? As the cogs in his brain worked, his eyes darted about the room, but they stopped, opening wide on seeing a cane lying on a side table.

"Oh, don't look so scared," Bullimore said after a moment. "As it's your first offence, I shall not overlook it, but store it in the recesses of my mind. But be warned, no boy ever avoids punishment a second time. My name isn't Bullimore for nothing." He rose and picked up the cane, flexing it between his fingers. Jamie jumped back as he swished it like a riding crop. Putting it back down, he picked up a piece of green cloth. "Instead, you may dust my books for your punishment. Jones, one of my fags, usually performs that chore, but he's poorly."

Phew, I've got away with it.

Jamie picked up the duster. "Where do you want me to start?"

The housemaster shrugged as if he'd lost interest, confirming Jamie's earlier thought. "Wherever you like." He took out a book and sat down to read. Jamie tried to see its title but, as he had already opened it, he couldn't see. He went along the shelves, taking out one book at a time and wiping it all over.

"You'll be all night doing it like that," he thought he heard Bullimore mutter from behind him.

He turned to face him. "But you said to dust them."

"I did indeed. They usually only receive a wipe across the top, but carry on. It's time they had a proper clean. Just be careful with the old ones. I should hate it if any of them came to grief." With a wicked glint in his eye, he picked up the cane again.

Jamie grimaced at the thought of being thrashed and resumed his task, humming as he took extra care.

"You have a lot of books written by Charles Dickens," he remarked after taking out the fifth one. "Is this one about Christmas? I love Christmas, don't you?"

"Shh, I'm trying to read."

"Sorry for breathing," Jamie muttered under his breath. Opening the book, he began to read, enthralled by the man called Scrooge who reckoned he didn't like Christmas.

He became aware of his housemaster standing in front of him. He hadn't noticed him leave his chair.

"You're supposed to be dusting, not reading." He yanked the book out of Jamie's hand and shook his head. "You may as well go now. Come back tomorrow and finish off."

"All right, but please may I…?" He'd been about to

ask if he could borrow the book but didn't think he should push his luck. Maybe next time.

The following morning he received a letter, not in his mama's writing.
Who can it be from?
Spreading out the paper, he looked at the signature—his father's. Why would he be writing? He began to read.
Dear Jamie,
I expect you will be surprised that I am writing instead of your mother, but I have some good news to impart and your mother is not well enough to write yet. But do not worry, she is not ill.
She has just been delivered of a child. You have a baby brother whom we have named Daniel.

Jamie looked up from the letter. A baby brother! Good news or bad? Pleased in a way, because much as he loved Alice and had loved Annabella, he decided a brother would be more special than a sister, but it would also mean he wouldn't be his mama's little boy any more. Would she love this new one more than him?

Putting the thought to the back of his mind, he reread the letter, to ensure he had the facts correct, folded it and put it in his treasure box with the others he'd received that term. His box contained items he'd brought from home—some birds' eggs, a sprig of ivy he'd found caught on his coat last time he'd seen Beth, a lock of Annabella's hair and a brooch belonging to his mama. Guilt made him bite his lip each time he took that out to watch the light glinting on the jewel in its centre, for he hadn't told her he'd borrowed it, and he hoped she hadn't missed it. Next time he went home he would own up and give it back. She wouldn't need it now she'd had the baby. He remembered she'd been forced to stay in bed for what had seemed like weeks after the twins had been born.

I wonder if he looks like me, he mused. The first time

he'd seen the twins, they'd looked like little, wrinkled gnomes, their faces screwed up. The new baby being a boy, though, shouldn't look quite so peculiar. Taking a look in the mirror, he examined his brown eyes and small nose and, baring his teeth, he ran his finger over their smooth surface. They looked white and even, but the baby wouldn't have any yet, so he wouldn't be able to compare them.

"Oh, my lord," he exclaimed, looking closer. A pimple had appeared on his chin. That hadn't been there last time he'd looked. "Ugh," he groaned, trying to rub it off. He'd seen one of the boys in the fifth form covered in spots and pimples. He prayed he wouldn't end up with an ugly face like his.

* * * *

Tillie turned over in bed and looked at her new baby, lying sleeping as usual in his cradle beside her. She sat up and lifted him out. He never cried for his feed, so she woke him when she deemed it the right time. Stroking his fair head, she flicked his heel to see if that would rouse him sufficiently to latch onto her nipple.

"Wakey, wakey, my darling, please take some milk," she crooned to him. "You only had ten minutes last feed, and even then you slept most of the time."

David came in, hobbled across to the bed and sat on the edge. "How's my little boy?" he asked, his face beaming as usual whenever he looked upon his son.

"He still won't feed," said Tillie, trying to attach him to her breast.

"Well, maybe he is not hungry."

"But he's hardly had anything all day. I'm really worried he isn't thriving."

"He looks fine to me. Surely, if he ailed, he would cry all the time." David stroked his son's face. "Is Nellie or the nurse concerned about him?"

"Nellie thinks he should be doing better but…" Why go over it all again? She'd been trying to explain her concerns to him since the birth, but he just didn't seem to want to take any notice of her.

"I'll leave you to it." Kissing her, he went back out.

"I hope he's right, my darling boy, but I'm convinced he is not," she whispered to the baby, who suckled quite energetically for a change. "Maybe it's just that you're so tiny and don't have the strength to suck very hard." But the twins had been even smaller than he, and she hadn't had any bother with them, not after the first few days anyway.

Ruby tapped on the door, poking her head around. "Phew," she gasped, rubbing her belly. "Those stairs seem to be steeper every day." She sat on the chair next to her sister.

"And you grow bigger every day, sis," remarked Tillie, transferring the baby onto the other side. "How much longer?"

"Another two months. I'll be as large as a horse by then. Sam says he thinks I'm having a foal, I'm so huge."

Tillie laughed. "Maybe it's twins."

"I keep thinking that. When I was little, I often wondered what it would be like to have a sister exactly the same as me." She smiled. "Not that anyone would want to be a replica of…"

"A–a–a," Tillie pointed her finger at Ruby. "What have I told you?"

Ruby pulled a face. "I know, I know. I still can't help myself at times. Sam becomes cross with me. He says I need to perk up my ideas before I have the baby, or it'll have no confidence itself."

"That's true." Tillie looked down at her baby, who had fallen asleep once more. "It looks like he's had enough." She put him over her shoulder and rubbed his back.

Hearing a little voice outside the door, she pretended she didn't know who it belonged to. "Who's that out there?" she called.

Alice ran in, followed by Nanny. "Me, Mama, Lith." It had taken some while before anybody had understood she had been trying to say Alice, and it had been Jamie who had realised it.

"So it is. Hello, my sweetheart. You look pretty. Green suits you."

Alice lifted up her white muslin pinafore and smoothed out the thick material beneath it. "Green."

"Where are you going?" Tillie straightened the headband holding back her daughter's long blonde ringlets.

"Horthy."

"To see the horses?"

The little girl nodded.

Ruby interrupted. "Yes, if it's all right with you, I thought I'd take her down to the stables. Sam's expecting us."

"Oh, yes, David's been thinking of buying her a pony. Has he already bought it?"

"Yes, a little palomino. It's so cute. She won't be able to ride it yet, of course, but I thought I'd introduce them to each other."

Tillie turned to the nanny. "Are you going as well?"

The nanny hesitated. "Well, I had not intended to."

"I think, in her condition, Ruby might need you." Tillie gave Alice a kiss. "You be a good girl." She received another nod in reply. "The weather is favourable today, not like yesterday, thank goodness, so off you go. Make sure she wears her hooded cape," she called after them.

Giving Daniel one more cuddle, she placed him in his cradle.

Needing to moisten her lips, she picked up a glass

from beside the bed, and drank what was left of the water, but it didn't quench her thirst. "I should have asked if Nellie or Betsy could bring me up a cup of tea," she moaned.

Maybe she could call one of them. Taking her dressing gown from the back of the door, she pushed her arms into it, went out onto the landing and looked over the rail.

"Mistress…Tillie…what are you doing out of bed?" Nellie's voice came from below.

"I'm so thirsty I could drink a river dry," Tillie called, leaning on the banister.

"Well, return to your bed, and I'll ask Betsy to bring you something." The housekeeper hurried up to her. "Come on, you shouldn't be out here."

Tillie realised the folly of her actions as she clung onto Nellie for support when a wave of dizziness washed over her.

"Tch, tch, I don't know. You're left for a moment and…You know you shouldn't even be out of bed, not for another week at least," Nellie admonished her as she helped her back into the safety of her comfy sheets.

Eventually allowed downstairs, Tillie entered the lounge. David folded his newspaper and patted the sofa next to him. "Sit here, my darling. I'll find a blanket for you."

"Thank you, David, but I'm not an invalid." She smiled.

"But you must not catch cold," he replied.

"I won't, I promise."

"I need to go out." He turned to Nellie, who placed a plate of sandwiches on the side table. "Do not let her do anything. She needs complete rest."

"Certainly, sir. I'll take good care of her."

"Where are you going in such a rush?" Tillie asked.

"I thought you might have sat with me for a while."

"It is nothing for you to bother about, just estate affairs."

She shook her head. He still wouldn't involve her in those matters. For a split second, she remembered Christine Wilson, but pushed the neighbourhood beauty to the back of her mind, for she had more important issues to bother about. "I want to organise Daniel's christening and my churching ceremony as soon as possible."

"Yes, we will discuss it on my return." He leaned down and gave her a peck on the cheek.

Not expecting a proper kiss, she wasn't disappointed when she didn't receive one, being considered unclean until she had been churched, but she thought her husband would be eager to organise the ceremony, especially the baby's christening, in case the unthinkable happened.

Shrugging, she picked up a sandwich as he followed Nellie out.

The baby stirred in the basket beside her. "Are you going to actually cry?" she asked him, but he settled again without doing so.

"Who would think I'd want a baby to cry?" she asked aloud. Ruby entered the room, holding Alice by the hand, their cheeks ruddy from the cold outside. "Are you talking to yourself again, sis?" she asked, taking off her gloves.

"Yes, that's what I'm reduced to. I know it's the first sign of madness."

Ruby laughed. "You're the sanest person I know."

"Well, I don't feel it. This baby is driving me to distraction. It just isn't natural not to cry."

Alice stood looking down at Daniel, her head to one side, and then put her finger into his mouth. "Baby," she said, but pulled it out again as he started to suck on it.

The look of disgust on her face made Tillie and Ruby laugh, as she wiped her wet finger down her coat.

"I wish he'd suck as hard on me," Tillie rued, pulling her daughter towards her and unbuttoning her coat.

"Let me do that." Ruby reached down and tried to take over.

"Ruby, I am not an invalid, as I keep telling everyone. I can sort out my daughter."

Her sister moved away, a look of rejection clouding her grey eyes. "I'm sorry," she murmured.

"No, sis, I'm sorry. Come here." She enfolded her in her arms, much as she would a child. "I know you're only trying to help, and you are—you're a great help to me, looking after Alice on Nanny's day off."

"Well, I need as much practice as possible, ready for this one." Taking off her own coat, Ruby patted her belly. "Can you feel him moving?" She took Tillie's hand and rested it on the place where a little bulge protruded.

"That'll be his elbow," Tillie said, drawing from her own experiences.

"Or his knee," Ruby added. "I sometimes think I'm going to give birth to an octopus with eight legs, each with an elbow and a knee."

"Ocputh." Alice waved her arms up and down in imitation of the sea creature. "Ocputh."

Tillie looked at her daughter in astonishment. "How does she know what they're like?"

Ruby shook her head. "Perhaps Nanny's been showing her pictures in a book."

"Yes, that must be it." She gave the little girl a hug. "Clever girl, you are learning a lot of new things, aren't you?"

Alice nodded as her thumb went back in her mouth.

"I do hope this baby's a boy," said Ruby, sitting down in an armchair. "Sam's longing for a son."

"But what do you yourself want?"

"I want what Sam wants."

"Ruby?" Tillie raised her eyebrows at her sister. "You have to have your own opinions sometimes. You can't go through the rest of your life doing whatever your husband wants all the time."

"I'm not, I…" Ruby shrugged. "Sometimes it's easier to do that, rather than have to think about things."

"Well, just be warned. You know your big sister knows best."

"Yes, sis, I always take notice of what you say, I always will. But Sam is my husband and…" She shrugged once again.

"Anyway, I think it's time for this little man's feed." Tillie looked down at the baby, who didn't look the least bit hungry. He slept quite contentedly.

"I'll take Alice up to the nursery and give her some lunch." Ruby stood up and leaned backwards, hands on her hips, moaning softly.

"Are you sure you feel up to it?" Tillie looked with concern at her sister. She seemed so full of aches and pains, more so than normal.

"Yes, of course. I'm just being mardy." Taking her niece's hand, she went out, as Tillie picked up Daniel and tried to wake him.

Chapter 8

Jiggling from one foot to the other, Jamie waited to hear if he had been chosen to play football for his school.

"And the final place goes to Dalton," the games captain pronounced.

"That's me," he yelled. "I'm in the team." Jumping up and down with excitement, he joined the rest of his team-mates. The boys who hadn't been chosen went back to the changing room—most of them, especially the sporty ones, looking dejected, but one or two followed the team in the hope they might be chosen as substitutes. Jamie tried to feel sorry for those who hadn't been picked, but so elated to be actually playing for his school, not just his house, the feeling didn't last very long.

"Have you played in the town before?" he asked the boy beside him as they walked out of the school grounds.

"Only once. It was spiffing."

Jamie had been longing to use that word again. He considered repeating it back to the boy but thought it would sound puerile, a new word he'd learnt from Latin, so he asked instead, "Really? Did we win?"

He didn't hear the boy's reply for he noticed Bullimore behind him. The housemaster had called for him to dust his books again and had let him borrow 'The Christmas Carol'. The previous study time he should have been learning some Greek words but hadn't been able to resist a peek at the first chapter and, once he'd started, he hadn't been able to put it down. When the supervisor had announced they could go, he'd looked up in amazement. The Greek words hadn't even been looked at.

Arriving at the playing field, Jamie limbered up with the rest of the team, trying not to slip on the frosty ground. Clapping his hands together as the games captain shouted his instructions, he watched his breath pour out of his mouth in the cold air.

They took up their positions, and the referee called for the game to begin. Jamie ran for the ball but a member of the opposing team kicked the back of his leg and tripped him up. The referee shouted again and the game stopped. Jumping up, Jamie chased after the opponent who had upended him, intent on revenge, but the referee yelled for him to stop, and one of his own team mates grabbed him, preventing him from catching the offender.

"Leave it be, Dalton. Don't cause a fight," the boy hissed in his ear, turning him around to face the play. Jamie recognised him as Oswell Peel, the boy he usually sat beside in class.

He obeyed but still seethed inside. "If he comes near me again, I'll kick him in the shins," he retorted.

"No, you mustn't," said his friend. "You'll be sent off."

"So how come that bully's still playing?"

He didn't receive a reply, for St Clements, as his friend was called, had already run to his position. The referee placed the ball for a free kick. Jamie thought he would be the one to take it, as he'd been the person who'd been fouled, so he lined up ready to take a run, but the referee pointed to a bigger boy.

"But it should be me," shouted Jamie.

"No arguing, carry on with the game," yelled the official.

He slouched off, but soon regained his good temper when he almost scored a goal, the ball skimming the side post.

As they sucked oranges at half-time, Bullimore came over. "You'd better curb your temper, Dalton. You're a good player, so don't spoil it."

"I...yes, sir."

The house captain, also the captain of games, gave

them a pep talk. "We can do it, chaps. We are only losing by one goal, but we can soon pull that back."

Jamie smiled at Peel. "We can, can't we?" Peel returned the smile. Jamie decided he would be his best friend, and wondered why he had been given the nickname of St Clements. He would have to ask him sometime.

Halfway through the second half, Jamie kicked the ball to his captain and ran forward towards the goal. In a prime position to score, he received it back, but just as he lifted his foot to kick it, the opponent who'd tripped him up earlier nudged him out of the way. Bitter bile rose into his mouth. Seething, he ran after the boy—much larger and taller than him, which made him all the more determined to have his revenge—he pushed him in the back with as much force as he could muster.

The player fell headlong onto the icy pitch. "Gotcha," roared Jamie as the referee stopped the game.

"You've had your warning. Off!" shouted the referee, pointing to Jamie.

"Me?" he protested. "But he fouled first."

"Off."

"That's not fair." Jamie had no option but to leave the pitch. He limped off. He must have hurt his knee when he'd tripped. Standing shivering as the game resumed without him, he wrapped his arms around himself, trying to find some relief from the cold air.

A shout went up from the small band of the other team's supporters. They had scored again. What an end to his first match! Dragging his feet, he made his way back to school. He didn't know if he should do so, on his own, but he'd freeze to death if he stood there any longer.

He went straight to the changing rooms and pulled down his trousers to examine his knee. Dried blood had stuck the material to his skin. He yanked it off, making him yelp, and the wound started to bleed once more.

Taking off the trousers completely, he pressed them against the bleeding knee and sat wondering what to do next.

Shall I wait for the others to come back? he pondered, but decided he would rather not be there when they did, so decided to visit the matron. Standing up gingerly, he found his clothes and, wrapping his vest around his knee, he pulled up his clean trousers and bundled the dirty ones into a ball.

He had not needed the infirmary before, but had met the matron.

"That's but a mere scratch," she said on examining him. The colour of her eyes matched that of his father's, but a shade bluer. They had a twinkle in them that put him at his ease straightaway. Sitting him on a chair, she began to wash the wound with some foul-smelling liquid. Jamie tried hard not to make a sound, gritting his teeth, and squeezing his eyes shut. When he opened them again, he could see a brownish mark on her forehead, just under her cap. It looked like a map of Australia. Only that morning, in the geography lesson, they had been learning about the large continent where the authorities sent prisoners. He had drawn a picture of it, almost the same shape as her mark. He wondered if she knew.

"There you are, my lad. All clean and shipshape." The matron straightened up and patted his head. "I'll find you a clean vest, then you can go back to your lessons."

"Do I have to? Can't I stay up here with you?"

"Nay, my lad, you need to…"

Jamie stood up. "Oo, I can't walk," he pretended, sitting back down. "It hurts too much." He was loath to face the rest of the team, knowing they would make fun of him for being sent off. "I'll have to stay 'til it's a bit better." He pulled the saddest, most pathetic face he could, looking at her with such pleading that she conceded.

"All right then, just for half an hour."

"Thank you," he said with the feeblest voice he had ever heard, amazing even himself at his play acting.

Unable to sit quietly for long, he began to tell her about the letter he'd received, informing him of the birth of his baby brother.

In the process of tidying up, she stopped. "And how do you feel about that?"

"I'm not sure, really." He looked her in the eye. "But my mama is wonderful. She tried to persuade Father not to send me here, so I know she'll still love me, even with a new son to look after."

"Of course she'll still love you. A mother has enough love to share, even if she has dozens of children."

"My little sister died, you know."

"Oh, recently?"

"In March. She fell down a well."

"How awful for you all."

While he had caught her in a sympathetic mood, he wondered whether to push his luck. "Do you think I'll be allowed to go home to see my baby brother?"

Matron rubbed her chin. Jamie noticed she had one finger much shorter than the others. It ended in a stump, without a fingernail.

"Oh, what happened to your finger?" he blurted out without thinking.

"I beg your pardon?" she asked, looking at her hand. "Oh, you mean this?" She waggled the finger. "I chopped it off."

Aghast, his eyes opened wide. "On purpose?"

"No, no, by mistake, years ago, dealing with an impudent scamp like you. You seem all right now, my lad. I think you might be able to walk." She helped him up and steadied him until he reached the door.

"Yes, it's a lot better, thank you." The bell rang for end of lessons. "It's definitely better," he called, almost skipping down the corridor, until he remembered he hadn't had an answer to his request to go home. Oh, well, it would soon be the Easter holidays.

Oswell Peel met him on his way to tea.

"Do you have any brothers or sisters?" Jamie asked as they sat down.

His friend shook his head. "No, my mother died giving birth to me, and my father couldn't cope without her. He sent me to live with my aunt, and we heard he'd committed suicide when I was seven."

"That's dreadful." Jamie couldn't imagine not having any parents. He'd only had his ma until he'd come to The Grange, and that had seemed enough at the time, but having had a father for the past four years he couldn't contemplate not having one. "So who do you live with now?"

"Still with my aunt, my father's sister."

"And doesn't she have any children?" Jamie bit into his sandwich. The football game had given him an appetite.

"No, she never married."

Jamie mulled that over. He thought all grown ups married. Even Miss H, his former governess, had, and she'd been really old, at least thirty five.

"That must be very lonely for you. Say…why don't I ask Mama if you can come and stay with us for the Easter holidays?"

"Oh, I don't know."

"I could send a letter today." Excited at the prospect of having another boy for company, Jamie thought it would offset the disappointment he would feel if his mama would be too busy with the new baby.

"But my aunt might be upset that I'd rather go to your house than back to her."

Jamie spread some more jam on his bread. His friend had a good point. A lonely old lady would probably welcome Peel's company after being on her own all term.

"But if she misses you that much, why did she send you here in the first place?"

"Because it's tradition in my family, and Papa left a trust to pay for me to come."

"Well, isn't it worth asking her, anyway?"

Jamie studied his friend's face for any sign that he might be willing. His eyes looked sad at first, then they began to brighten up, and a smile spread over his face. "I would rather like to come."

"It would be spiffing, wouldn't it?" There, he'd managed to use the word again.

"Yes, it would. I'll write to her this evening."

In bed that night, Jamie thought about all the things he could do with Oswell during the holidays. They might even see his buzzard. That would be extra spiffing.

Disappointment washed over him, however, when he received his reply from home. His father said it would be too much for his mama to have another person, a stranger, in the house.

He wrote straight back.

'Dear Mama,

I beg you, would it not be better for me to have the company of someone my own age? We would stay out of your way and be on our best behaviour. I could show him the library and the lake. Oswell is the nicest, kindest, quietest, goodest boy in the class.

Please reconsider.'

He didn't receive a reply for a few days. Peel had already received a reply from his aunt saying she would be happy for him to go, so they waited on tenterhooks each time the master distributed the mail. Time began to run out, with only three days left before the end of term. What if he didn't receive an answer? What would they do? Peel's aunt might have made other arrangements.

Finally, on the day before they broke up for the holidays, the answer came.

"Hooray," he shouted. "He can come." Skipping down the corridor to find his friend, he waved his arms in the air. "Hooray," he sang over and over until he saw a prefect in the distance and slowed down, trying to look dignified until after he'd passed him, then speeding up again.

* * * *

It began to rain as the train pulled into the station. Covering their heads with their coats, they ran across the platform and into the dry building. Sebastian would be making his own way from there. Jamie hadn't had a chance to speak to him, and hadn't liked to broach the subject with Peel listening, so didn't know if his mother had run off with her lover. The older boy had barely spoken all the way. He had sat staring out of the window, looking very downcast.

Pushing their way through the other passengers sheltering from the rain, Jamie peered out of the station entrance, and could see Fred waiting for them with the pony and trap, his hair plastered to his face and his coat shiny from the rain pouring down on him "Oh, no," he wailed to Peel. "He hasn't brought the carriage. We'll be soaked."

"Can't we wait in here for a while until it stops?" his friend suggested.

"Better not. Fred won't be best pleased if he has to sit out there becoming even wetter, waiting for us."

"Come on, then, let's go."

They ran and climbed into the trap just as a clap of thunder split the air. Jamie could see Sebastian pulling away in a brougham with the hood up. Should he jump out and stand in front of it and ask if they could have a lift? By the time he'd thought about it, it had disappeared down the lane.

A blaze of lightning lit up the sky as they pulled away. "Can't we shelter somewhere?" he shouted to Fred, but didn't hear a reply as another clap of thunder seemed to explode from the clouds. In different circumstances, at home in the dry and warm, Jamie would have loved to sit at the window and watch the storm but, actually out in it, he felt differently. He and Oswell crouched down as best they could in the bottom of the trap, covering themselves with their coats.

He felt them stopping and looked out. He didn't recognise the stable barn. "Where are we, Fred?"

"At the Major's. I thought we'd better shelter here until it stops." Climbing down, Fred took a rag from a nail on the wall and wiped down the pony. Steam rose from her flanks and the smell of wet horse filled their nostrils. "Your father's gone out in the brougham to visit Mister Hodges on estate business. The rain hadn't started when I left home. Tom had warned me it would, but I hoped we'd be back in time."

"Tom's our gamekeeper," Jamie explained to Oswell. "He always knows what the weather's going to do." His friend nodded as they shook their coats.

A pigeon flew down from the rafters and pecked at the oats in the stall. "Who lives here now?" Jamie asked, looking up to see other birds in the roof. "Isn't the Major still in the asylum place?"

"Yes, he is, so nobody lives here, it's deserted." The stable boy pulled at a big cobweb woven across the front of the adjoining stall. A large spider ran up and began to repair it.

Oswell jumped back, cringing.

"Don't you like spiders?" asked Jamie. "They're fascinating creatures if you look closely at them."

Oswell shook his head. "No, I don't." Turning, he walked to the door. "It's still raining," he called, sticking out his head before pulling it back in quickly.

School for Jamie

Jamie stood watching the antics of the spider. "Mama will be wondering where we are."

"I expect she'll know we're sheltering somewhere," offered Fred, giving a handful of oats to the pony, who nickered her thanks.

"What'll happen to this house," asked Jamie, "if nobody comes to live in it?"

"I don't know. I suppose it'll go to wrack and ruin."

Jamie turned to Oswell. "Shall we come and explore it tomorrow?" His friend didn't look too eager, but Jamie thought it would be a spiffing idea. "Will we be allowed to, Fred?"

"The house is locked up. You won't be able to enter inside and, anyway, it would be trespassing."

Jamie sighed. Another good idea shattered. He might come and see, anyway, just in case.

Not having heard any thunder for a while, he went to look out. "I think the storm's over, Fred," he called, so they clamoured back into the trap and set off once more. Their coats too wet to put back on, the boys tried to keep warm by wrapping their arms around their bodies and thumping their hands together.

Chapter 9

Tillie entered the nursery. Nanny usually insisted on Alice putting away one toy before taking out another, so she could not understand why she could see toys scattered across the floor. Stepping over a train, it registered in her mind that it belonged to Jamie, and she didn't think Alice played with it. She put it to the recesses of her brain, worried about Daniel who had been uncharacteristically fractious all day. She took him from the nanny and gave him a cuddle. "I hope he isn't coming down with something." She stroked his red cheek. "He doesn't have a rash anywhere, does he?" She unfastened the buttons on his jacket to examine his back and neck.

"No, ma'am, I've checked." Nanny picked up Alice, who vied for her attention by tugging her pinafore. The little girl reached over to the baby. "No, don't touch him, just in case."

With no sign of a rash, she refastened his clothes. "I'm sure he has a fever. If he isn't any better by this afternoon, I'll call for the doctor, to be on the safe side."

"I haven't heard of any illnesses going around the area." Nanny put Alice back down to play and picked up the untidy toys in a hurry, as if she'd only just noticed them.

Tillie sat in the chair, preparing to feed the baby. She noticed some paint peeling off the ceiling. The yellow wallpaper looked very shabby as well, with several bare patches. Another job to be done. She sighed. David didn't seem to have any interest in the everyday running of the house. She would have to mention it to Nellie. The sight of Annabella's doll, sitting on the tallboy, reminded her of Jamie and the fuss he had made when he had thought the nanny had thrown it away. Dear Jamie. How she still missed him, although he should be on his way home.

Glancing towards the window, she watched the rain beating down. A loud burst of thunder made Alice jump and run to her. "It's all right, sweetheart, it's only the angels beating their carpets." She remembered telling Jamie that years before.

Actually, shouldn't he be home by now? And he's bringing a friend.

"I don't suppose you know if Sam has left to pick up Jamie yet?" she asked Nanny, who, having tidied up the toys, sat at the table, sewing.

Nanny looked up, a puzzled expression on her dour face. "Um, I thought Sam had taken the master to see somebody."

"So who's picking Jamie up then?"

Nanny shrugged, looking as if she couldn't care less.

Tillie looked down at Daniel, who suckled half-heartedly. "Oh, come on, darling," she tried to coax him into speeding up. "I need to check if anyone's gone to pick up your brother. Your big brother—he's coming home today. I wonder what he'll make of you."

She really hoped Jamie wouldn't feel put out. He shouldn't do, he'd loved the twins the minute they'd been born.

"Have you finished?" Putting him over her shoulder, she rubbed his back until he gave a tiny belch. "That will have to do." She laid him on his tummy on her knees while she adjusted her bodice, then took him over to Nanny. "Please settle him down. He seems fine at the moment, much cooler, but we'll need to keep our eye on him." She knew she sounded overprotective, worrying at the slightest hint of anything untoward, but she couldn't help it. After losing Annabella… "I'm going down to see about Jamie."

Alice looked up from the doll she had been undressing. "Jamie," she shrieked. "Jamie."

Bending down to pick her up, Tillie swung her

round. "Yes, sweetheart, he's coming home today. Isn't that wonderful?" She thought she heard Nanny snort but, glancing at her, she seemed to be concentrating on the baby. It must have been him, belching again.

Putting her daughter down, she told her, "You stay here with Nanny while I go and see if he's arrived."

Another clap of thunder shook the room, and Alice grabbed her leg. "Me go."

"All right, come on then." She really hoped her older son had not become caught in the storm. Not that he would be afraid, but he would be drenched, and his chest still played up sometimes in bad weather.

She found Maisie alone in the kitchen. The little scullery maid had completely recovered from her bout of illness, and seemed happy to be back working with Freda. Betsy bustled about, setting the table in the dining room, and she could not find Nellie.

She entered the lounge and walked over to the window. The rain seemed to have abated. Alice pointed down the drive. "Jamie," she yelled.

Tillie had been so intent on the dark clouds scudding across the sky that she hadn't noticed a cart in the distance. "So it is." Running to the front door, she yanked it open. A cold draught blew in and, shivering, she picked up Alice as they waited on the front step.

It seemed an age before the pony and trap pulled up, Jamie waving madly. Tillie tried to take a look at his friend, but he had his head down so she couldn't see his features. They both jumped out as soon as it stopped, and she ran to them, giving Jamie a hug and shaking hands with his friend, before hurrying back inside.

"You're drenched," she stated. "Come on in near the fire." Giving their coats and hats to Purvis, who as always seemed to appear as if by magic, they ran into the lounge.

"Are you going to introduce us?" she asked as they

stood warming their hands in front of the roaring fire.

"Mama, this is Oswell Peel, known as St Clements. Peel, this is my mama and my little sister, Alice."

They shook hands again, both saying, "I am pleased to meet you."

"I've been meaning to ask you about your nickname, Peel. Why do they call you St Clements?" Jamie asked, giving his sister a squeeze.

"It's something to do with the song 'Oranges and Lemons'." Jamie didn't look any the wiser at first, then a grin spread across his face. "Oh, orange peel, I see. That's good, isn't it, Mama?"

"Yes, dear, very appropriate." Tillie didn't know what to say to the stranger. He seemed very polite and well-spoken. What more could she ask for? "What would you like us to call you while you're here?"

She didn't fancy calling him Peel or St Clements, so was pleased when he replied, "Oswell, if that's all right, ma'am."

"Oh, good, but you don't have to stand on ceremony, my dear. Missus Dalton will be fine."

The boy smiled, a lovely smile that lit up his whole face. His short hair still showed signs of the rain where his hat hadn't covered it. Alice went across to him and put out her hand. He looked at Jamie, his blue eyes filled with panic, clearly unsure what to do.

"She likes you, Peel." Jamie bent down to his sister. "This is Oswell. Say hello."

She took her thumb out of her mouth and said, "Othwell."

"That's it, good girl."

His friend still looked uncomfortable, so Tillie suggested, "Jamie, why don't you take Oswell up to his bed chamber, the yellow one, now you've thawed out. Your trunks arrived this morning, so you can both change out of those wet clothes. Then you can show him around the house."

"Good idea, Mama. Come on, Clemmy." The boy gave Jamie a sour look at the new nickname as they went out.

Jamie didn't even ask about his new baby brother, she thought, picking up Alice, and following them out of the room.

* * * *

"This house is enormous," exclaimed Oswell as Jamie showed him into the music room a short while later. "My aunt's house only has three bedrooms."

"I used to think like that. Before I come here, I lived in a travelling caravan, apart from a little while when I lived with a lovely old lady called Missus Curtis." Bad memories returned of the fire that had killed her and Maisie's mother.

When he went quiet, his friend asked, "How did you come to live here then?"

"I…I'll tell you about it some other time." Jamie shivered, putting the thoughts to the back of his mind. He couldn't bear to think of that day and the resulting week, not when he had someone of his own age to play with. "What do you want to do tomorrow?" he asked, eager to change the subject.

Oswell shrugged. "What do you propose?"

"Oo, 'propose', that's a big word."

"My aunt uses it all the time. I suppose I…" Oswell grinned. "Oh, it rhymes—suppose, propose. We could write a poem."

"I ain't…I mean, I am not very good at poems." Jamie grimaced. His friend spoke so well, he thought he had better try as well. "I did one for English, and it didn't turn out very good…I mean, well."

This is going to be hard work, trying to talk proper.

School for Jamie

"But I love making up poems, they're easy." Oswell put his finger up to his lips. "Let me see. How about...*In what manner, do you suppose, would a man in love, down on one knee sweetly propose?*"

"With a rose," yelled Jamie, jumping up in glee that he'd found a word to rhyme.

"Well, yes, although the next line did not need to rhyme, but never mind, you have the idea."

"Oh." He thought he'd been so clever. Deflated, he walked over to the window. It had started raining again, so they couldn't go down to the lake.

"Do you play?" asked Oswell.

Turning back, he saw his friend running his fingers over the smooth surface of the piano.

"Me? No, do you?" Jamie had heard boys having piano lessons in the room below his dormitory. He loved listening to one particular piece, and longed to know its title. When Oswell nodded, he asked, "Do you have lessons at school?"

"Yes."

Jamie lifted up the lid. "Go on, show me."

Oswell hesitated. "Are you sure? Won't your parents mind?"

"No, Father's out, and Mama's too busy with the baby."

"When will we see it?"

"What?"

"The baby. Is it a boy or a girl?"

Jamie felt guilty that he hadn't been up to see him. He had intended doing so during the tour but, somehow, they had missed the nursery. "It's a boy. His name's Daniel. Show me what you can play and then we'll go and see him, if you want."

Oswell sat down and splayed his fingers. "Are you really sure? My aunt won't let me play hers without asking permission first."

"Yes, it'll be fine." Jamie had never had any inclination to try, so didn't really know. He couldn't lose face now, though, by changing his mind.

Jamie stood beside the piano as Oswell began to play. He had only managed a few notes when Nellie came rushing in. "Who…?" She stopped, looking at Jamie with raised eyebrows.

His friend seemed oblivious to the interruption. He carried on, the lilting tune filling the room. Nellie stood and listened, her head moving in time to the music, one hand on Jamie's shoulder, pointing with her other finger, as if conducting an orchestra. When he finished, they both clapped.

"That was beautiful," the housekeeper said. "It's such a pity nobody plays this anymore."

"Will you learn me, Peel?" Jamie asked. "I'd love to be able to do that."

"Well…" his friend hesitated, standing up.

Jamie ran his fingers across the notes from end to end, creating a discordant sound.

"It's not that simple. You need to practise for hours every day."

"Oh." *Maybe not such a good idea, then.* "Hours?"

"Yes, if you want to be proficient."

"Pro?"

"Really good."

"I don't think I'll ever be procient at anything." Deflated, Jamie closed the piano lid.

Nellie patted him on the shoulder. "You're the sort of person who's jack of all trades but master of none," she said, as if that was supposed to cheer him up. "Anyway, have you been up to see your baby brother yet?"

He shook his head. He'd been putting off the moment as long as possible.

"He looks a lot like you," she continued.

"Does he?" Maybe he wouldn't be such a monster after all. "Does he really?" He had better go upstairs and check that Nanny hadn't been pinching him. Being a girl, Alice escaped harm, but with the baby being a boy... "Come on, Peel. Let's get it over with."

They left Nellie running her fingers over the top of the piano and muttering about the amount of dust she could see.

"Oh dear, poor Betsy'll be in trouble," Jamie alleged as they went upstairs.

"Who's Betsy?" asked his friend.

"The parlour maid. She's a lovely girl, but I don't think Nellie's very happy with her work. I heard her complaining last time I came home that she slap dashes."

Tapping on the nursery door, they went inside without waiting for a reply. His mother sat in her chair. She had clearly been feeding the baby as she lifted him up, exposing her naked breast.

"Jamie!" she exclaimed, trying to cover herself, turning away from them.

Jamie looked at his friend. His cheeks had turned the colour of beetroots, and his mouth exuded peculiar noises.

"It's nothing to be embarrassed about," he explained. "It's natural."

But Oswell, having taken one step inside, edged his way back out of the door, his eyes looking as if they would burst out of their sockets.

"Come back later, Jamie, when I've finished." His mother held the baby in front of her to shield herself from his friend's view.

Jamie followed Oswell out. He hadn't even had a proper introduction to his new brother. Why did everything have to go wrong? It dawned on him that his friend wouldn't have ever seen a woman breastfeeding before. "You don't have to feel awkward, you know. It's how the baby's fed."

"I'm sorry," Oswell said with tears in his eyes. "I've spoiled your introduction to your brother." He turned to go back downstairs. "I shouldn't have come. I'm so really sorry." He ran down, taking two steps at a time. Jamie thought he could hear him sobbing as he tried to catch up. The faces of his father's ancestors on the walls seemed to be mocking as their eyes followed him. He tried not to look at them but, feeling unsettled, he slipped and fell down the remainder of the stairs, landing upside down on the small square of landing that divided it from the next flight. One of the pictures of a man in a funny hat definitely laughed at him.

Oswell stopped and looked back. "Are you hurt, Dalton?" Hurrying back, he helped Jamie to his feet.

"Of course not." Jumping up and straightening his coat, he heard someone running upstairs. "Auntie Ruby!" he cried with delight.

"Jamie, I thought I heard someone fall. Let me look at you." Fastening his top button, she ran her hands down his arms, muttering something about him being hurt, but could only take in her enormous belly. It looked like it would explode any minute. Surely his mama's had never been that big, even when expecting the twins.

He looked into her grey eyes, wanting to hug her, but afraid it would squeeze out the baby. "I'm fine, Auntie Ruby, really, I am. How's Sam?"

"Sam's very well, thank you, but aren't you going to introduce me to your friend?"

Being a squash on the little landing, Jamie continued downstairs as he made the introductions.

"So, how are you enjoying your stay so far?" Auntie Ruby asked Oswell as they reached the hall. Grimacing, he wrung his hands, but made no reply.

At that moment, Betsy came out of the dining room in tears. Taking one look at the trio, she stuffed her handkerchief in her mouth and ran into the kitchen.

"Why's Betsy crying?" Jamie started to go after her. "She's usually so cheerful. I don't like seeing her like that."

"There's no need to concern yourself, Jamie. You look after your friend. He doesn't look very well." Auntie Ruby steered the boys into the lounge, where they sat down as she pulled the bell. As they waited for the maid, she turned to Jamie. "What do you think of your new brother?"

"Well..." What could he say?

Betsy came in, her eyes still red. "Would you bring some lemonade for Master Jamie and his friend, please, Betsy," Auntie Ruby asked. The maid bobbed a curtsy and went out.

"He has a look of you around his eyes," his aunt continued.

"That's what Nellie said," he replied, wanting to change the subject. "Do you think Sam will mind if we come down to the stables tomorrow?" He could see his friend still seemed very unsettled. "Do you like horses, Peel?" he asked him.

Oswell shook his head, keeping his gaze down. "Not much."

"Do you ride at all?"

Another shake of his head. That scuppered that idea.

Betsy returned with the drinks, and his aunt stood up, rubbing her belly. For a split second of panic, Jamie thought the baby would be born there and then. His face must have given away his thoughts for she smiled and patted his shoulder. "Don't look so worried, the baby isn't due yet. Enjoy your drinks, and I'll see you later on."

Oswell sneezed as she turned to go. "Bless you. I hope you're not coming down with a cold."

"I think I might be. I feel very unwell." He took out his handkerchief and blew his nose, muffling what he said after that. It sounded something like going home.

But he's only just arrived. Surely, he can't want to leave already?

Jamie jumped up to try to make him change his mind, but his aunt put her hand on his arm. "It would be for the best, especially with your brother being so little. He isn't very robust." She put her hand on his friend's forehead. "I didn't think you were well. Where do your parents live?"

Feeling guilty that he hadn't realised Oswell felt poorly, Jamie blurted out, "He don't have no parents. He lives with his aunt." He turned to Oswell. "She lives in Derbyshire, don't she?"

Oswell nodded. "In Buxton."

"Well, that's too far to travel today. We'll have to sort things out for you to return tomorrow."

Jamie lay in bed, his throat sore, his eyes streaming. *I hope Peel doesn't feel as bad as I do*, he thought. Thank goodness his friend had gone home. Two poorly boys in the house would have put too much strain on the household. He couldn't go out of his room in case the baby caught his illness. His mama popped her head around his door occasionally, but didn't come right in, the same with Alice, who waved from the doorway, and he'd only seen his father twice since he'd been home. What holidays they had turned out to be!

A few days later, Nellie came in. "You may leave your bed today and sit near the window."

"Hooray," he tried to yell, but his voice hid in the back of his throat somewhere. Pushing aside the covers, he stepped out. Nellie quickly laid a thick, warm blanket around his shoulders. "You mustn't catch cold," she chided.

It took ages to reach the chair near the window. "This reminds me of when I first come," he managed to whisper.

"That's long enough. Back to bed." Nellie pulled him up after a few minutes, a look of concern on her face. He willingly climbed back into his still warm bed, snuggled into the soft sheets and went to sleep.

Looking out of the window a week later, he saw the grounds covered in a sprinkling of snow. "Fiddlesticks," he moaned as Nellie changed his sheets. "Just as I'm betterer, it starts to snow, so I s'pose I still won't be able to go outside."

"No, young man, I'm sorry to say you definitely will not."

"Why are you whispering?" he asked, concentrating on fastening his shirt buttons.

"I'm not, I'm speaking normally." She turned to face him. "Is your hearing worse again? The infection must have damaged your ears." She sighed. "I'll ask Freda to warm up some olive oil." She patted his head. "Just as it seemed to be improving. It's always one step forward and two steps back with you, isn't it, me lad?"

He nodded in agreement. "When do I go back to school?" he asked, pulling on his jacket.

"If this snow continues, it won't be for a while." She resumed her task, shaking the white sheet and laying it flat on his bed.

Hoping it would snow for weeks, he went to the window, pulling the brown curtains back for a better view, the ground below rapidly disappearing under a blanket of whiteness.

Nellie smoothed out the counterpane. "Do you like it there?"

"Pardon?" He turned to face her.

"At your school? Are you settling in?"

"It isn't too bad, I suppose."

"Your friend was very personable—what we saw of

him, at any rate. Do you have many others?"

"Not really. Most of them think I'm... It don't matter. What's for dinner? I'm starving."

The housekeeper smiled. "You must be feeling better."

Chapter 10

Tillie untied the ribbons on Alice's blue bonnet and took off her own hat. "Show Papa your red cheeks." The little girl ran to her father, sitting in the armchair with a glass of brandy in his hand.

"It's rather early for that, isn't it? Is everything well?" she asked him.

"Don't start lecturing," he snapped, putting the drink on the table at his side. He lifted Alice onto his knee. "Have you had a nice walk?" he asked, warming up her small cold hands with his large warm ones.

"Lamb," she said. "Baa."

"Yes, Papa, we saw lots of lambs," Jamie added.

"Did you?"

"A whole flock of them, ewes as well, all huddling up to the wall, trying to keep warm." Jamie went across to look out of the window. "I hope they'll survive out there in the snow."

The door flew open and Sam came rushing in. "Please, mistress, come quickly, it's Ruby."

"The baby?" Tillie asked.

"I think so."

"Have you called the midwife?" Tillie put her hat back on and refastened her coat.

"Yes, she's on her way."

"You haven't left her on her own, have you?"

"No, a neighbour's with her."

"Can I come?" asked Jamie, to which he received a resounding 'No'.

Tillie turned to David. "Shall I take Alice up to the nursery?"

"No, I am quite capable of looking after my daughter. You go and see to your sister."

"Are you sure?"

"Yes," he barked.

"There's no need to shout." Telling herself to ignore her husband's bad mood, Tillie followed Sam out, and they ran up the lane as fast as possible in the slippery snow.

Arriving at the cottage, they found Ruby, moaning on the bed in the throes of labour. "Oh, Tillie, thank goodness you've come," she cried. "You didn't tell me it would be as painful as this."

"Just be brave, little sis. It'll be worth it in the end." Tillie flung her coat on the tallboy and went across to calm her sister. Taking a flannel from a bowl beside the bed, she wiped Ruby's brow, crooning to her as another contraction took hold. Sam lit up a cigarette and went to wait in the passage, where she could hear him pacing up and down.

After two hours, Tillie could feel her breasts filling with milk. "I shall have to go, my darling," she said. "Daniel will be fretting for his feed. But I shall return as soon as I can."

Her sister nodded, clutching her hand as if she couldn't bear to let her go. Much as she didn't want to leave her sister in the lurch, Tillie had to attend to her own baby. She didn't have time to arrange for a wet nurse at such short notice.

After going through this procedure several more times, exhaustion set in, even though Sam took her in the trap after that. Blinking to try to keep awake, her head began to nod when she heard the midwife call, "Hear it comes," and, with one tremendous push, a baby girl arrived.

Ready to give a shout of joy, Tillie noticed a worried look on the midwife's face. The baby didn't cry when she smacked her bottom, and she looked distinctly blue.

Tillie and Ruby watched in silence, but after a few minutes, the midwife wrapped the little body in a towel.

School for Jamie

"I am so sorry."

"May I see her?" asked Ruby, sounding calmer than she clearly felt. Tillie knew she would be torn apart inside.

"No, mistress, I don't think it would be a good idea."

Tillie turned to go and give Sam the bad news, but Ruby moaned, "I want to bear down again," and another tiny head appeared.

"There's one more. Push, lass, push," the midwife cried as a second girl made her entry to the world.

This one howled as soon as she drew breath. "Thank God," panted Ruby, craning her neck to see the baby.

"I wonder if there are any others in there," joked Tillie, in an attempt to hide her fears, relieved that at least one of the babies had survived.

The midwife swaddled her in a blanket and handed her to Tillie before pressing on Ruby's belly. "I don't think so," she said. "You may rest now."

Once the midwife had finished her duties, Tillie handed the baby to Ruby and called Sam to come in to see his daughter.

"Isn't she beautiful?" said Ruby, turning the baby so he could have a good look. "But I'm sorry..." She began to cry.

"Sorry for what? Please, my darling, don't cry." Sam looked across at Tillie, clearly nonplussed.

"There were two," Tillie explained, "But one didn't..." She couldn't bring herself to complete the sentence.

Sam looked at the midwife with the bundle. "You mean...?"

The midwife nodded and went out, saying, "I shall be back in the morning to check you over, mistress. Good day to you."

Sam turned back. "This one's healthy though, isn't she?"

"Yes, yes, can't you tell?"

The baby began to wail at the top of her voice. "She has a good pair of lungs on her, at any rate." Sam bent to kiss Ruby as she prepared to feed her. "What shall we call her?"

"I thought Eleanor, after your mother," Ruby suggested, once the baby started to suckle.

"Yes, that would be nice."

Now the excitement had died down, Tillie could not keep her eyes open. "I must go home."

"Let me take you," said Sam. "You can't walk all that way on your own in the dark."

"No, I couldn't drag you away from your wife at a time like this."

"I'll ask the neighbour to come in and sit with her. Wait just a moment." He turned to Ruby. "That's if it's all right with you, darling?"

"Yes, of course. I couldn't let you go on your own, sis. You must be shattered and, anyway, I think I'll have a sleep now." She looked down at the baby with such tenderness that Tillie's eyes filled with tears. She couldn't be happier for her sister. Despite the sadness of losing one twin, maybe this baby would be the making of her, dispel some of her feelings of inferiority, and prove her worthiness of being a mother.

* * * *

Yawning, Jamie waited for his mother's return. She'd said she shouldn't be long the last time she had come back to feed Daniel, and that had been ages ago. He tried to concentrate on his book, 'Treasure Island', but Long John Silver couldn't hold his attention.

He put the book down on the table and stood up, "Father, would you teach me to play chess like you promised the other day?"

School for Jamie

"Not tonight, Jamie. I am too tired and would not do the game justice." His father had also been reading. He closed his book. "Anyway, should you not have been in bed hours ago?"

"I want to wait for Mama, to make sure she's safe. How long does it take for a tiny baby to be born, for heaven's sake?"

"Oh, Jamie." His father smiled. "There is no way of telling when a baby will arrive, more is the pity. We men just have to wait it out patiently. You will find out one day."

"Do you think I'll ever be married, Father?"

"I do not see why not. What makes you ask?"

"Well...you and Mama are happy, aren't you?"

"Yes, of course."

"It's just that Sebastian's parents...his mother..."

"Yes, I heard."

"And you...well..."

"Come on, boy, out with it." The candlelight played on his father's angular face, causing his blue eyes to look severe.

Jamie wished he hadn't begun the conversation. He didn't want to upset his father by accusing him of anything, but... "You seem to snap at Mama all the time." There, he'd said it.

His father's face seemed to crumple and he sat back in his chair, wiping his hand across his mouth. "I am sorry if that is how it seems, Jamie, but I have things on my mind, things you do not need to concern yourself about." He shook his head. "Jamie, it does not mean I do not love your mother, please be assured of that." He took a cigar out of its case and lit one. The smoke drifted across to Jamie. It smelled intriguing, and he wondered if he dared ask to have one, but decided not to. Maybe next time he came home.

Still not entirely convinced by his father's words, but

knowing he would have to accept them, he stood up. "Shall I go and meet Mama? Surely she'll be on her way home by now?"

"I do not want you wandering around in the dark on your own, son. Just be patient, please. How about a game of cards?"

"Yes, can we play cribbage?" He hurried to the sideboard and took out a pack of cards and the cribbage board. "May I deal?"

His father nodded. The pouches under his eyes made his grey face look sad. Jamie wondered if he should let him win to cheer him up, but once the game started, his natural inclination overtook his concern. "Fifteen, and one for his nibs. I win." He won the first game hands down.

"Are you looking forward to returning to school tomorrow?" After Jamie had won the second game as well, his father sat back and pushed his black hair off his face.

What could he say? He shrugged.

"You will miss your brother, I expect. You have only just become familiar with him."

He'd only seen Daniel a few times, and couldn't really call that becoming familiar. Once he'd reassured himself that Nanny had not hurt the baby—he'd seen her bending over him, but it hadn't looked as if she pinched him—there hadn't seemed much point revisiting him. "I'll miss Alice. She's growing up so fast, isn't she? She can talk for England now."

His father nodded as the door opened and Betsy came in to put some more logs on the fire and light some more candles.

"Would sir like anything else?" she asked, bobbing a curtsy, her face aglow from the fire.

"Well, while you are here, pour me a brandy."

"I could've done that, Father," Jamie protested.

"Please let me do it."

"Very well. You may go, Betsy."

Jamie poured his father's drink and handed it to him. "Have you noticed she isn't as joyful as she used to be?"

"Who?" His father drank the golden liquid down in one mouthful and handed Jamie the glass to be refilled.

Pouring another one, Jamie replied, "Betsy. I saw her crying earlier."

"It is probably women's problems. Pray, do not worry about it. Do you have everything ready for the morning?"

"Yes, I think so." The brandy looked inviting. Jamie licked his lips, wondering what it tasted like. Should he sneak some while his father rested his head back on the chair with his eyes closed?

As he picked up the decanter, his father's voice echoed around the room. "Do not even think about it."

How did he know? "Can't I just have a taste?"

"No, son, a taste becomes a liking and a liking becomes a habit. Much better not to try it in the first place. There will be plenty of time when you are older."

The door opened once more. Jamie swivelled around, expecting it to be his mother, but Nellie came in with a pile of napkins that she put away in the sideboard drawer. "You're up late, Master Jamie, and you're going back to school tomorrow, aren't you?" She turned to go out.

Why did everybody keep reminding him? They all appeared eager to be rid of him.

Before he had time to reply, his mother walked through the door.

"Mama," he cried, running to her.

"Thank goodness that's over with." She dropped down into the nearest armchair.

"Has she had the baby?" Jamie perched on the arm of the chair and rubbed her cold hands.

She nodded. "A girl." She seemed about to say something else but closed her mouth.

"Let me make you a nice hot cup of tea," said Nellie.

"That would be lovely, thank you."

"A sandwich as well?"

His mother shook her head.

Looking at her with concern, his father asked, "Are they both well, Ruby and the baby?"

She merely nodded.

"Well, young man—" He turned to Jamie. "Now your mother is home, safe and sound, I think you should go up to your bed. Say goodnight."

Jamie reached down and kissed her. "Goodnight, Mama, see you in the morning."

The next day, he sat at the kitchen table eating his breakfast, chatting to Maisie.

"I wish I could learn all them things, instead of slaving away in here," she moaned, peeling another potato.

"Well, next time I'm home I'll learn you—I mean, teach you—how to read, if you want." Jamie stuffed a sausage into his mouth, savouring the spiciness. The ones they had at school didn't taste nearly as delicious. "I should have thought of it earlier. We could have done it...oh, no, I've been poorly, haven't I? There wouldn't have been time. Anyway, you can write, can't you?"

"Only me name, and I sometimes do that wrong."

Freda came out of the pantry, carrying a sack. Jamie jumped up to take it from her as she dropped it, and doubled over with a strangled moan, almost falling to the floor. Maisie quick-wittedly pushed a chair under her and she landed on it, slumping forward onto the table.

"That's the third time this week," said Maisie. "I keep telling her she ought to see the doctor, but she refuses."

School for Jamie

"Does Mama know?"

The maid shook her head. "I'm not sure. Nellie does."

"Well, I'm going to tell her."

"No," croaked Freda, "I'll be fine in a moment. There's no need to worry her."

Maisie rubbed the cook's back. "That's what you always say, but it happens too often."

"Please, I don't want to be a burden."

"You'll be more of a burden if you're too ill to work. How would I manage on my own?"

Freda stood up, a little shakily. "See, I'm perfectly well now. Come on, those potatoes need peeling."

Shrugging, Maisie looked at Jamie, her lip caught between her teeth. "What can I do," she whispered, "if she won't seek help?"

Should he at least hint to his mama? But Freda might think Maisie had snitched on her, and give her a hard time. He put his hand on the cook's arm. "Freda?"

"Jamie, I'm perfectly well, please don't fret. You go off to school and forget what you've just seen. Now, where did I put the butter?" She disappeared back into the pantry.

Jamie turned to Maisie. "I think you ought to tell someone if it happens again, no matter what she says."

"I will."

Nobody had said anything about the cook having a baby. He wondered if Maisie would know. "Is Freda…?" he began, but stopped when she came back out.

"I'd better go and collect my things and say my farewells," he said instead. "Sam should be here soon to collect me." Reaching over, he gave his little friend a hug. "And don't forget those reading lessons when I return."

Her beam of pleasure stayed in his mind as he said goodbye to his parents and Alice and Daniel.

"Give Auntie Ruby my love, and your baby," he

called as Sam dropped him off at the station, ready to start another term.

* * * *

"Have you finished 'The Christmas Carol'?" asked Bullimore, lounging in his armchair as Jamie toasted a crumpet.

"Almost. I didn't dare take it home for the holidays in case I forgot to bring it back. I read 'Treasure Island'. Have you read that? It's about a…"

"I know what Treasure Island is. Mind you don't burn that."

Jamie had turned to his housemaster to listen to him, and hadn't been concentrating on the toasting fork. He quickly pulled it back from the fire as smoke began to rise from the crumpet. It had only suffered singing on one side, thankfully. He buttered it and handed it over, holding his breath.

"It's just as well I like them well done. One more minute and you would have been in trouble."

Phew. He put another one onto the toasting fork and leaned back on his haunches, savouring the delicious tang of the crumpet as it heated up, releasing its yeasty smell. He would have liked one himself but knew there to be no possibility of that. Pulling it away before it could burn, he dolloped some butter on top and gave it to Bullimore.

Biting into the crumpet, butter ran down the housemaster's chin. "Did you have a good time in the holidays?" he asked as, reaching over and picking up a napkin, he wiped it off.

"Well, I was poorly most of the time." Jamie stood in front of him, unsure whether to do any more toasting.

"I understand Peel went home with you?"

"Yes. How do you know?"

"Ah, we housemasters know everything that goes on

School for Jamie

with our pupils."

"He didn't stay long."

"No, so I heard. Tell me why." Handing Jamie his empty plate, Bullimore wiped his hands and sat back, his arms behind his head.

"He became ill." Still unwell, his friend had not yet returned to school. Jamie had already been tormented by his classmates, saying he'd given him the pox.

Best to change the subject. "Would you like any more?"

"No. What's wrong with Peel?"

"I don't know. I thought he just had ifflunza."

"You mean 'influenza'?"

Jamie shrugged. Hadn't he just said that? "May I go now?"

Bullimore stroked his chin, looking thoughtful. "I hope you haven't brought any germs back with you."

"How could I bring Germans? I only brought my birds' eggs and other treasures."

"Haven't you heard of 'germs'? They can kill you." At Jamie's look of shock, he continued. "Off you go, then, *à tout à l'heure*."

Jamie hesitated, wanting to know more about those things that could kill, but Bullimore shooed him out. He wandered down the corridor, trying to imagine what they could look like. Why hadn't he ever heard of them before? Maybe the dictionary would tell him. He hurried to find it, but couldn't find the word 'jurms'. Maybe he could ask one of his tutors. Which one would know about killers? His first-year head, Mister Sumpton, probably would. With his bald head he looked a bit like a killer himself. He would have to sound him out when a chance arose.

The following week, having learnt all about the tiny things called bacteria that had only recently been discovered, he had a cricket lesson. He knew he would be good at it, for he remembered playing on his birthday some years before. He had beaten everybody, even his papa, and he'd had two good legs then. After all, you just needed to hit the ball as hard as you could, and run.

He tried not to be disappointed when the other team won the toss to bat first. With his position being near the boundary, the ball hardly ever came near. Daydreaming about what they might have for dinner, he became aware of shouting, and looked up to see it spinning towards him. Moving to his left, he cupped his hands and the ball fell neatly into them.

"Hoorah," his team members shouted. "Well done."

Strutting forward, he threw the ball to the bowler, barely able to contain his jubilation. How proud his father would be again. However, it didn't come close for the rest of the innings, so he resumed his daydreaming.

The other team scored a meagre one hundred and ten before being bowled out, and his turn to bat arrived.

"This should be easy," he said to the other batsman. "We'll beat them hands down."

"Don't be too cocksure, Dalton," the boy replied. "We still have quite a fight on our hands."

"Don't be such a wet blanket, we'll walk it."

"Just pay attention and keep your eye on the ball," the games master called.

He stood in position, tapping his bat on the crease line, eager for a good score. The first ball went over his head, and the second one went wide. "I bet the bowler's scared of me—he knows I'll do well," he murmured, lifting his bat to hit the next one. He whacked it with all his might and it flew over the boundary for a six.

"I knew I'd be good," he turned to say to the wicket-keeper but, turning back, he saw the next ball already coming towards him, and didn't have time to adjust his bat. The ball hit the stumps near the top, knocking off the bails.

His shoulders slumped, Jamie stared at them as they tumbled to the ground. How could he have been so unlucky? The bowler should not have thrown until he'd indicated his readiness. Maybe if he picked them up and put them back, he would be allowed to have another try, but the umpire called him to leave the pitch, so he had no option but to slouch off with his tail between his legs.

"I told you to keep your eye on the ball," the games master said.

"I'm sorry, sir."

"Remember next time." He patted Jamie's shoulder. "Well done for scoring the six. You could do well, but you have to concentrate."

"Yes, sir, thank you, sir." He'd had such high hopes of scoring the most runs, so the praise came as little consolation for being out so soon.

The following week, he performed better and scored twenty-two. "I kept my eye on the ball like you told me last week," he said to the games master on their way off the field.

"Yes. Dalton, well done. You'll make the first eleven if you keep it up."

The first eleven, how spiffing would that be!

"You just need to concentrate on your balance. You almost fell over playing that last shot."

"Yes, sir, I will."

On his way back from his fag master that evening, he rounded a corner in the corridor and almost ran into Silas Brown, the last boy he wanted to meet. Keeping his head up, he tried to ignore the bully from the football field, as his cronies surrounded him like a pack of wolves. They began to taunt Jamie. "Well, look who we have here. The boy who almost killed his best friend."

Determined not to rise to their jibes, he tried to walk past them, but felt his coat being pulled. He turned to see a particularly ugly boy whose name he couldn't remember. His jutting jaw and long nose looked just like a wolf. The boy sneered, pointing to a window. "Bet you couldn't climb out of that without falling."

"Prob'ly not," replied Jamie, still trying to push past them.

"Oo, prob'ly not," the boy mimicked in a high voice, as he pulled Jamie towards the window and opened it. "Let's see you try."

"No, I don't want to."

"We don't care what you want. *We* want to see you do it, don't we, chaps?" Silas joined in with his crony as he turned to face the others. Most of them nodded, urging Jamie closer. Panic bells began to sound an alarm in his head.

"Bet he won't dare," one of the others said, poking him in the ribs. "He doesn't have the guts. He's a mother's boy."

"I expect his mother's a whore," another boy taunted. "What do you think, chaps? Only a whore would beget a coward like him."

At the reference to his mother, his fear vanished. From the boy's sneering voice he could tell a whore would be something insulting. Jumping up onto the window sill, he leaned out. A wave of dizziness made him hesitate as he looked down, seeing a sheer drop to the quadrangle two floors below. He couldn't back out now, though. He had to clear his mother's name. Clinging for dear life onto some ivy growing up the wall, he edged his way out onto the outside sill.

He'd thought that would be it, and started to climb back in, but the window slammed shut. Having nothing to hold onto, he fell, away from the look of horror on the faces of the boys behind the glass.

Chapter 11

"Don't try to sit up."

Whose voice is that? Where am I? Jamie tried to open his eyes through the excruciating pain in his head, but could only see blackness. Putting his hand up to his face, he felt soft cloth.

What's that smell? Clean, pure air blew in, probably from an open window. But something else, something he had smelled before hung in the atmosphere. Then he remembered—the infirmary. *Is that matron's voice?* He couldn't be sure.

Then another voice spoke, so softly he could barely hear it. "My poor Jamie, my little boy. Thank goodness you're awake."

That's Mama. What's she doing in the infirmary?

A hand stroked his. He grabbed it, pulling her closer. The scent of her familiar perfume filled his nostrils as she kissed his cheek.

Then another, deeper, voice. "You are lucky, my boy. What on earth made you climb out of a window?"

Father.

But how could he answer? He couldn't explain what the bully had said, not while his mother sat beside him.

Fortunately, he didn't need to reply, for she said, "Never mind that now, David. We need to concentrate on his recovery."

How long have I been here? It must have been quite a long time if his parents had come.

His body ached all over.

Good news, though, he could move his arms perfectly well. One at a time, he tried lifting his legs. The left one didn't hurt. *So far, so good.* Pain shot through the right one, though, when he moved it.

He tried to sit up, but someone gently pushed him

down.

"Matron said…" he couldn't hear the rest.

"But I need to know if my back hurts," he replied.

"Your back seems fine, son. Lie still." Fortunately, his father had a much louder voice. "Hopefully, you have only injured your head and your leg."

"But why are my eyes covered?"

"As a precaution."

"But when will I have it taken off?"

"Tomorrow. Now rest."

Jamie lay back. That sounded like a good idea. He just wanted to sleep.

"We shall come back in the morning. Good night, son." He felt his father's bristly chin rub against his cheek and then his mama's soft, silky skin as they each kissed him goodbye.

"Is Alice here?" he asked dreamily.

"No, Nanny is looking after her."

"Make sure she doesn't pinch her," he whispered. "She's a naughty nanny sometimes."

"Don't you worry about Alice. Just sleep."

Pain stopped him sleeping very much. Because he couldn't see, he couldn't distinguish morning from night. He thought he heard Matron asking him if he wanted something to eat. His stomach rumbled, so he nodded and tried to sit up.

"Let me help you," offered a different, higher voice. He couldn't fathom who it belonged to. It seemed really odd to move his head and not be able to see anything, even when he opened his eyes and blinked. Usually, if he awoke in the middle of the night, his eyes would gradually become accustomed to the dark, and they would eventually make out shapes, but this blackness never wavered.

"Open up," the boy said. Jamie assumed it to be a

School for Jamie

boy. Opening his mouth, he felt a spoonful of something soft and claggy put in—probably porridge, but it didn't really taste like anything—and tried to work out where he'd heard the voice before. The scene at the window rushed through his mind, then the football pitch. It sounded like Silas Brown, but what would he be doing feeding him porridge in the infirmary?

After eating a few more mouthfuls, he shook his head. "No more, I think I'm going to be sick." Before he could prevent it, the contents of his stomach rose up and spewed out of his mouth. He lay back, shivering. Different voices hissed and moaned around him, while hands wrapped him in blankets and turned him over and back and over again. The motion set off his stomach once more, and he vomited again. The bitter taste in his mouth increased when someone fed him some foul-tasting medicine. He almost choked on it, until some welcome water followed.

Eventually, he lay still. The rolling had stopped, and his stomach felt more settled, even though it still gurgled.

"Jamie," called someone he took to be Matron. "Can you hear me?"

"Yes, Matron."

"Your parents will be here soon. When they arrive, we will take off the bandages."

Nodding slowly, he tried to imagine what could be beneath them. *Am I blind? Is that why she wants to wait until my parents arrive?*

It certainly seemed like it.

He tried to poke his finger under the bandage to relieve an itch, but couldn't reach high enough.

"What are you doing?"

"It's itchy. I need to scratch it."

"Please don't." Her breath felt warm on his hand as she dragged his away. "I know it's frustrating, but you really must not pull off that dressing."

He shivered. Clenching his jaw to try to ignore the irritation, he dropped his arm and felt for the counterpane to cover himself.

Then he remembered. Silas Brown.

Sitting up, he called, "Silas, is that you?"

"Yes, Dalton. How are you feeling?"

"What are you doing here?"

"Well…I thought I'd come and see how you were."

What a cheek! He pushes me of a window and then comes here, as bold as brass… But maybe he is concerned.

The bully's voice hissing in his ear dashed that thought. "Don't you dare snitch on us, or your life won't be worth living."

That's more like him. "What? I can't hear very well." Best to pretend.

Matron rescued him. "Off you go now, Brown. Thank you for dropping in. You can see your friend is recovering."

Friend? If only she knew.

Brown shook his hand. "Goodbye then, Dalton. Don't forget what I said. See you later."

Not if I see you first. But he might not be able to see. "Matron, why aren't my parents here?" The sooner those damned bandages came off, the better.

"They'll be here very soon. Don't fret."

Don't fret? What else does she expect me to do?

"How's the stomach? I could give you some more medicine?"

"Oh, no, not if it's that foul stuff you gave me earlier. Please, don't give me any more."

"But it did the trick, didn't it? You weren't sick again."

He had to admit the truth in her words, but prancing horses would not make him tell her so. Nothing on earth would persuade him to have any more of that evil stuff.

Tillie grabbed her husband's free arm, trying hard not to cry as they made their way to the infirmary. "Oh, David, it was worse than I had envisaged. My poor boy."

"We need to stay positive and focus on his recovery."

She helped him up a step. "Don't you think we should take him home with us?"

"I have been thinking about that, but have come to the conclusion that he would be better off staying here."

Disappointed, although she had known in her heart of hearts that would be his reply, she remained silent.

"We can stay for a few more days to make sure he is recovering. The inn is quite comfortable," he added.

"Oh, thank you. After all, it's his birthday soon. Could we stay until then?"

"I am not sure about remaining here that long. The estate does not run on its own. Maybe I could leave you and the children here and come back for his birthday."

"I shall have to be content with that." She would still have preferred him to stay with them. The image of the beautiful Christine Wilson, whom she had thought he had been about to marry four years previously, came into her mind. Could she be the reason David seemed so eager to rush home? *Don't be so mistrustful,* she told herself. *Put that idea out of your head.* "I wonder what time the doctor's coming. I'll have to go back to the inn in an hour or two to feed baby Daniel. I hope Nanny is taking care of him and Alice."

"Of course she is."

"I wonder what Jamie meant yesterday, when he called her 'a naughty nanny'."

"Delirium, my dear. Don't take any notice of the ranting of a sick boy."

"I suppose you're right." She couldn't help feeling a little anxious, though. Jamie had never seemed to like the nanny. "You don't think I told him too much of a white lie, saying Alice wasn't here, do you?"

"Oh, Tillie, do stop. You did not tell a lie. Jamie asked if she was here. Well, she is not here, is she? She is at the inn."

She pulled on his arm. "Oh, David, please don't be out of sorts with me. I'm just worried about him."

He turned to her. "I know you are, and I am too."

As they walked through a quadrangle, Tillie looked up at the leaded windows, all closed. "I wonder which one he fell from. How could he fall out of a window, David? It isn't as if it's the middle of summer and they would be open to let in a breeze. In fact, I feel a definite chill in the air, so it just doesn't make sense." She pulled her plaid shawl around her shoulders.

"I shall have to find the reason once he is better. It does not make sense to me, either."

* * * *

"Ah, Mister and Missus Dalton." Jamie hadn't heard the door open but sat up on hearing the matron's welcome.

"Mama, Papa!" He could feel his eyes filling with tears, and it struck him that if they could do that, surely he couldn't be blind. A sob escaped him as his mother's soft arms enfolded him, the scent of her warm body engulfing him with homesickness.

His mother sniffed in his ear, and he guessed her tears flowed as well.

"How are you feeling today, son?" asked his father in a gruff voice.

He couldn't reply, just nodded, biting his top lip in an effort to stop crying.

"Did you sleep?" his mother asked and, without waiting for a reply, continued something about friends coming to see him. He caught the phrase, "Saw your friend... So pleased you have made friends... important..."

If only she knew!

"And...Oswell? Has he been in?"

He shook his head, opening his mouth to offer her an explanation of why his friend could not come, but she continued to chatter on. Finding it almost impossible to listen, he switched off until he heard, "Ah, Doctor."

"Well, now, young man, the moment of truth."

Oh no, I can't tell them who made me climb out of the window? Please, don't make me.

"Let us take off these bandages."

Jamie breathed a sigh of relief. He wouldn't have known what to say. He would have had to lie.

Sitting up straight, he tilted his head forward as the doctor began to unravel the bandage. The pain in the top of his head made him cringe, and he waited with bated breath while his mama squeezed his hand.

They were off. *Dare I open my eyes?*

"Well, Jamie, can you see?"

Very slowly, he opened the left eye. Blackness. He quickly opened the other one. Hazy shadows danced in front of him. Nothing clear.

"Jamie!" his mother shrieked. "Can you see anything?"

Gradually, the shadows changed to shapes. Something came closer, but he couldn't quite make it out. "Are you wearing a red hat?" he asked.

"No, son, but I am wearing a red tie." His father's voice sounded rather funny as he continued, "Can you see any other colours?"

"Something blue."

"That's my coat. Oh, thank God." His mother's arms engulfed him so he couldn't see anything at all for a moment, just smell her familiar scent again. He wanted to cling onto her, but she pulled away, crying. Jamie had learnt that she often cried when happy.

His father patted his hand. Blinking hard, Jamie could make out the wrinkles at the sides of his blue eyes. How welcome he found them.

"You still have that mole on your cheek," he remarked, causing the other occupants of the room to burst out laughing.

"What's funny?"

"Nothing, my darling, we're just so relieved you can see so clearly," he thought his mama said.

He put his hand up to his forehead to see why it hurt so much. It felt lumpy.

"Don't worry about that," Matron pulled his hand down and sat him straight, smoothing out his bed covers, her white apron very clear. "That will soon heal."

"May I have a look in the mirror?"

"I don't think you should, not until it's healed."

All sorts of images flashed through his mind. Had his head been cut in two? He needed to know. "Is my brain sticking out of my skull? Please, let me see."

"It's nothing like that, no, no." His mother turned to the matron. "Maybe it would be better to let him see."

"I don't usually advocate patients being shown their wounds but, maybe in this case, it would be advisable." She fetched a small hand-mirror from the cupboard on the wall and held it in front of him.

He didn't know if he wanted to look once the moment of truth arrived. Squinting so he could only see small amounts, he could just make out a red patch. Feeling braver, he opened his eyes wider.

"Ugh," he exclaimed. A large reddish-brown scab that looked like a tortoise covered his forehead and cheek, extending into his hair.

"It should heal quickly." Matron quickly removed the mirror.

"Please let me have one more look." He reached out

to take it back, half of him not wanting to see it again, but the other half fascinated.

Matron hesitated. "Well, just a quick one, then." She didn't let him hold it, just held it in front of his face for a few seconds. It didn't seem any worse than the first time, but no better either.

"Will I be able to get up tomorrow? Am I cured?"

"Well…" began the bespectacled doctor, "I wouldn't quite put it like that. You will have to wait a while until your leg mends."

Tillie hurried across to take Jamie's hand. "But will he heal?" she asked.

"Oh, yes, I'm sure of that. May I have a word outside?"

Tillie gave Jamie a kiss. "We won't be a moment." She followed David and the doctor out of the room.

* * * *

"What do you need to say, sir, that you cannot say in front of the boy?" asked David, taking off his gloves. His pinched, pale face betrayed his concern as they stood in the corridor.

"It is nothing to do with this injury, sir, it is rather his hearing. Has he always been slightly deaf?"

"No," David said.

Tillie looked at him. "We have been concerned since he caught the measles last year." She nudged her husband. "Haven't we?"

David looked puzzled. "Have we?"

"Yes, I told you before he went to school, and Nellie's noticed it as well." She turned to the doctor, who had been watching them.

"Let's find somewhere for you to sit down, sir." The doctor took his elbow. "It can't be comfortable to stand for long periods with that crutch."

"I am quite used to it now, but it would be easier if we could."

They found an empty room, and the doctor asked David how he had incurred his injury. Too polite to interrupt when she just wanted to continue the conversation about her son, Tillie sat patiently while David recounted the events of the accident. After what seemed like an age, they eventually returned to the subject at hand.

"So, doctor, do you think it will go away—Jamie's deafness?" Tillie asked. "We hoped it would just be a temporary disability."

The doctor took off his spectacles and wiped them with the hem of his cloak. "There's no way to know for certain. Sometimes it can last forever. Only the other day I heard of a case of a young man who had suffered from measles, or was it meningitis? I'm not sure. Anyway, it sent this unfortunate man crazy, and he attacked a policeman. He ended up being locked away in an asylum."

At Tillie's gasp, he added, "I apologise, ma'am. I don't know what made me tell you that. That is an extreme case. I am not saying your son comes into that category, no, not at all."

She let out her breath in a soft whistle. "You had me worried there for a moment, doctor. I thought you were going to tell me my son was mad."

"Oh, no. I'm so sorry to have worried you like that. In fact, your son is very rational. He will not tell me how he fell, though. I am most concerned about the incident. When I asked him, he became tongue-tied and talked a load of drivel. I am sure there is more to it than meets the eye."

"Yes, I agree. We haven't had a chance—" She turned to David, who had his eyes closed "—have we, David, to question him?"

School for Jamie

Her husband's eyes opened. They looked pained as he shook his head. "No, not yet, but we will do before we return home."

"Well, I do not want to pressure the boy until he has fully recovered. I'm sure it will all come out in the wash, as they say." Replacing his spectacles, the doctor stood up, shook David's hand and then bowed to Tillie. "I must leave you now. I have another boy to look in on. I bid you good day."

When he had left, Tillie turned to David. "We'll go back in for a little while, and then you need to be in bed." At his raised eyebrows and look of anticipation, she added, "Not in that way. You soon perked up. A moment ago, you seemed to be half asleep."

"I am rather weary, but I could be persuaded to 'perk up', as you put it."

He reached out and took her hand. "We haven't made love for ages."

A thrill of desire pulsed through her, surprising her. Fancy feeling that way in that cold, bare room, of all places! "Not here!" she croaked.

"My darling wife, even I would not be that bold." He laughed, his eyes creasing at the sides.

Tillie just wanted to kiss those creases. "We'll say our goodbyes to Jamie, and then, when I've fed Daniel and put him down for his nap…" She looked up at the clock ticking on the wall. "He'll be fretting, his feed is overdue, then we'll say we need a rest and…" She reached forward and kissed his lips seductively.

"I can't wait, my darling. You won't change your mind, will you?"

"No, no matter what happens. I promise."

Chapter 12

Arriving at the inn, they were shocked to find Alice wandering around outside on the pavement, with no sign of the nanny. Loud voices could be heard from inside. Tillie jumped out of the carriage before it had even stopped and scooped up her daughter. "What on earth are you doing out here on your own?" she shrieked.

A scruffy woman of indeterminate age lounged against a wall a few yards away, with two small children clinging to her apron. "She's bin there ages," she sneered. "I was starting ter think she were lost. I seed a young gentleman eyeing her up not long back. I thought for a mo that she belonged to 'im, but 'e saw me watching and sloped off."

David had been helped from the carriage and, without acknowledging the woman, hurried into the inn.

Tillie debated whether to answer her, but rushed after her husband. They found the nanny shouting at the landlord. Tillie looked around for her baby. "Where's Daniel?" she screamed.

The pair who had been arguing became aware they had company and stopped, staring at Tillie and David as if they thought them to be apparitions. The nanny looked around her, as if she had forgotten where she had put him.

"Where's my baby?" Tillie yelled again.

Alice took her thumb out of her mouth. "Lith take him for walk."

"What?"

The little girl pointed outside. Tillie almost dropped her as she ran out. The woman who had been talking to her earlier stood just outside the door, holding a perambulator. "This belong to you an' all?" she sneered. "My, my, yer must take better care of your kids, lady, or

School for Jamie

yer'll lose 'em. There's lots of thieves about these parts." She reached inside the perambulator and tickled the baby under his chin. "Cute little thing, ain't 'e?"

Tillie grabbed the handle and yanked it away from her, cringing at the thought of the woman's filthy hand touching her baby. As she pushed it inside, the woman whined, "Don't I gets no fanks, then, for rescuing yer nipper? A pretty little thing like 'im, dressed in them fancy togs, could 'ave fetched a nifty price down the market."

Aghast at such a thought, Tillie didn't know what to do. Should she pay the woman? She had her children back now, so why bother?

The woman pulled her shawl from her shoulder, though, as she tried to continue inside. "Too proud, is we, to fank a kindly lady?"

Lady? No-one on earth would describe her as one of them.

David came out. His eyes narrowed as he saw the woman holding onto Tillie's shawl. A toothless grin appeared on her dirty face as she let go of the shawl and patted Tillie's arm.

"You 'ave a good 'un 'ere, mister," she drawled. "She were just about to reward me fer saving yer young 'uns. Weren't yer, me darling?" Her mouth closed and her eyes widened as they dropped to David's footless leg. The expression on her face changed as if she was trying to work out how she could gain some extra money.

"Just give her some money, David, please," Tillie begged. Daniel screamed, and she just wanted to hurry inside and feed him, away from the beggar.

His hand delved into his trouser pocket, but came out empty, so he tried his jacket. "I do not seem to have any coppers."

"Silver'll do, me luvly. I ain't proud," the hag cackled. Tillie looked down at the children, still clinging to the woman's apron. Green snot ran from their red noses and their tangled hair crawled with head lice. Feeling sorry for them, she said, "Just give her whatever you have, David."

I could have ended up like that wretched, unfortunate woman if David hadn't taken me in, she thought as she pushed the perambulator through the door, *so I must not judge her.* But she still flinched at the thought of the woman touching her baby.

Taking Daniel out, she brushed past the nanny, who picked up Alice—the landlord had disappeared—and hurried through the bar to their room at the back of the inn, where she rinsed out the flannel from the wash basin and wiped his yelling face, still cringing. Once his raucous cries had been silenced, she tried to relax as she fed him. Her breasts were engorged from being late, and her sore nipples made relaxing out of the question.

She contemplated her fate. How lucky she had been that Jamie had found his way to The Grange when she had been imprisoned. It just didn't bear thinking about what would have happened otherwise.

David came in, dragging Alice by the hand, and closed the door behind him. "Where's Nanny?" she asked. He shook his head, his lips pursed. When he didn't reply, she asked, "What on earth was going on? Why was she arguing like that? And, more to the point, what could she have been thinking of, letting Alice take the baby outside on her own? She can barely reach the handles of the perambulator. I shudder to think what might have happened."

He sat down in the other chair and lifted Alice onto his lap. "I have told Nanny to go and sort out her differences with the landlord. We do not want him evicting us."

"We should sack her." Tillie rubbed the baby's back.

"We cannot, we need her. How would you manage? We cannot take the children to the school each day."

She sighed. "I suppose you're right."

Alice climbed down and sat on the rug, playing with her doll. David sat back, taking off his gloves and hat. "Anyway, nothing untoward happened, so we have to be thankful for small mercies."

"I know, but I don't know if I can trust her again. What if that horrible woman out there had…?" Tillie shuddered and changed Daniel over to the other breast.

He looked purposely towards the bed. "I fear there is no likelihood of what we spoke about earlier happening now, is there? So much for your promise."

"What? Oh, that." She reached forward to touch him, but he shrugged her off. "Don't be like that, David. It isn't my fault. I'm as disappointed as you. I was truly looking forward to it."

"Really? Or are you just trying to appease me?"

"Honestly, David. Maybe we'll be able to find an opportunity later." She didn't want him running to Christine Wilson for what she, his wife, would not give him.

They both jumped as a knock came on the door. As Tillie had finished feeding the baby, she looked at David before calling, "Come in."

The nanny poked her head around. "I am so very sorry about all that." She gestured behind her.

Standing up, David picked up his crutch. "I shall let you sort it out, wife. I am going to the bar for a drink."

"We could ask the maid to bring one in here." Tillie couldn't bear the thought of him going off in a mood. Why had he called her 'wife'? He had never done that before.

"No, I need some time on my own." He picked up his hat and opened the door.

Alice jumped up and grabbed his coat tail. "Me come, Papa?"

Bending down, he replied, "No, not this time. You

stay with your mama," and he went out, closing the door as she began to cry.

Tillie sighed. "Come here, sweetheart. Papa will be back soon." At least, she hoped he would.

About to hand Daniel to the nanny, she thought better of it. He needed his smelly nether regions changing, but she had to mollify her daughter first, so she laid him in his makeshift cot.

The nanny stood twiddling with her bonnet, a defiant set to her mouth. *She knows I can't give her the sack because I'm reliant on her.*

Not feeling in the mood for an argument, she picked up Alice and cuddled her, saying to the nanny, "Just make sure it doesn't happen again. I don't want to know what caused your argument, and we'll put it behind us this time. I really cannot cope with all this stress, with Jamie being so poorly, and everything else."

"Yes, ma'am, sorry, ma'am." She dropped a curtsy. "Do you need me now?"

"No, just leave my sight."

"Yes, ma'am."

After she had gone, Tillie remembered the nanny hadn't even asked after Jamie. It was as if she couldn't care less about him. Maybe his dislike of her needed investigating.

They called back to the school later that evening, but Jamie had fallen asleep, so they left without speaking to him. David departed the following morning after calling in to see him.

Tillie felt abandoned, and tried to persuade him to stay a little longer, but to no avail. She had given in to his attentions the night before, but not with much enthusiasm. He had rolled over afterwards and fallen asleep without saying a word, but she had lain awake for ages, worrying about her earlier thoughts.

And the nanny. Before they had left the inn, she had

School for Jamie

made her promise to pay extra special attention to the children, but Tillie's nerves remained on tenterhooks, wondering what she would find when she returned.

Jamie seemed subdued. "I have to stay in bed 'til my leg's better," he moaned. "Will I have to have it cut off, like Papa did?"

"No, no, my darling. It's only a fracture, nothing like your father's injury."

"Well, I could have a crutch like his, couldn't I? Then I can get up sooner."

"I'm sorry, Jamie." Tillie turned from looking out of the window, watching her husband drive away, as she rubbed her tired eyes. "If the doctor says you need to stay in bed, then…"

"I'll go and find some games," suggested the matron. "What sort do you enjoy playing?"

"Any." Jamie perked up. "What do you want to play, Mama?"

"Something like draughts would be ideal." And wouldn't need too much concentration.

"I'll have a look." The matron left the room.

Tillie still needed to be convinced his sight had not been damaged. "Can you really see, Jamie?"

"Yes," he drew his arm up level with his shoulder, "but my shoulder don't half hurt, especially when I do this." Extending his arm, he reached up.

"Well, son, you know the answer to that." She smiled. "Don't do it." She brought his arm down, rubbing it in a caress.

"I ache all over really, but Matron said it's quite natural after…" He looked sheepishly down at the floor.

"Jamie, how…?"

"Oh, look, here she is. What did you find?" he asked quickly, not looking at Tillie.

"Draughts and chess. Do you play chess?"

"No, Papa never learnt me." He screwed up his face.

"But I love draughts." Taking the box, he set it on the small table at the side of his bed. The sleeve of his dressing gown caught one of the pieces and knocked it on the floor.

"I'll find it," he cried, lifting his blanket as if ready to climb out of bed.

"Jamie, stay there, I'll pick it up." Reaching under the bed, she retrieved the piece. "Let's make you more comfortable." She moved the table to one side and helped him sit straight.

They played one game. Tillie couldn't concentrate, and Jamie won easily.

"Mama, you let me win. That doesn't count."

"No, son, you won fair and square. I just have a lot on my mind."

She could see his eyes struggling to stay open.

"You need to rest, my lad."

"But what about another game?"

"We can play that later. Does your head still hurt?"

"Only a bit."

"You sleep now, and I'll return in a short while."

"Can you bring Alice to see me?" Tillie had told him earlier about her being at the inn.

"No, my darling, it wouldn't be advisable. Not yet, anyway."

"Not even for my birthday?" he asked sleepily.

"Hopefully, we'll all be home by then. We'll have a special party. Just sleep now."

Should she have raised his hopes by mentioning a party? Too late, she had already said it. It would give him something to look forward to, to speed his recovery. She pulled his blankets over him, and walked the short distance to the inn, tying her bonnet ribbons tightly to stop the cool wind blowing it off, and clinging onto her shawl.

Holding her breath, wondering what she would find,

she entered the inn, and found the nanny playing with Alice quite happily, the baby still fast asleep. She need not have worried. The nanny had promised there would not be a repeat of the previous day's performance. Tillie still didn't know what she had been arguing about and didn't want to. She just wanted her children to be looked after safely. Surely it was not too much to ask for?

Chapter 13

Jamie's swift recovery allowed him to go home the day before his birthday. His leg seemed to have healed without any sign of a limp.

Tillie fretted because she didn't have time to prepare a proper party for him.

"We'll cope," said Nellie when she voiced her concerns.

"I know, but Freda seems even more poorly than before I went away. Has she seen the doctor?"

The housekeeper filled the lamp with oil and set it on the sideboard. She looked up, her dark eyes full of concern. "No, she flatly refuses."

"She's lost weight, hasn't she?"

"Yes, I think so. But what can we do? We can't take her forcibly to see the doctor, and she won't have him come here." She shook her head. "She's my dearest friend, but she's so infuriating at times."

Tillie didn't know what to suggest. "Well, if *you* can't persuade her, then I'd have no chance." She picked up a pile of napkins. "Anyway, we need to organise Jamie's party. Just a small affair. He isn't up to anything grand."

"I'll have a word with young Maisie. She's becoming a great help, and I'm sure Mistress Ruby will be along later. She could leave baby Eleanor with Nanny while she mucks in."

"Um…" A good idea? Tillie didn't want to be a tittle-tattle, but she felt Nellie ought to know what had happened at the inn. She regaled the housekeeper with the facts.

"I can believe it," Nellie replied when Tillie had finished. "I don't like gossiping, but I heard she had a disagreement with one of the shopkeepers in the village a few weeks back."

"I wanted to sack her there and then, but the master made me see sense. I shall start looking for a replacement as soon as Jamie's better, though."

* * * *

Jamie sat at the head of the table, feeling like a king, surrounded by presents. His father sat opposite, his auntie next to his mama, trying to calm her baby. "Auntie Ruby, why does Ellie cry so much?" he asked. She had such a loud cry he could barely hear himself think, let alone what people said.

"Her name is Eleanor. Please don't shorten it. I know you like…" The baby yelled again, and he didn't hear the end of her sentence. Ruby jogged her up and down, and she stopped. "She cries because she's a greedy little beggar, aren't you? And I can never fill her." Giving her a kiss on her cheek, she held her out. "Do you want to hold her, Jamie? She's quiet now."

"Only if she doesn't wriggle too much or touch my poorly head." Sitting Eleanor facing him on his knee, she gave him a beaming smile. "She likes me," he gushed. Not like his brother, who rarely smiled.

Alice climbed down from her chair and came to join in the attention. "Me hold Ellie."

Ruby groaned. "Now see what you've done. Your sister's shortening her name as well."

"Oh dear, I'm sorry. But she wouldn't be able to say her full name, would she?"

Auntie Ruby bent down to her niece. "Say 'Eleanor'."

Alice tickled the baby's cheek, then pulled off her mobcap and ran across the room with it.

"Alice," his mama cried. "Bring that back here."

The little girl stood dangling the mobcap, her blue eyes wide and defiant.

"Lithy's," she lisped.

"No, it isn't yours, it's the baby's. Now bring it back."

When she didn't move, Jamie asked. "Shall I fetch it, Mama?"

"No, Jamie." His father held out his hand to her. "Your sister must learn to do as she is told. Alice, please give the hat back to Auntie Ruby."

Her thumb crept into her mouth, and she walked slowly back and did as she'd been bid.

"Thank you." His father smiled. "Now, come and sit on Papa's knee and be a good girl."

In vain, Jamie tried to put the mobcap on the baby, so Auntie Ruby took her and laid her in her basket.

The door opened, and everyone turned to see Nellie and Maisie carrying plates of food. Betsy came in with a cake covered in marzipan.

"Is that for me?" Jamie asked, his eyes lighting up.

"Yes, of course." Betsy placed the cake in the centre of the table.

"Can I have some now?"

"Not yet." His mother shook her head indulgently. "We'll have the sandwiches and pies first." She turned to Nellie. "Do you have a candle we could put on the cake?"

"I'll fetch one, ma'am." The housekeeper turned to go, but his mother caught her skirt and whispered in her ear. All Jamie could make out were the words 'Daniel' and 'Nanny'. Nodding, Nellie went out as the maids brought in some more food.

"You've done us proud, thank you so much," his mama gushed when Nellie returned. The usually austere housekeeper's face beamed.

Jamie began to worry once more about the nanny. Surely, she wouldn't hurt a baby? He put the thought to the back of his mind as they tucked into the delicious array of pastries, sweetmeats and small cakes.

"May we cut the cake now?" Jamie asked. He loved marzipan and couldn't wait to taste it.

Nellie lit the candle from a taper.

"Close your eyes and make a wish," said Auntie Ruby.

"What sort of wish?" He just wanted to try the cake.

"Whatever happy event you would like to happen in the next year."

What a tricky question. There were so many. "I wish…" he began.

"Don't say it out loud."

Opening his eyes, he looked at all the faces watching him expectantly.

"We don't need to know. It's your own secret wish."

Squeezing his eyes tightly shut again, he silently wished to see Beth again, that his head would heal quickly, and a general happiness for all his family, hoping that three things did not count as being greedy.

"May I cut the cake now?" The least they could let him do.

His mother came around the table to help him. "Just the first slice, then."

* * * *

"How do you feel today?" his mother asked him a week later as they sat in the lounge, and he tried to teach her how to play chess. His father had taught him a few days before, and even though he didn't feel confident, he knew the basic rules.

He moved his knight into position. "All right, I suppose."

"Are you still having those headaches?" She moved her rook.

"You can't do that. The rook can only move straight ahead or sideways."

She sat back. "I'll never remember all these rules. Anyway, you didn't answer my question."

He shrugged. "Only a bit." He didn't want her to worry.

"Well, do you feel strong enough for a certain person to come?"

"Who?" He tried to imagine who she meant. "Sarah?"

"Possibly. But only if you are up to it."

"Yes, yes." He jumped up, almost knocking the chess board over. "Of course, but..." Would her awful mother be coming? He didn't think he would be able to cope with her.

"But what? I shall put her off if you're not sure."

"Oh, I am sure about Sarah. You know I love her. It's just...never mind. Yes, please. Should I write to her?"

"If you want, although your father has already done so."

"I ought to have written before. I'll do it now, unless you want to finish the game?" When she shook her head, he continued, "Does she know about...?" He pointed to his head. It had almost healed, but he wore a cap, even indoors, to hide the remains of the unsightly scab.

"Yes. Maybe you will feel able to tell her how it happened, as you don't seem able to tell us, your own parents."

He kept his gaze down, feeling guilty. But how could he? Leaning down, he kissed the top of her head. "I'll go and write my letter."

* * * *

Sarah arrived two days later, alone. Jamie breathed a sigh of relief. She made a huge fuss over Daniel, cooing and blubbering.

I thought she was coming to see me!

School for Jamie

She soon handed the baby over, though, when he filled his nappy. His little face screwed up, turning as red as a beetroot with his efforts. Jamie found it rather funny.

"Do you think your mother will have another baby to replace George?" he asked once they reached the library.

"No, I asked her that, but she said she couldn't. I don't know why." Taking out a book, she blew the dust off the top and opened it. "Do you read much, Jamie?"

"Oh, yes." He took out a large red, important-looking one. "All the time." He could barely lift the heavy tome and dropped it onto a small table, pretending to read it. The lists and facts did not interest him at all, but he ooed and aahed, hoping to impress his cousin.

"Do you know if you have any Jane Austen novels in here?" She walked up and down the rows, carrying the book she had taken out. "I still haven't read 'Mansfield Park', and I would so love to do so."

"Um…I'm not sure. Let me see." Mansfield Park? He'd seen a map book showing towns and villages in Derbyshire, but didn't know where Mansfield was, let alone its park. "The atlas type books are on this shelf. P'raps it'll be with them."

Sarah laughed. "No, silly, it's a novel."

"Oh." *I was only trying to help. She didn't have to say it like that.* "We'll ask Father when he returns," he muttered.

"Yes, it would probably be quicker."

"Shall we do something else? It's stuffy in here."

Jamie turned towards the door, and Sarah began to follow. "Shouldn't you put that book back in its place first?" she asked.

Oh drat! "I'll ask one of the maids to do it. It's rather heavy." He put his hand up to his head as if it hurt and began to limp, even though his leg had healed completely. "I mustn't tax myself."

"Oh, no, of course not. Let me do it."

"No, Sarah, honestly. The maid will be only too pleased to help." Which one should he ask? Who would be the least likely to moan? He would have to ask when Sarah had gone to her room, just in case.

"If you're sure," she said.

They met his mother in the hall. "How would you like to go to Scarborough for a holiday?" she asked. "Your father and I have been discussing it, and he thinks the sea air would benefit us all."

"Oh, Scarborough, that would be spiffing. Isn't that where we went on the train when I was little?" exclaimed Jamie, spinning around to see Sarah's reaction. She grinned.

"Yes, that's right," replied his mother. "Although I wouldn't say you are that big now."

Trying to make himself tall, he turned to Sarah and took her hands in his. "Oh, Sarah, you'll love it. A man had a little monkey, and…oo, a show with peculiar people that we didn't go in 'cos, we didn't have time, and Mama thought it too unnatural. Maybe, now I'm grown up, you and me would be able to go on our own?" Turning back to his mother he asked, "Do you think so, Mama?"

"We'll see."

"And will Alice and baby Daniel be coming?"

"Yes, the whole family."

"And…Nanny?"

"Of course. How else would we manage?"

That put a damper on the idea. "What do you think, Sarah? Do you want to go?"

"Yes, please, it sounds really exciting."

"Have you ever been there?"

"I don't think so. I remember going to the seaside once, when I was very small, but I couldn't tell you where it was."

"That's settled then." His mother turned towards the door. "I shall go and start making the arrangements."

At dinner that night, the conversation buzzed around the forthcoming holiday. "When will we...?" Choking on a piece of pheasant pie, Jamie couldn't finish his question.

Sarah patted his back.

"That serves you right for speaking with your mouth full." His father picked up his napkin. "I thought we had taught you better manners."

"I'm sorry," he managed to say once he had recovered. *Drat and double drat!* Why did he always show himself up in front of his cousin? She always showed good manners and never seemed to put a foot or a finger wrong.

"Anyway, to answer your question, we shall be leaving at the beginning of next week," his father continued.

Jamie quickly swallowed the food in his mouth before replying, "Oh, spiffing." He had wanted to yell out something much more appropriate but, by the time he'd finished his mouthful, the moment had gone. "That's great, isn't it, Sarah?"

"I can't wait." She beamed, clearly as excited as him, but sat demurely with her hands in her lap. Then her face dropped. "Will we be hiring one of those bathing machines I've read about in Mama's magazine? I don't have a suit."

"Well, yes, we are hoping to," said his mother. "But don't worry. I shall need to purchase one as well, so we can go shopping together."

The smile returned to Sarah's face. "Thank you."

"Will I need one?" asked Jamie, not relishing the idea of visiting a tailor's shop. He hated shopping. He found it the most boring thing in the world, and couldn't understand why ladies enjoyed it so much.

"Well, yes, of course. But you will only have to be measured. That won't take long. I know how much you abhor going into shops."

Abbror? What a lovely word. Another one to add to his list.

"Thank you, Mama, yes, I do abbror shopping." He looked at Sarah, hoping she would be impressed by his use of the word, but she smiled in a peculiar way, as if trying not to. Had he said it wrong? It had sounded the same as when his mama had said it. *Drat, drat and triple drat.*

In a bid to change the subject of shopping, he looked towards his grinning father.

"No, Jamie, I will not be bathing. I do not think my crutches will stand up in the sand."

"Oh, no, of course not. What will you do, then, Father?"

"Do not worry, son. I shall find plenty to amuse me." He began to stand up. Jamie always wanted to help him, but knew his efforts would be refused, so sat still.

"If you will excuse me, I shall retire to my study."

After he had left, Jamie asked, "What about Alice, Mama? Will she be able to bathe?"

"I'm not sure. We shall have to see once we arrive. Anyway, would you two like to play a game or, as it's still light outside, do you want to go for a walk?"

Jamie looked at his cousin, wanting her to suggest a game, but she dashed his hopes. "Actually, Aunt Tillie, I was wondering if there was a particular book in the library, called 'Mansfield Park' by Jane Austen. I've wanted to read it for ages."

He stood up. "Well, if you're going to read, then I'll go and…" What could he do that might make her change her mind?

"No, Sarah, I don't think we have that one." His mother came to his rescue. "That will be something else we can do in Scarborough—browse the book shops."

"While I do something with Father," Jamie quickly

School for Jamie

added. Looking around bookshops would be even worse than haber…thingy shops.

"Why don't you have a game of chess, then? You do play, Sarah?" His mother stood up as Betsy came in to clear the table. The parlour maid grinned, back to her usual self. "Is your brother recovering?" his mother asked her.

"Yes, thank you, ma'am. They think he'll make a full recovery."

"Why, what happened?" asked Jamie.

"He caught his arm in the plough and we thought he would lose it. He nearly died, but he's much better now."

"I'm sorry. I didn't realise. No wonder you've been…" Jamie felt awful that he hadn't known anything about the accident. "Not Fred? I'm sure I saw him yesterday."

"No. Bertie, the oldest. His wife is expecting a baby any day."

Jamie watched the maid scurry out, laden with dirty dishes, and offered up a silent prayer to thank God for saving her brother.

He wondered if any of the servants would go with them to Scarborough. Maisie hadn't been out with them since the day at the zoo the previous year. "Will Maisie be coming with us, Mama?"

"No, dear, not this time."

He felt guilty he hadn't made time for his former friend, the truth being she had settled so well into her role as a maid, she just seemed like another servant. He supposed that page in the book of his life had been turned. But he still felt guilty.

His mother continued, "We shall be staying in a hotel, and they'll have their own staff."

"So, will they have a nanny? We won't need to take ours, then."

"No, they won't. Why don't you tell me why you

dislike her so much?"

He couldn't—couldn't risk going to hell. Maybe he could find a way of disgracing her. Pretending he hadn't heard his mother, he turned to the cupboard and, taking out the chess board, tried to think of a plan as to how he could do so, but once into the game, he found his concentration slacking, so had to abandon the idea. Daily becoming more adept, he didn't want to risk having a bad game. His king in check, for a moment he thought he'd lost, but he moved a knight to protect him, and eventually won.

The following day, the household hummed with action. Tillie sent Jamie and Sarah outside to play, although Sarah, being a young lady, didn't 'play' any more. They took a walk around the lake, Jamie hoping to see the buzzards. He longed to show one to Sarah, although she hadn't seemed very enthusiastic when he'd told her about the one he'd seen killing the crow. His father let them take the binoculars. Jamie had promised he would take extra special care of them.

Chapter 14

Daniel would not settle all day. He still didn't seem to be thriving as well as he should, being small for five months old, but David had convinced Tillie the sea air would be very beneficial. Each time she tried to start something, he would cry. Nanny had left him with her, saying she had enough to do, preventing Alice from taking the clothes out of the suitcase as soon as she put them in.

Sitting in her nursing chair, she cuddled the baby, trying to imagine what Jamie's aversion to the nanny could be. She seemed perfectly amiable with the younger children. Maybe she had a side she didn't show. Tillie hadn't forgotten the incident at the inn. She would give her one last chance during the holiday.

Excited, but also stressed that she couldn't help with the packing or organisation, she walked up and down, trying to soothe her baby. "What's the matter, sweetheart? Why won't you go to sleep?"

He replied with another yell.

"I hope you're not coming down with some illness, not today of all days."

She laid him in his cradle and stroked his forehead. Not particularly feverish. "Are you growing some teggies?" His gums didn't feel hard, though, so teething didn't seem to be the problem.

He sucked hard on her finger. "You can't possibly be hungry again. I don't relish the idea of hiring a wet nurse, not at this late stage, but I'm evidently not satisfying you. I think I shall have to ask Freda to start making you some weak oatmeal."

She fed him, gave him some Mother Baileys' Quieting Syrup, hoping it would do the trick, and laid him back in his cradle. Eventually, he slept.

The next day, the seamstress called to bring the new clothes Tillie had ordered for the holiday. David had said they could manage with what they had, but she had insisted they needed some new ones.

"We can't be seen in our old, shabby things all week," she had insisted.

"My, how you have changed," he had answered with a wry grin. "To think that when you first came here, you only had one spare dress in your bag."

"Yes, don't remind me, and that a hand-me-down from Becky."

She had kissed him, long and passionately, before saying, "And I have you to thank, my darling husband, for my deliverance from who knows what awful fate. I frequently shudder when I think what could have happened to me and Jamie."

Thinking about Becky, the baker who had saved her life, she felt guilty that she hadn't been in touch, and determined to write to her, if the chance arose at the seaside.

Trying on the pink dress, she marvelled at how quickly the dressmaker had finished it, as well as a matching one for Alice. If they had had more notice, she would have insisted on two outfits each, but had to be content with the one. Nellie and Betsy had stayed up half the night, sewing a new shirt for Jamie, while the nanny had concocted a dress for Daniel that Tillie didn't particularly like, but which would have to suffice.

Jamie spoke of nothing else but the holiday during dinner. Tillie noticed his hearing seemed to be worse when in a state of excitement. She tried to remember if it had always been the case. Several times, he asked Sarah to repeat what she had said, but then she always had been softly spoken.

* * * *

They finally arrived at the hotel. Jamie stared in amazement at the grand yellow building. "It's enormous, even bigger than I imagined. Won't we get lost inside?" "Well, it isn't as large as your school, and you find your way around that, don't you?" His mother held his hand, also looking up in awe at the huge hotel.

He would not admit it to her, but now and again, he did have to ponder which direction to take.

They went through the large doors into a bright hall with two wide staircases leading up either side of the far wall, meeting in the middle. Large candelabras, lit by dozens of flickering candles, hung from the tall ceiling.

"Good day to you and welcome to our hotel." A man with a bald head and bushy whiskers came towards them. "You must be Mister and Missus Dalton. Mister George Lighten at your service." He gave the deepest bow Jamie had ever seen.

"He doesn't look like a George," whispered Jamie to Sarah, hiding behind his mother. "Do you think your Georgie would have looked like that in fifty years' time?" Jamie giggled, his hand in front of his mouth, but his cousin didn't look amused.

"Jamie!" his father yelled. "Be quiet."

Oh dear, another blot.

Mister Lighten snapped his fingers and two bellboys appeared. "Show our guests to their rooms." When he spoke, his nose twitched, showing two rabbit-like teeth. Sorely tempted to put his fists up to his mouth and pretend to be one, like he had taught Alice to, Jamie knew he would be in even more trouble, so contented himself with thinking of a nickname to call him—Bunny? No, too babyish. Rabbit? No, too ordinary.

"Whiskers."

Everyone turned to look at him. "I beg your pardon," his father said, glaring at him.

Had he said it out loud? Oh, fiddlesticks.

"Sorry, I just…" He looked about him, desperately trying to find something to use as an excuse. "That picture up there…" He pointed to a portrait on the wall. "I thought he had whiskers, but he hasn't…"

"Just pick up your bag and follow us," his father said, crossly. "And keep your mouth closed."

"Yes, Father." He thought he saw a glimmer of a smile on his mama's face as they were shown to their rooms.

Through his window, a brick wall obstructed the view of the sea, and he hoped Sarah would be able to see it from the one she shared with Nanny and Alice.

Putting his bag on the bed, he went out into the corridor. He could hear his parents arguing in their room, with his baby brother crying in the background, but couldn't make out the words, just their raised voices. Should he interrupt or wait? The voices stopped, so he knocked. His father called, "Come in."

Opening the door, he saw his mother, looking dejected on the edge of the bed, and his father standing by the window with his back to her. Jamie tried to see the outlook through the window, but his father's body blocked his view.

"Jamie." His mama's face cheered up. "How is your room?"

It would be ungrateful to complain, and he didn't want to add to her woes, so he merely shrugged. "May I go out and look at the sea? Can you see it from your window?" He walked farther into the room.

His father moved to one side. "There it is. Satisfied?" Jamie hoped his bad mood hadn't arisen because of his earlier behaviour.

"Caw, you have a good view, there's even boats over there." He could see blue sea stretching for what seemed like miles, rounding a bend to his left, and cliffs reaching

School for Jamie

up to the sky to his right.

"That's the harbour where the fishermen go out to catch your dinner." He put his arm on Jamie's shoulder, seemingly in better spirits. "Go and unpack your bag and, once your brother has been fed, we will all go for a walk along the beach."

"That would be spiffing."

His mother smiled. "You like that word, don't you, Jamie?"

"Aye, it's great."

"Make sure you put your clothes away neatly, or would you prefer Nanny to do it?"

"No, I'll be careful. I don't need *her* looking after me."

"That's what I thought. Now you're thirteen, it's time you were given more responsibilities." She picked up Daniel, his cue to leave.

It didn't take him long to put his clothes into the wardrobe and stack his two books on the shelf. Sitting on the bed, he twiddled his thumbs. What could he do while he waited? He hadn't brought his treasure box, so couldn't check on his eggs. Read a book? *That's why you brought them.* Not in the mood for reading, he yearned to be out in the fresh air.

Maybe Sarah had finished her unpacking. He could go and see her. But the nanny would be there.

He paced up and down the small space between the blue bedspread-covered bed, the wardrobe and small table bearing a candle, washbasin and a jug, and stopped at the window. Maybe, if he peered right around the corner of the wall, he might see the tiniest bit of blue sea. But another wall hid everything. If he looked right up, he could just make out a tiny piece of sky above a chimney. At least that was blue.

Unable to stay cooped up any longer, he went back to his parents' room and called through the keyhole, "I'm just going outside, Mama. I won't go far," without waiting for a reply.

Stepping out into the fresh breeze, he wished he'd put on his scarf. It hadn't seemed that blowy when they had arrived. Should he go back and fetch it? No, he might bump into someone who would tell him to stay inside.

Finding himself on the promenade, he walked along, breathing in the salty air and listening to the raucous cries of the seagulls. One swooped down, and he could feel the rush of air as its wings only just missed his head. It picked up what looked like a piece of bread from the beach, flying up to sit on a lamp post to eat it.

He wondered if buzzards ate bread. Maybe he could lure one down when he returned home, and see it close up. That would be great. But he knew buzzards only eat other birds or small mammals, so maybe not.

Small boats bobbing on the water enticed him downwards. How he would love to have a ride in one, to go bouncing up and down, feeling the wind blowing in his face, although he wouldn't lean out too far. He didn't want a repetition of his last boat ride.

Before he knew it, he had arrived at the harbour. Angry voices drifted up and, looking down at the sands below, he saw two burly, bearded fishermen arguing. For a moment, it seemed as if one would punch the other, but he threw down the rope he had been holding and stalked off, brushing Jamie's arm as he passed, almost knocking him over. The other man shook his head and continued mending his nets, seemingly uncaring of the other man's bad manners.

Disgruntled at being pushed in such a way, Jamie wondered whether to run after the burly man and demand an apology, but then remembered he'd said he wouldn't go far. Looking back the way he'd come, he tried to remember the name of the hotel. The great? No. The enormous? No. Something more grand than that.

That's it. 'The Grand'.

"I s'pose I'd better go back," he muttered to a large gull sitting on the railing. Its beady eye blinked before it spread its large wings and rose up into the sky. "I'll ask Father if we can come back this way again. It looks really interesting."

Hurrying back the way he'd come, he couldn't see any hotels along the beach, only up on the cliff. Could his be up there? Had he really come all the way down that slope? He'd been concentrating on the boats, and didn't remember doing so.

A couple with two small children approached, so he decided to ask them. "Good day to you, ma'am." He used his best voice, bowing as low as the hotel owner had done. "Excuse me, but please could you tell me where I might find The Grand Hotel."

As he bowed, the wind caught his cap. He ran after it, picked it up, shook off the sand, and turned back to the family. They had continued with their walk. A young man strolled along ahead. He ran and stood in front of him, holding tightly to his cap and asked, "Excuse me, sir, but please could you direct me to The Grand Hotel?" Did that sound polite enough?

"Why, yes, young sir." The man's pleasant face smiled as he pointed up the cliff. "I do believe that is The Grand, that large yellow building with the four towers."

"Oh, fanks, I mean, thank you, sir." He remembered, then, seeing the towers on the top when they'd first arrived. Running backwards, he called, "Good day, sir." He might run into the man again, and didn't want to leave a bad impression.

Wheezing and puffing, he reached the top of the cliff where, tidying himself up, he put his cap back on. He had carried it to make sure it didn't blow off again. He walked through the front door, his head high, whistling as if he had not a care in the world—at least, he hoped he gave that impression.

The lobby thronged with people—mothers and nannies with screaming children, fathers lounging around, smoking, but no sign of his parents. Should he wait there until they came down, or go to their room? Surely, the baby had been fed. He'd been gone ages.

But could he remember the number of their room? Wishing he'd taken more notice, he thought it had a three in it but couldn't be sure.

He knew they'd turned right when they'd followed the bellboy so, easing his way through the smoke and the mass of people, he went down the corridor. It had definitely not been the first room, but he stopped and listened at the second door to see if he could recognise his parents' voices. Silence. No voices at the third either. Bending down to look through the keyhole, he heard behind him the one voice he hated.

"What are you doing, boy, snooping at strangers' doors? And where have you been? Your parents have been frantic."

He didn't need to turn. He knew, even before she grabbed his earlobe and gave it the hardest pinch she had ever inflicted, digging her nails in so it felt as if they met in the middle.

"Leave me alone." Wriggling out of her grasp, he touched his ear, sure it would be bleeding.

As she reached forward to grab him again, Sarah appeared. "Ah, Nanny, you've found him."

Clutching his bloody ear, he tried to reach his cousin, to put her straight, but the nanny grabbed him and put her arm around his shoulder. "Yes, the poor mite lost his way, but Nanny saved him, didn't she? Poor diddums," she crooned as to a young child.

Revolted at her touch, he twisted out of her grasp, about to contradict her, when a door opposite opened and his mother came out. "Ah, Jamie, did Nanny find you? Thank goodness. You look a little windswept, have you been out?"

"Yes, Mama, I told you I was going. But *Nanny*—" He said the word with as much contempt as he could "—didn't find me, she…"

"Never mind the whys and wherefores, he's safe now," the witch interrupted, turning him to face the opposite direction. "Off you go to your room and wash your hands before we go out." She half turned her head to speak to his mother. "He told me he scraped his ear when he slipped on a patch of rough shingle, so it needs cleaning."

"You've hurt yourself?" his mother asked anxiously.

"It's only a scratch, isn't it, dear?" Nanny butted in before he could reply. "I'll help him wash it. Come on, darling." She almost pushed him down the corridor with his arm up his back, hissing in his ear, "Keep your foul mouth shut."

"We'll see you in five minutes," he heard his mother call behind him.

He tried to call back, but the witch's hot breath on his cheek silenced him. They rounded the corner to his room. Once he saw the number, he remembered it—121, and his parents'—123. How could he have forgotten such a simple number? Yanking his arm free, he pushed the nanny so hard, she fell on the floor. He opened his door, ran in and closed it behind him, leaning against it, panting, full of the worst anger he had ever experienced. His tongue stuck to the roof of his dry mouth. He could barely breathe.

He felt the doorknob move, and looked down to see a key in the lock. Quickly turning it, he bared his teeth. "You're not coming in," he shouted.

"Jamie, darling, Nanny only wants to help you. Please let me in." She sounded so sweet, but he knew better.

The doorknob rattled again.

"No, go away. I don't want to see your ugly, fat face ever again."

Her voice changed to a deeper tone. "You know what will happen if you blab."

"I don't care. I'm telling Mama, no matter what."

"I don't think you will. You won't want to bear the consequences."

He heard a rustling sound, and then silence. Had she gone? He leant against the door, too afraid to move in case she managed to enter somehow. He imagined her turning to a jellylike mass and squeezing through the keyhole, so turned the key a half turn to block it up. Then he ran across to the window, made sure it was locked and drew the thick curtains. He didn't want her climbing in there. But that threw the room into darkness, so he opened them a tiny chink, just enough to let in sufficient light to see his way to the bed.

Sitting down, he took a deep breath and felt his ear again. It had stopped bleeding. He stood up, poured some water into the basin and washed his hands. Then he looked in the mirror on the wall, but could hardly see. He'd noticed a candle earlier, but what could he light it with? Unable to find anything, he went back to the window, and listened hard, before opening the curtains a little more.

He almost jumped out of his skin when a loud knock came on the door. "Jamie, are you in there?" Sarah. Phew, he thought *she'd* come back.

The doorknob turned. Blowing out his breath, he pulled back the curtains, calling, "Yes, Sarah, I'm coming."

Should he check the mirror first or unlock the door? Mirror. Grabbing the flannel, he dipped it in the water and wiped it over his ear, satisfying himself that no blood could be seen, before throwing it into the bowl and unlocking the door.

"We're all going out now," she said with a puzzled look on her face. "Are you well?"

Turning back to pick up his cap, he replied casually, "Yes, of course. Where are we going?"

"Just for a walk. Your father can't go far, as you know, but he wants to come."

Taking her by the arm, he replied, "That's good. He'll need his warm coat, though, it's very nippy out there. So will you. I'm glad to see you have your bonnet well tied."

She gave him a weird look as they made their way to the lobby, where his parents sat in the easy chairs near the door, with no sign of Alice or the baby or…

"Where are the little ones?" he asked, hoping against hope that they'd gone out with *her*.

His father grinned. "The *little ones*, as you call them, are having a nap. Nanny is staying in to look after them."

Thank goodness for that. Should he mention what had happened? But he couldn't wipe the smiles off their happy faces—not yet, anyway.

His mother pulled on her gloves. "She said she'll bring them out if Alice wakes up shortly. I suppose we could have brought Daniel with us in his pram. The fresh air would do him good." She put her hand on his father's arm. "Shall I go back for him, David?"

"No, dear, let us be away from this bustle. He will be fine. Like you said, the nanny will take them out later. Come on."

Outside, the wind seemed to have abated. They all took deep breaths and began walking. Taking his mother's hand, Jamie smiled up at her.

"Where did you go earlier?" she asked.

"Oh, just down to the boats. Do you think Father will let us have a ride on one? Lots of people seemed to be enjoying a ride."

"We'll see, later in the week." When she used her favourite expressions, 'we'll see', it usually meant 'no', but he hoped it didn't this time.

"So did you…all the…down there?" she asked as if surprised, but the breeze blew some of her words away. He nodded, but his father began to lag behind, so they waited while Sarah went back to him.

"I'm…right, you carry…" They waited anyway, and let him overtake them.

"He won't manage the slope, will he, Mama?" Jamie asked as they approached it. "He should have let John bring the wheelchair."

She shrugged. "You know your father…"

Letting go of his mother, he hurried forward. "Father, if you want to go down to the beach, I could be a crutch, if you put your arm around my shoulder."

"Thank you, Jamie, but no. I'll sit on this bench and watch you all."

His mother caught up. "Are you sure, darling? I thought you'd manage a little farther than this."

"Go, and stop fussing. I need a sit down. I will be fine."

Wrapping his legs in the checked blanket she'd been carrying, she kissed his cheek, and the three of them went down the slope, turning every now and again to wave.

Walking along the promenade, his mother pointed to the beach. "That's all sand, Jamie. Whereabouts did you fall?"

Oh, what had the witch said? "I beg your pardon?" he stalled for time to think of a reasonable reply. He really ought to admit what had happened, but he felt so useless, allowing her to continue to intimidate him, and what a rumpus it would cause. He couldn't ruin his mama's holiday.

"Your fall?" She stopped and examined his face. "What did you hurt? Didn't Nanny say you'd cut yourself?"

"Oh, it was nothing." He hoped she'd forgotten what had been said, her memory being bad at the best of times.

She seemed satisfied, so they continued walking. The breeze did not feel so severe down there, and the sun warmed their skin. "I should have brought my parasol," his mother said after a while. "I can feel the sun burning my face. I think we had better return."

"Oh, Mama, not yet. Can't we stay out a little longer?" Jamie turned to Sarah, who stood looking out to sea. "You don't want to go back yet, do you?"

She merely smiled.

"You two can stay, but I must return to your father." His mother waved back up the slope and his father waved back. "Don't be late for dinner, though."

"I don't have a watch. Do you, Sarah?"

"Yes. I'll make sure we are in plenty of time, Aunt Tillie."

Further along the promenade, Sarah stopped to look in a shop window. Jamie didn't want to waste the afternoon in shops, so walked away, hoping she would follow.

She soon caught up. "There's a lovely little ornament in there my mama would love. Next time we come out, remind me to bring my reticule, so I can buy it."

Not while I'm with you, he thought. "I'm hoping we can go for a ride on a boat," he suggested instead. "Would you like to?"

She pulled a face. "Maybe."

They continued down to the harbour, and stood watching the fishermen bringing in their catches, until Sarah said they should start going back.

"Do you like it here?" Jamie asked. "I absolutely love it. P'raps I'll be a fisherman when I grow up."

"I'm afraid you won't have the chance, my dear

cousin."

"Why not?"

"Because the estate will be yours when your father dies, and…"

"But he won't die for a very long time. He's only…" He worked out his father's age "…thirty-nine or forty. I know that sounds old, but your mama is older than that and Uncle Victor is even older than her and they're still alive. And one of our masters at school has a whole head of white hair, so he must be ancient."

"That's not the point."

"Anyway, I don't want to talk about that now. I'm on holiday."

He took her arm and they started to make their way back. In the distance, coming towards him, he spotted the fisherman who had earlier barged into him. He gasped. What if he did it again? What if he jostled Sarah and hurt her? Holding his breath, he stood in front of his cousin.

"What's the matter, Jamie?" She tried to urge past him.

"I'm protecting you," he whispered.

"What from?"

The man walked past without acknowledging their presence. Jamie let out his breath, feeling rather foolish. He wiped his hand across his mouth and pulled at his collar. "I thought that man… But it don't matter. Come on. We don't want to be late."

Maybe I won't be a fisherman, after all.

At breakfast the following day, his mother looked through the window. "The weather has changed today. It looks like rain. What shall we do?"

The maid serving them leaned closer. "If I may be so bold, ma'am, there's a new store opened in the town. It's enormous."

Jamie groaned inwardly.

School for Jamie

"Oh, thank you." His mother turned to his father and asked, "What do you think, David? Could you manage that?"

His father raised his eyebrows at Jamie. "I think it would be better if you two ladies looked round the shops while Jamie and I did something different."

She turned to Jamie. "That sounds reasonable. What do you think, Jamie?"

Does it 'eck as like? "I think that's a spiffing idea." Both his parents laughed.

"That's arranged, then. Oh, Sarah, I didn't ask you what you wanted to do. Would you like to go and see this store place, just the two of us?"

Her eyes lit up and she nodded, grinning. "Yes, please, Aunt Tillie. I'll take my reticule in case I see something I would like to buy."

Sarah and his mother continued discussing the virtues of what a large store could contain, but Jamie had lost interest. He finished his breakfast staring out of the window, watching the seagulls wheeling around above them, wondering what he and his father could do. The big, old, ruined castle he'd seen glimpses of up on top of the cliff looked interesting, but his father wouldn't be able to make his way up there. What else?

As they stood up to leave the dining room, his father put on his hat. "I think I shall order a carriage to take us for a ride around to the other bay."

"Oh, David." His mama's face dropped. "I had hoped to do that later in the week. Could you postpone it?"

"My dear, you are doing what takes your fancy. I shall do what takes mine, and today I want to take a ride."

Jamie could see his mama trying to accept his father's words. "We could all do that again another day, couldn't we?" he tried to pacify her.

"Of course we could, Jamie. There is absolutely

nothing to stop us taking a ride every day, if we so wish." His father smiled at him and then raised his eyebrows at his mother.

"Yes, of course. I am just being silly. Thank you, Jamie." She adjusted her shawl. "I think I'll wear my coat today, instead of this. I shall just go and change."

Sarah hurried after her. "And I shall fetch my reticule."

His father put his arm on Jamie's shoulder. "Do you need to change your jacket or fetch anything, son, or may we proceed?"

"No, Father, I'm quite ready." Pulling on his cap, Jamie straightened his back and followed his father outside. The drizzly rain could not deter his spirits on such a rare treat, having his father to himself. He could forget about everyone else—the witch, the baby and the females—and have man-to-man time, just the two of them.

They soon found a carriage willing to take them. The driver, a cheery fellow who never stopped talking, helped John assist his father inside, and Jamie climbed in behind him.

"The rain's eased off, sir. Would you like the top down?" The driver doffed his cap and bowed, drawing circles with it.

"Oh, yes, please may we, Father?" Jamie grinned at the funny man. "We'll be able to see so much more." Standing up, he imitated the driver with his own cap. "Sir."

"Sit down, Jamie, the carriage will overturn." His father smiled, turning to the driver. "Yes, please, young man, if you would be so good." He seemed to be in much better spirits than he had for a long time. *It must be the sea air*, thought Jamie. *It's already doing him good.*

Setting off once the top had been secured, with John settled beside the driver, they both took deep breaths. "I can smell …what is it? It's sort of fishy." Jamie looked down into the foot well to make sure no dead fish lurked near their feet.

"The seaside has its own particular aroma. It always reminds me of when I was a boy, and my parents brought me and Aunt Annie here. I remember that as one of the best days of my childhood."

His father didn't often speak about himself, so Jamie sat and listened, enthralled. Sitting opposite him, he could hear most of his musings, in between taking it in turns to answer the chatty driver every now and again, and the few words he couldn't hear, he made up. He tried to imagine him as a young boy. Watching his features light up as he spoke, he tried to make them fit into a small boy's face.

A seagull flew close, squawking loudly, making Jamie look to his right, over the sea. As they went around a long bend, he could see another beach in the distance.

"We are rounding the promontory now." His father turned his head to look behind him. "You should be able to see the North Bay in a moment."

"I already can. What did you say we're going round?"

"The promontory."

Another new word, 'promtorory'. He'd be able to try that one out on Sarah later.

"And you should be able to see the ruins of the old castle up on the cliff." His father pointed up to his right.

"I noticed that yesterday. Who do you think lived there?"

"Well, I understand it was first built in the twelfth century, the most important fortress on this coast."

"The twelfth century? By gum, what a long time ago." He tried to remember his history lesson. Which king ruled then?

"King Henry the Second would have been on the throne around that time." His father beat him to it. "But I think it was built just before his reign."

Drat, he had been about to say that. Then he remembered something really important, and said it quickly before his father could outdo him again. "He was married to Queen Eleanor, wasn't he? She had the same name as Auntie Ruby's baby."

"You are right. I had not made the connection. Well done."

Jamie puffed out his chest, thrilled he had been able to impress his father at last.

* * * *

Tillie and Sarah found their way to the town centre. Tillie had never seen such a large collection of shops. She realised what a sheltered life she'd led.

On the other hand, accustomed to living in Harrogate, Sarah did not find them such a novelty, but she enjoyed herself as they spent a happy hour looking in the windows and browsing around the larger stores.

"You'll have to come and stay with us some time," she suggested as they rested their legs, sitting in a café, drinking coffee. "I would love to show you around our town. And Mama…well, she revels in shopping trips. She can't have enough of them."

"Thank you. Your Uncle David and I have been meaning to pay a visit, but there just never seems to be the right moment. One thing after another crops up—usually a disaster of some sort."

Sarah reached over and patted her hand. "You do seem to lead an eventful life, Aunt Tillie. Mama has a very easy one compared with yours."

"I mustn't complain." Tillie took another sip of the strong, bitter coffee. Sarah had insisted on treating her, so it would be churlish to leave it.

Forcing down another mouthful, she looked around.

"Isn't this a lovely little café? The pretty blue gingham curtains at the windows match the blue tablecloths. We shall have to come here again." It felt so good to have a moment away from the everyday chaos of her life, and just sit and relax, glad, after all, she hadn't gone with David. He had seemed so grumpy that morning, even though they had made love passionately the night before, and he had held her closely until she had fallen asleep.

"I suppose we had better be making tracks." Sighing, she put down her half-finished drink. "Baby Daniel will be wanting his feed." She called the waitress over for the bill, hoping to pay without Sarah realising, but her niece immediately took out her purse. "I'm paying, Auntie, I told you it was my treat. I insist."

"You are a good girl, thank you. I hope your mother appreciates what a marvellous daughter she has." Knowing full well that not to be the case, she just wanted her niece to know how well she thought of her.

Black clouds blotted out the sun but the rain held off as they made their way back towards the hotel. "What would you like to do when we arrive back?" she asked. "I'm afraid you're going to be very bored until Uncle David and Jamie return. I can't see them being back for a while."

"Oh, don't worry about me. I shall probably find a quiet spot and read my book."

"Oh, we didn't find a book store, did we? What's the name of that one you were hoping to buy?"

"Mansfield Park, but it doesn't matter. I have two others I have yet to read."

Tillie looked up to the sky. "It's a pity the weather isn't more clement. You could have gone down to the beach. The hotel seems rather noisy and smoky. Maybe we should have booked you a room of your own instead of you having to share with Nanny and Alice."

"Oh, no, I don't mind. It would have been an

unnecessary expense. It's good of you to bring me at all."

Tillie debated whether to ask her niece if she had ever noticed anything untoward about the nanny. Maybe she could spy on her. But that would be unfair on the girl. She decided to wait a few days until she had been in her company for a while, and then sneak something into a conversation. She also wanted to ask her if she could try to wheedle out of Jamie how he had come to fall out of the window. Would it be too much to ask of her, though?

They soon arrived at the hotel and went their separate ways. Baby Daniel still slept, so she could have spent a while longer at the shops. They had found a place that specialised in making bathing suits, so had both been measured, and she had given Jamie's and Alice's sizes, as theirs didn't need to be exact. She had arranged to pick them up two days later. She hadn't bought anything else, but Sarah had found a lovely trinket for her mama, so at least her niece had had a fruitful trip.

* * * *

The following day, Jamie jumped for joy as his father granted his wish to have a ride on a boat. Daniel stayed once more with the nanny, but this time they allowed Alice to accompany them.

The skipper announced, "All aboard," and everyone took their seats.

"It isn't very speedy. I thought it would whizz along," Jamie moaned.

"It is fortunate it does not," replied his father, "for I should not be able to enjoy the ride if it travelled any faster."

"Why not?" Jamie hadn't noticed until then that his father's face had turned a peculiar shade of green.

"I think your father is feeling seasick," his mother remarked, before running after Alice, who would not stay still.

Sarah took the little girl from her. "Come and sit on my knee." She turned and shaded her eyes from the sun. "Look over there, is that a dolphin?"

Jamie jumped up. "Where? Where's a dolphin?" *Drat. Why wasn't I the first person to spot it?* That would have been the best achievement of the holiday, better even than actually seeing one.

Sarah pointed over to the other side. "There, look, it's just surfaced." Everybody on the boat craned their necks, and those across the other side stood up, oohing and aahing, to see the unusual shiny, black creature as it rose out of the white-flecked water, and dived back in.

"There's another one," cried Jamie. At least he'd been first to notice that one.

"Are you sure they are not porpoises?" his father asked. He seemed just as interested as everyone else, his face having returned to its usual colour.

"What's the difference?" asked his mother, but nobody seemed to know.

They watched the dolphins' antics for a few minutes until they disappeared, and everyone sat down again, murmuring about the exciting event.

Once more back on dry land, Jamie asked, "Can me and Sarah go and see what's on that pier thing?"

His mother closed her eyes and pursed her lips. *Did I say something wrong?* he wondered.

"If you ask properly, young man," his father replied, "Then yes, you *may*."

Sarah must have thought she would rescue him, for she asked, "Please may Jamie and I go to the pier?"

Blowing out his cheeks, he seethed inwardly. *That's what I said, only just a bit different. Why does it matter how it was said?*

"Yes, you may," his father replied. "But make sure you stay together. I would hate to bring your mother's wrath down on my head, Sarah, by having to inform her that you had gone astray."

She kissed him on the cheek. "Yes, Uncle David, of course we will."

His father sat in the wheelchair which John, his valet, had waiting for him at the quayside, and he and his mother and sister went in one direction, while Jamie and Sarah turned in the opposite.

* * * *

Three days later, Jamie put on his bathing suit. "But, Mama, I won't know what to do. I can't go bathing on my own."

"Well, males and females have to use separate machines, so you can't come with me and Sarah, and your father can't go, of course."

"Couldn't John come in with me?"

"No, silly, he's a servant. Anyway, he isn't likely to have a costume. And what would your father do without him?"

He stood looking in the mirror at his reflection. What a sight! "I don't think I want to be seen in this, anyway. It looks daft."

"Well, we all do, I suppose, but it's the price we have to pay if we want to go in the water."

"Why can't I just roll up my trousers and paddle like I've seen other people do?"

"If that's all you want to do, then that's your choice, but I'm sure once you're in the sea, you'll love it and not want to come out. At least, that's what the lady in the room down the corridor told me."

"Maybe we can find a gentleman who's on his own and ask him if I can share his hut."

"Yes, that's a grand idea. We'll do that. Change back into your own clothes, and we'll go down to the beach in about half an hour."

She went out, leaving Jamie to take another look in the mirror. What a good job none of his mates at school could see him! They would have a proper laugh. Taking off the one-piece, long-sleeved, woollen bathing suit that only left his hands and feet exposed below the neck, he dressed in his old trousers and shirt.

His ear had completely healed, and he had been able to avoid the nanny since that first day. He needed to check on his baby brother to make sure he didn't have any marks, but never found the opportunity to be alone with him—his mother or the witch always guarded him—so he couldn't think when he would have an opportunity. One would arise sometime. He would just have to be patient. He still hadn't come up with a plan to disgrace her, either.

His mother had been right. He loved splashing about in the sea. The kindly, elderly gentleman with whom they had found to share sat in the hut with his valet most of the time, just venturing out now and again, as far as knee-deep, taking large breaths of air before retiring back inside.

The water's ice-cold chill had taken Jamie's breath away when he had first jumped in, but once he'd become accustomed to it, he found he could swim a little by flapping his arms and kicking his feet.

He could just make out his mother and Sarah farther along the beach in the female section, swinging Alice by the hands. They seemed to be having a good time. He hadn't seen their bathing costumes, but they appeared to be fully clothed, for when they went into the deeper water, the material billowed out like hot air balloons.

"Young man," he heard the gentleman call about half an hour later. He swam up to him, showering him with spray. "I shall be leaving in about ten minutes. I'm going in to change. You be very careful while I can't see you, and no mischief. Understand?" He shook himself like a dog.

Aw, I don't want to leave the water yet. Jamie swam away, wondering whether he could swim as far as his mother. What would the other ladies say if he, a male, turned up in their section? Wouldn't it be great to see the looks on their faces? Dare he do it? No, better not, his mama would be embarrassed, Sarah, too.

A moment later, he realised his feet couldn't touch the bottom. *Just keep swimming back to the beach,* he told himself. After a few strokes, he tried to stand once more, but the seabed had disappeared. Where had it gone? It had been there a minute ago. He tried again, but still couldn't. He flapped his arms even harder, but they began to tire. Surely he had reached the shallows. But the people on the beach seemed even farther away.

From behind him, a gigantic wave engulfed his whole body. The roar of the waves hurt his ears as he sank, spiralling around and around, deeper and deeper. At last, he reached the hard, solid floor of the seabed. But he couldn't breathe, his lungs wouldn't work.

I'm going to die. I'm never going to see Mama or Father again. Please, God, help me. I'll be such a good boy...

Chapter 15

Jamie opened his eyes as a fit of coughing overtook him. *What's that bright light? Am I in heaven?* He couldn't hear any angel music, though, only a soft murmuring and the constant crash of waves. *Waves? In heaven?* He closed his eyes again.

"Jamie," a voice cried, and a little hand touched his face.

"Hello, Annabella," he squeaked. "Fanks for meeting me."

A deeper voice said, "Thank God."

That can't be God, then. He wouldn't thank Himself, would he?

"Is that you, Papa? Not God?"

"Oh, Jamie, yes, it is me, your father."

"Not my father in heaven, hallowed be thy name?"

"No, Jamie." His mama's voice.

"Mama?"

"Yes, my darling." Her face tasted salty as she squeezed him tight, kissing his cheeks and pressing his face to hers. "And here's Alice."

"Not Annabella, in heaven?"

"No." Her breath came out in short, sharp gasps. "You're safe...alive. But you nearly drowned. We nearly lost you."

Memories of being swirled about in the waves, and not being able to breathe, made him shudder as he lay back.

But at least he wasn't dead.

His throat felt full of sharp needles as he began coughing again.

"Wrap him up," his mama yelled. "He's shivering, poor lamb."

His vision began to clear, and he saw hundreds of

people surrounding him. He tried to sit up, but the faces all merged into one blur. "How...?"

"Don't try to speak, my sweetheart." He could tell by the juddering movements of her body as she held him close once more that his mama had started crying again.

"We need to help him back to the hotel now we know he's..." Over his mama's arm he saw John and Sarah help his father ease himself down onto the sand, clearly too overcome to continue.

"You, too, Uncle David," Sarah said, crouching down beside him.

It dawned on Jamie that she, as most of the other people, still wore her bathing suit. Oh no, he would be blamed for the ladies' state of undress. The shame of it! He hid his head in his mother's bosom. How could he make it up to them?

"I'm sorry," he blurted out.

"No, Jamie, it's our fault. We shouldn't have left you on your own." His mama clutched him to her again.

"But I wasn't...that old man?" He looked for the gentleman who had shared his bathing machine, and saw him at the back of the crowd with his valet.

Jamie waved to him, but he turned away and hid his face. He didn't wave back.

"He blames himself," his mama said. "He knows he shouldn't have left you in the sea. He should have made you come out when he did."

"But..."

His father tried to stand, but the shifting sand hampered his efforts. "Do you feel able to walk, Jamie?"

"Yes." He stood up, trying vainly to hold in another cough. His mother held him until it stopped.

"Shouldn't you take him to the hospital?" a voice from the crowd called.

"No, please, I'll be..." Another bout welled up in his throat. *Swallow it back, don't let it come out. I don't want to go to no hospital.* He managed to contain the spasm enough by turning his head and spitting into the sand.

"Jamie!" his mother gasped. "That's rude."

Well, it was either that, or cough like a barking fox and be took to hospital.

The crowd parted to let him and his mother through. His father still sat on the sand, with little Alice beside him.

"I need to help Father."

"Sarah and John will do that. We need you back first."

"But we can't walk through town dressed in these silly clothes."

"Oh, my goodness. I hadn't thought of that." His mother dragged him back to where his father tried to gain a foothold. "David, we need to go back to the bathing hut to change. We can't be seen away from the beach in these ridiculous costumes."

"Of course." His father finally managed to stand.

Jamie's clothes had been left in the old man's hut. They all looked the same. The man's valet appeared. "Let me help the young man, ma'am. It is the least I can do." He took Jamie's arm.

"Yes, Jamie, you go and change while I take Alice and Sarah..." She pointed in the direction of their own hut.

Taking off the wet suit, Jamie quickly dried himself, put on his clothes and took a step outside.

"Don't forget your bathing suit, young sir." The valet wrung it out and handed it to him.

"I don't want to ever see it again in me whole life," he retorted, throwing it into the corner. "I hate it." He ran out, grabbing his cap, forcing it onto his wet hair. "And I never want to see the sea or any other type of water ever again."

The valet ran after him. "Please, young sir, wait. You

are going in the wrong direction. Your mother is that way."

He stopped. Of course. Wrapping his arms around his body, he shivered again. How could he be so cold when he could feel the warm sun?

The valet placed his own jacket around Jamie's shoulders. "You've had a nasty shock, young sir. You need to keep warm."

"I would if it weren't so cold."

"There's your father and, oh…it looks like your mother and sisters are ready as well."

"My sisters?" Had Annabella actually come back from the dead? Then it dawned on him. "Oh, the tall one's not my sister, she's my cousin."

The ladies hurried to him, looking very dishevelled indeed. "Mama, your bonnet is skew-whiff." He grinned. "And your coat is buttoned up wrong."

"You seem to have recovered your good spirits," she replied, unfastening her coat. "I've never dressed so quickly in my whole life. Sarah had to…but never mind. You need to be back in the warm." She turned to the valet. "Thank you, sir. Is this your jacket?"

He nodded. "Return it later. My master and I are staying at The Grand Hotel."

"So are re." Jamie's teeth were chattering so much, he couldn't speak properly. He pulled the jacket around him, but it didn't seem to hold much warmth.

His father came closer in his wheelchair. "I'll sit on that bench, and John can take Jamie back in my chair." Standing up, John helped him onto the bench, and Jamie gratefully sank into the chair, snuggling under the blanket as the valet pushed him up the slope.

"How come you were there, Father, when they pulled me out of the water?" Jamie asked later as they sat down to dinner. A rest in his comfy bed had perked him up. Mister Lighten, the hotel owner, had heard of his escapade and had instructed the maid to warm it with hot water bottles.

"We were just enjoying the sunshine when I heard someone shout that a boy had got into difficulty. For some reason, I cannot think why, I immediately suspected it to be you."

Jamie frowned. "Oh, Father!"

"Well, you are the most accident-prone boy I have ever known. You seem to fall foul of every situation you are in."

"Um, s'pose I do." He grinned. "But who rescued me? I need to thank them." It dawned on him that he could hear quite well. It must have been all that water clearing out his ears.

"It was that valet," his mother replied. "Well, not him, exactly. He was helping his master undress when he realised he couldn't see you, and he ran out and shouted for help. A young man nearby swam out and pulled you back to the shore. What on earth were you doing so far out, when you can't even swim?"

"But I can swim now…though I don't ever want to do it again." Shuddering, Jamie looked down at his arms, visualising himself trying to draw them backwards and forwards to save himself.

"No, me neither," said his mama. "I just want to go home."

"But we haven't seen the freaky show or been on a donkey or…"

"I know, but I just feel…" She shrugged.

"Papa? Do we have to?"

"I think it would be best, Jamie. Maybe we can come back another time and complete the list of entertainments."

Jamie finished his meal in silence. *It's my fault we're cutting the holiday short. As usual. Everything's always my fault.*

Chapter 16

Back at school once more, Jamie attempted to settle down, trying, as best he could, to steer clear of Silas Brown, dodging around corners and hiding whenever he saw him and his cronies coming towards him.

Joining the choir, he loved the release singing gave him. He'd always loved to sing, and found learning new songs an enjoyable challenge. Some of them he pigeon-holed for teaching Alice in the holidays, for she loved singing as well.

He excelled at art. One day the art master picked up one of his drawings and showed it to the class. "Can anyone tell me why this picture is so commendable?" he asked the class at large.

At first, nobody put up their hand. Unsure if the question included him, he looked around, as a voice from the back said, "The perspective, sir?"

"Yes, correct, anything else?"

Pleased somebody had said something positive about his picture, Jamie tried to remember what perspective meant. He certainly had not been aware of using it. The master hadn't told the boys the name of the artist, to ensure there would be no prejudice but, even so, when Jamie turned to the back and saw Silas Brown put his hand up, he expected him to say something scathing about the colour of the sea, or the size of the people on the beach.

"The overall impression of movement, sir." Wow, a compliment from the bully. What a surprise. Of course, he hadn't known whom he praised, and Jamie hoped the master wouldn't tell them. It would spoil the effect completely.

"Well done, Brown, my thoughts exactly." The master put down the picture and picked up someone else's, asking different questions. Jamie sat basking in the glory of the pleasing comments, not really taking notice of what they said about the others, until the master asked him a specific question, and he realised he hadn't heard what he had been saying.

Drat, I've done it again.

"Um…"

"Does anybody else know?"

Several boys put up their hands. Phew, a lucky escape.

The rest of the lesson they had to create a design of different patterns in a box shape. *This is easy peasy. I could do this standing on my head with my hands tied behind my back.* Chuckling at the image of himself trying to do that, he looked up and saw the master glaring at him.

Pulling his face straight, he carried on with his work, wondering if he should challenge Silas Brown, next time he saw him, with the fact that it had been his picture the bully had flattered. Would it make him friendlier? Not arriving at any conclusion when the lesson ended, he hurried out before everyone else, so he could avoid him.

"Jamie, do you want a game of hopscotch?" Oswell Peel asked at break time. Although still not very strong, he had recovered from the bout of glandular fever.

"If you want," he replied, looking over at one of the older boys he had seen earlier, watching him. "Do you know the name of that boy over there?"

Peel took his turn. He reached number two. Craning his neck to see who Jamie had indicated, he dropped his leg and his turn ended. "You mean that one with the piggy eyes?"

"Piggy eyes? He doesn't have piggy eyes. He's rather handsome, in my opinion."

"I think his name's Alexander Bank. Why, you don't have a crush on him, do you?"

"No, of course not." Nobody admitted to having

crushes on older boys, although practically all the younger boys had one. "It's just that he keeps looking at me in a funny way."

"Well, maybe he fancies you."

Jamie tried to take a sneaky peek at the older boy, standing casually talking to a friend. Maybe he did have small eyes, but he had a lovely smile.

"Come on, Dalton, it's your turn. Drag your eyes away from Pigface if you want to carry on playing. If you don't, I'll find someone else who does," Oswell nagged.

"You're not jealous, are you?" Jamie asked, throwing his stone into number four.

"Don't be so stupid. Why on earth would I be?"

"Because you don't have anybody to love?" Jamie hopped up to the top, turned back and, bending down to pick up his stone, lost his balance and fell sideways.

"Serves you right," declared Oswell, stalking off and leaving Jamie to dust himself down and walk away as if nothing had happened, hoping Alexander Bank hadn't seen him fall.

"Dalton, how's the head?" The voice of one of Silas Brown's cronies called. *Ignore him*, he told himself, pulling his hat on tighter.

"Climbed out of any good windows lately?" A ripple of laughter went through the group.

Jamie didn't know whether to carry on or challenge the bullies, but a different voice, silky and deep, came from behind him. "Leave Dalton alone, you bully." Turning, he saw Alexander Bank and his friend right behind him.

"And what will you do if we don't?" Half-hiding behind one of his gang members, Brown didn't look quite so cocky.

"Do you really want to find out?"

Picking up his coat tails, Silas walked away without replying, followed by the rest of his mates.

Jamie turned to his hero. "Oh, thank you," he gushed, looking into the darkest eyes he'd ever seen.

"I don't think they'll bother you again."

"Thank you," he repeated, unable to think of anything else to say.

"I heard about you falling out of the window. I'll bet it had something to do with those bullies, didn't it?"

His eyes wide, Jamie opened his mouth but closed it again, looking down at his shoes. Dare he admit it? Even though Alexander said he wouldn't be bothered by them again, he still couldn't risk it.

"I admire you for your reticence, but you really should report them."

Jamie covered his forehead to hide the scar. He didn't know what reticence meant, but he couldn't own up, not with Brown's threats when he had been in the infirmary still ringing in his ears. His life wouldn't be worth living.

"Maybe we'll persuade you. Come to my room this evening after study."

Jamie looked up. The older boy smiled at him with such a look of…he couldn't quite decide how to describe it, but it made his insides turn to mush.

He remembered he should have been shining Fenner's shoes or some other task—he wouldn't know until he arrived—at eight that evening. Dare he not go?

"I…" Oh, what a decision. He couldn't turn down such an invitation. Maybe he could send word to his fag master to say…what? He could just see Fenner's green eyes narrow and feel the edge of his whip if he did so.

"I expect you have duties to perform." Bank clearly realised why Jamie didn't give him an immediate reply. "Come to think of it, so have I. We'll make it another day, then. I'll let you know when I'm free."

Jamie really wanted to say he'd go, no matter what. As Alexander turned away, he kept his hands in his pocket to stop himself tugging at his champion's jacket, and saying he'd changed his mind. With a heavy heart, he lined up as the bell went, and followed his fellow pupils into school.

* * * *

Maisie picked up a towel from the kitchen floor and shook it. "What's that doing down there, and where's Freda? It isn't like her to be late. She's usually the first one down." Frowning, she went to look in the pantry. It was empty.

"I s'pose I'd better make a start," she murmured, poking the range into life.

Betsy came in, yawning and pulling on her mobcap. She sat at the table and yawned again. "Where's Freda?" she asked, resting her head on her arms.

"Don't know. Haven't you seen her either?" Swishing hot water into a teapot, Maisie poured it back out and put in two teaspoons of tea and boiling water. "Do you know where the tea cosy is?"

Receiving an "Uh?" she realised she would not receive any help from the parlour maid, so went in search of it herself.

She jumped when Nellie's voice yelled from behind her, "Get up, girl. What do you think you are doing?" Thinking the housekeeper addressed her, she jerked around, but saw Betsy being pulled up from the chair.

"I'm sorry, Nellie. I'm just so tired," moaned the parlour maid.

"And why is that?"

"Something kept me awake all night. Some noise. I don't know what it was."

"Yes, I kept hearing a strange sound," Maisie added. "Sort of moaning-like."

"Well, that's no excuse for slacking. Where's Freda?"

School for Jamie

"We haven't seen her," Maisie replied, taking out the heavy frying pan. "You don't think she's ill, do you? Could it have been her making the noises?" She dropped the pan onto the range. "I'm going to see." Wiping her hands down her apron, she ran past the housekeeper, not waiting for her approval.

Taking the back stairs two at a time, her heart in her mouth, she prayed, "Please, God, let her be well, just a bit late."

She listened outside the cook's door.
Silence.
She knocked.
No reply.
She knocked again.

When she still didn't receive an answer, she slowly turned the knob. Peeping inside, she expected to see the chubby cook standing there, fastening her apron, or adjusting her mobcap. Instead, she saw a shape under the covers in the bed.

Tiptoeing across the room, she held her breath and tapped her shoulder. "Freda?"

No response.

She tried again. "Freda, please wake up."

The cook's stone-cold face stared up at her.

* * * *

Trying to decide what to write in his letter home, Jamie chewed the end of his pencil and picked up the letter he'd received that morning, reading the same sentence over and over again. *'I am afraid I have some bad news. Freda passed away yesterday.'*

Passed away? Did that mean she'd died? Surely not? She wasn't that old. Passed away? It must mean that, what else could it be? And what about the baby?

Maybe he could ask Oswell if his mother had 'passed

away'. But his friend hadn't spoken to him since the incident in the playground. He had befriended one of the black princes from Africa. Jamie hadn't actually spoken to any of the three members of royalty in his year. He'd heard one of them speaking, and couldn't understand his accent, so steered clear of them.

Who else could he ask? Alexander Bank? That would be a good excuse to seek him out, although, how could he bring up the subject? He couldn't just walk into his room and blurt it out. But he needed to know for certain before he wrote his letter. It would be awful if he said how sorry he felt that Freda had died, and she stood in the kitchen, cooking pies or baking bread, as usual. How bad would that look?

He tried to imagine home without her. It just wouldn't be the same. And Maisie—she would be so upset. Maybe she'd be promoted to Freda's job. But, nay, he knew she would be too young and inexperienced.

Where had he left his dictionary? It might say what 'passed away' meant. He tried to remember where he'd put it. If only he could be tidy, he'd know where to find everything. Deciding it must be in his desk in the classroom, he gave up the idea.

He decided to ask Fenner. Folding his letter, he stood up. But he'd already been to his room and made his toast earlier. Why hadn't he thought of it then?

It would have to be Alexander. His hero had said he would arrange a meeting some time. What better time than this?

Knocking on his door, he heard shuffling noises inside the room. Should he go in? As he tried the knob, the door flew open and Silas Brown ran out, pulling his jacket on with one hand, and holding his cap on his head with the other. Jamie hadn't realised Brown had become one of Bank's fags. He couldn't be. In the playground the other day, Alexander had definitely…

"Come in," called Bank.

Puzzled, Jamie stood watching the fleeing back of his enemy hurry away.

"What was Brown doing?" he asked as he went in.

"Brown?" Bank straightened his coat. "Never you mind. What brings you here? I didn't realise we had arranged a meeting."

Still trying to work out what had been happening, Jamie shook his head. "We hadn't, but I didn't think you'd mind. You see, I have a problem." He produced his letter. "Does that mean that she…?"

"That she what?"

"Well, I hope it doesn't, but I think it means she's dead."

"That's right, she's snuffed it, dead as a dodo, breathed her last."

"Oh." He didn't need to say it so bluntly. "Thank you. Sorry for bothering you." Jamie turned to go. At least he knew, but he rather wished he'd found out in a different way. Maybe the older boy could not be called such a hero after all.

Dragging his feet along the corridor, he wondered if he would be allowed to go home for Freda's funeral. Matron would be the best person to ask. Speeding up, he went towards the infirmary and searched through the empty wing, surprised to find nobody in any of the beds.

He finally tracked her down, sitting in her office drinking a cup of nasty-smelling coffee. "No, Dalton, not for a servant. A member of the family would be different," came her reply.

"But Freda is almost family." He wanted to hold his nose to avoid the bitter aroma drifting up from the steaming cup, but knew she would deem him to be unmannerly, so merely held his breath.

"Almost isn't enough. Now off you go." She shooed him out.

Although dissatisfied with his fruitless petition, he couldn't wait to leave. Grimacing and blowing out his held breath, he almost ran out, vowing never to have coffee in his house when he grew up, wondering why anyone would want to drink such muck.

He did not have time to write his letter, Wednesday being his weekly bath night. He would have liked to relax for more than the allocated fifteen minutes, even though at home he jumped out as soon as possible, but time meant something at home, he didn't want to waste it. He had to make do with small mercies, though. Freda often used to say that. But she would never say another thing, not ever again. She was dead, just like George and Annabella.

Sitting in the bath, half-heartedly splashing water over his body, he wondered if she had been expecting a baby. Could that have been what killed her? Why did people have to die, especially when they weren't even old? Freda had been quite old, and so had Great Grandmamma, but little Annabella…

* * * *

With Jamie back at school, the house lacked spirit. Tillie wandered around like a lost soul. She had pleaded with David to let him stay at home. After the incident in the sea and the one at school, she felt even more that he should not be sent away. Her husband had been adamant, though, and wouldn't be swayed.

If only she could have a say in something—anything. Why should wives be treated as if they didn't have a brain, or an opinion? Nellie had more say in household matters than she did.

Ruby came into the hall, carrying Eleanor. "What are you doing, sis?"

"Absolutely nothing."

"Oh, why's that?"

"Because that's all I'm allowed to do. I have no… But never mind, I'm just feeling sorry for myself, as usual. What with Freda's funeral and baby Daniel being sick all over me this morning, I'm fed up to the back teeth."

Eleanor reached out to her, a beaming smile on her face. Tillie took the baby. "You're a little beauty, aren't you? And you're really thriving. I think you must be almost as heavy as Daniel, and you're two months younger."

Ruby took back her daughter. "Did you call the doctor out to him again?"

"No, what's the point? He just tells me to persevere. I know I don't have enough milk to satisfy him, but he can't seem to keep down the mashed food we give him."

"Well, is he asleep?" At Tillie's nod, she continued, "Let me make you a nice cup of tea. I'm sure you could do with one right now."

Tillie followed her sister into the kitchen. Maisie looked up from sweeping the floor. "I'm sorry it's such a mess, mistress. I'll catch up, I promise."

"Don't worry, Maisie. It isn't your fault." Tillie sat down at the table, then stood up again. "What you really need until the new cook arrives tomorrow is some help. And that is something I can do. Where are the carrots?"

Maisie blinked her eyes in horror. "No, ma'am, I can't let you do that."

"I did it before I was married, so there's nothing stopping me now."

Ruby agreed. "Do you think your nanny would object to looking after Eleanor for a while? I could help as well."

"I'm sure she won't, and if she does, she'll have me to reckon with. She's on her last chance, so just tell her I said she must."

Ruby hurried out as Tillie rolled up her sleeves. "Do

you have a spare apron? I'd better not soil my black frock."

"Please, mistress, it don't seem right. What would the master say?" Maisie stood with the sweeping brush in her hand, a look of anguish marring her pretty violet eyes. Clearly uneasy, she tucked a curl into her mobcap.

Taking the brush from her, Tillie patted her arm. "Please don't upset yourself, Maisie. The master's out on business, so he doesn't need to know. And, anyway, I'm sure he would applaud my ingenuity. Anything that helps with the smooth running of the place can only be a good thing. Maybe I'll cancel the new cook and take over myself."

At the scullery maid's swift intake of breath, she reassured her, "I'm only joking. I haven't even arranged for a lady's maid yet. Now, what needs doing first? Peeling the potatoes? That's right up my street."

Ruby returned and picked up a bunch of carrots still attached to their greenery. "I can scrub the carrots, or do you peel them?"

Maisie shook her head, but clearly eager for the help, she murmured, "Peel."

An hour later, the dinner prepared and the kitchen as pristine as it had ever been, Maisie opened a drawer and put a stray spoon away. "Freda doesn't... didn't like anything out of place. She..." She burst into tears.

Seeing her so upset, Tillie's eyes filled. "There, there," she tried to console her.

Clearing her throat, Ruby picked up the kettle. "I thought we were having a cup of tea."

"It's not fair," wailed Maisie, burrowing her face in Tillie's bosom. "Why didn't she go and see the doctor? She might still be alive now."

"You know Freda, as stubborn as a mule." Tillie cuddled her until her tears subsided. "We tried to persuade her enough times."

"Surely, she knew she had something serious." The little maid dried her eyes with her apron and set her mobcap straight. "What did they say it was? A carcin…?"

"A carcinoma of the womb." Tillie sat down, wiping her hands across her face.

The smell of baking bread filled the kitchen, reminding her that life goes on relentlessly. People die but those left behind have to carry on, and normality, whatever that is, has to be resumed. But she couldn't prevent another tear creeping down her cheek for her own baby daughter.

Chapter 17

Doodling while he racked his brain to think of something else to write about, Jamie began to draw pictures of the teachers. "He-he, that's a good one," he chuckled quietly. "Old Fishy." But he needed a bigger nose. Rubbing out the tip of the headmaster's nose, he elongated it. His bald head needed to be a bit higher. "That's better." Putting the paper to one side, he started another drawing. Who should he do next? Mister Sumpton. He drew a round face and long, greasy black hair and added a large mole to his cheek. A few more? He put one right on the end of the nose. "He-he, I love it."

"What's so funny, Dalton?" the prefect in charge of the study period called.

Jamie had been so absorbed in his pictures, he hadn't realised he'd been chuckling aloud. He quickly hid the drawings under a book. "Nothing, I was just coughing." He gave a loud cough to confirm his statement, but it set off a real bout.

The prefect jumped back. "Now, now, there's no need for histrionics." Jamie couldn't stop. He could barely breathe. The boy behind him thumped him on his back, but it didn't help. Panicking, Jamie tried to stand, knocking his papers onto the floor.

"I'll fetch some water," one of the other boys cried, before running out. Jamie coughed so much he began to heave, but the boy soon hurried back and, grabbing the glass, he emptied it in one gulp, slumping down into his seat, taking in a vast lungful of air as the spasm calmed down.

The prefect picked up the papers that had been knocked off. Jamie moaned as he stood looking at them.

"Well, we seem to have a budding artist in our midst," the prefect jeered. "Is this supposed to be our

School for Jamie

venerable headmaster, Mister Lancelot Trout, by any chance? Oh, and who is this? Surely, not our Head of Year One, Mister Tristram Sumpton?" He held up the pictures for everyone to see. Jamie reached up to try to grab them back.

"No, no, they're…" He could still barely speak. The other boys whooped and cheered.

"I think Mister Trout would be very interested in these, don't you, boys?" The prefect waved them in the air.

"No. Please, don't." Jamie jumped up to try once more to seize the papers, but the fair-headed prefect, being a lot taller, held them just out of his reach, his large brown eyes taunting Jamie.

"What do you think, boys? Shall we take them to old Fishface or save Dalton's bacon?"

"Fishface, Fishface," the boys chanted.

Jamie sat down, his head in his hands. "I didn't mean no harm." He sat up again. "Please, don't."

"What's it worth?"

"What d'yer mean?"

"Well, if you want us to give you back the caricatures, we want something in return, don't we, boys?" The prefect nodded his head, egging on the others.

"Pay, pay," they shouted.

"What sort of payment? I don't have much money." At least he had an option, but at what expense?

Raising his hands, the older boy quietened the class. "Shush." Once the room hushed, he asked, "Any ideas? What would be fair retribution for our silence?"

The room exploded with everyone shouting out ideas. Jamie couldn't bear the noise any more. He jumped up. "Do what yer want. I don't care," he yelled and ran out.

Halfway down the corridor, he stopped, wondering

what would happen if they did show the pictures to the headmaster. Would he be expelled? Maybe he should go back in and see what they'd decided. He stood chewing his fingers.

Hearing voices coming from the other end of the corridor, he saw a group of boys coming towards him, one of them a crony of Silas Brown's. Not waiting to see if the bully followed behind, he turned back towards the study room. He didn't want to leave his letter for them to read.

Waiting a moment, he listened outside the door. It seemed quiet inside, so he opened it and ran in, grabbed his things and rushed back out before anyone could say anything. Closing the door behind him, he saw that the group he'd seen earlier had already gone by, so turned in the opposite direction. Once around the corner, he took a moment to check the papers. *Are the pictures amongst them? No. Drat, drat and treble and four times drat.* He'd really hoped they'd relented and put them back.

Oh, well, at least if I'm expelled I'll be able to go home. But his father would be so disappointed in him. Not just disappointed, he would be livid. Although, his mother wouldn't be at all upset. She'd welcome him home with open arms.

Hopefully, he wouldn't have that option and it would all die down with nothing coming of it. He would just have to wait and see.

The next morning he awoke with a thick head. He'd tossed and turned all night, worrying about his carcitures—or whatever the prefect had called them—and if he would be expelled. Every time he'd heard a noise, he'd expected a hand on his collar, dragging him out of bed, but the morning had arrived with him still there. Nobody had said a word about them at supper, although, each time he'd looked across at one of his classmates, he'd run his forefinger and thumb down his nose as if to elongate it. He'd tried really hard not to look, but somehow his eyes had been drawn to him like a magnet.

That particular boy didn't sleep in his dormitory, sparing him the humiliation of seeing him first thing. *Just ignore him*, he kept telling himself. *He'll stop eventually.*

The day passed without incident. Jamie wondered whether to find the prefect who had his pictures and ask for them back, but decided to let sleeping wolves lie. Wolves? *No, you idiot, it's dogs. 'Let sleeping dogs lie'—that's the expression.*

* * * *

Exasperated, Cecelia, the nanny, picked up Alice. "You naughty girl. I've told you not to dip your biscuit in your drink. Now, look what you've done, spilt it all down you. I only put that dress on clean this morning, now I'll have to change it. You deserve a good slap."

She raised her hand. The child began to cry.

Red anger boiled up inside her. How had she ended up as a skivvying nanny? She could have been a baroness. If only Humphrey hadn't been killed in the riding accident the day before their wedding.

The baby woke up and started to cry as well. "And you can shut up, you little..." She closed her mouth quickly before anything came out that Alice could repeat to her parents. Picking him up with one arm, she sat them both on her knees, trying to placate them before the mistress heard the hullabaloo and came in to admonish her again.

"Mistress High and Mighty thinks she's a cut above us. At least I was born into nobility. She's just a trumped-up trollop, saved from the gutter by the kindness of the master."

Alice's thumb had gone back into her mouth, and

she had stopped crying.

Cecelia put her down with her rag doll and rocked the baby. "I should have been doing this to my own child." Tears sprang into her eyes. "I'll never have the chance to bear children, and I wanted a whole brood."

'Stop feeling sorry for yourself, Cecelia.' Her ailing mother's words rang in her ears. 'You have to make the most of your life. You know your father, God rest his soul, always said you could overcome any obstacle with your strong character.'

"Oh, Mama, why did you have to die as well?" she whispered.

Sitting rocking the baby, her thoughts drifted back to the inn where they had stayed after Jamie's accident. The landlord had recognised her from when she and her mother had frequented it on their travels, and had been taunting her with her downfall. No wonder she had retaliated. Anybody in her position would have done so.

Daniel had gone back to sleep so, giving him a cuddle and a kiss, she put him back in his crib, regretting her earlier outburst. She had to bestow her motherly affections on someone, so who better than the helpless little baby?

In the meantime, Alice had found the tablecloth she had been embroidering and had wiped her wet dress with it.

"No, not that." She yanked it off her, but the damage had been done. "God give me strength," she moaned, her hands once more itching to slap the child. Spreading the cloth out, she ran her fingers over the intricate stitches. How many hours had she sat weaving the pink and blue flowers?

"Argh!" Screwing up the tablecloth in frustration, she flung it across the room. It landed on the rocking horse, making Alice laugh. She ran across, pulled it off and tried to repeat the action herself. As angry as Cecelia felt, she didn't want her handiwork spoiled beyond repair, so she stormed over and grabbed it.

"When your mother comes to feed the baby, I'll take you for a walk, young lady. You've been cooped up too long."

Replacing the little girl's wet dress with her best green one, the only other clean one she had, she wondered why she couldn't feel the same love for her as she did for Daniel. *Maybe because you hadn't known her from a baby.* And as for that Jamie... She only had to look at him and her hackles rose. He rubbed her up the wrong way all the time. Thank goodness he'd been sent away to boarding school. *I wish he would stay there all the time, but then Madam flipping Matilda would be in an even worse mood,* she rued.

The door opened, and the object of her scorn came in. "Isn't Daniel awake yet? I thought he would want feeding by now."

"He did wake earlier, ma'am," *nice and sweet,* "but went back to sleep. I'll bring him to you when he does, then I'll take this little lovely out for a walk." She pointed to Alice, who lifted up her arms to her mother to be picked up.

"That sounds like a good idea, doesn't it, my sweetheart?" the mistress cooed, cuddling her daughter, then added, "But if you want to go now, I'll wait here."

She nodded. "Thank you, ma'am. I'll fetch this little lovey's coat." The sooner she left the house, the better.

Wrapping herself in her shawl outside, she took a deep breath. If she'd had to stay one more hour in that place, she would have gone mad.

Taking hold of Alice's hand, calm crept over her, as the sun came out from behind a grey cloud, until Alice shouted, "Bird," and pointed to a magpie flying past.

She looked in vain for its mate. "That's all I need, a harbinger of doom. 'One for sorrow...' Come on, child, let's hurry to the village. I need some diversion." She dragged Alice along the lane, her little legs barely touching the ground. They arrived in the village, out of breath.

Seeing a sweet shop ahead, she decided a lollipop would keep the child quiet if she dared go into the inn for a drink. She opened the door, making the bell tinkle.

"What colour would you like?" she asked the child.

"Red."

"Make it two," she said to the young girl behind the counter. "That will keep her quiet for twice as long."

"Pop," said Alice, her eyes lighting up, as she held out her hand.

"Not yet, wait until we are outside."

The assistant wrapped the lollipops in a paper bag, and Cecelia paid for them.

"Pop," the little girl demanded again, her eyes blazing.

Cecelia could see the shop girl looking at her as if gauging whether she would give in. The bell over the door pinged again as another customer entered, so she grabbed Alice's hand and pulled her outside.

Bending down to the child's level, she took one of the lollipops out and held it just out of her reach. "You can have this as soon as we are inside that building," she pointed to the inn, "and not before." Standing up, ignoring the child's wail, she almost ran towards her destination.

So many people crowded the street that she couldn't see The Dog and Duck at the far end of the village. *Of course, it's market day. The inn will be packed.* Maybe she would be able to smuggle Alice in without her being noticed.

Reaching the inn, she found it packed indeed. Had she the gall to enter an inn alone? But how dry her mouth felt. The frothing ale beckoned, overcoming her reluctance. It would only be for a minute or so.

School for Jamie

Taking one of the lollipops out of the bag, she handed it to Alice, who immediately stopped howling. Bending down, she looked the child in the eye. "Now, sweetheart, I want you to be a very good girl, understand? You must not make any noise whatsoever, just stay right beside your nanny, as quiet as a little mouse."

The smell of the ale and the sweaty bodies inside the inn almost made her gag, and she could see her charge wrinkling up her face. "I know it doesn't smell very nice, but we won't be long. Just suck your nice red lollipop, all right?"

Taking a deep breath, she entered the noisy inn, wrapping her skirt around Alice. Jostling and pushing her way through to the bar, she wondered if the hassle would be worth the effort, but the lure of the drink drew her closer. It seemed an age before the barman looked her way, and she debated whether to leave, for she could feel Alice wriggling at her side, but then he placed it in front of her. Licking her lips in anticipation, she lifted up the glass. The man beside her knocked her arm. *No! Not now I can practically taste it.* Half the drink poured over the bar but she righted the glass and put it to her mouth. Oh, the joy. Drinking the paltry remains, she held out the glass to be refilled, glaring at the man who had nudged her, but he seemed oblivious, chatting to his mate. Should she challenge him? After all, he'd cost her the price of half her drink. No, she didn't want to cause a fuss, not with little Alice hiding under her skirt.

Alice? She felt down. The child had gone. She looked about her frantically, but the mass of bodies prevented her seeing anything below waist high.

"Alice," she called, "Alice."

"Who you looking for?" a man with black teeth and bad breath asked.

She couldn't admit she'd brought a child into the inn. Pressing her fist to her mouth, she squeezed by him through the throng of laughing customers. At the door, she expected to see the child waiting for her. But not a green coat in sight. *She must still be inside.* How on earth would she find her in that mêlée?

Pushing her way back in, saying, "Excuse me, excuse me," to everyone she bumped into, she searched the inn. But no Alice, no sign of her charge.

What should she do? Pretend she'd lost her outside and ask if anyone had seen her wandering in? That seemed a good idea. "Excuse me," she shouted, trying to be heard above the clamour of voices. "Has anyone seen a little girl in a green coat?"

One or two people near her shook their heads and continued their conversations. That did not work. Shoving people out of her way, she reached the bar again. "Excuse me," she shouted once more, but everyone ignored her, so she climbed onto the bar itself.

"Hey, lady, what do yer think yer doing?" the bartender called.

"Has anyone seen a little girl?" she repeated.

"Aye, I seen lots," jeered an old man with a long moustache. Everyone laughed.

"Me, too," called another. "There's half a dozen up at my 'ouse. You can 'ave any one of 'em." The laughter echoed around the room again.

The bartender reached up to her. "Come on down, miss. You're making a show of yourself." He helped her down. "Why would anyone have seen a child in here, eh?"

Making her way through to the door, she rubbed her brow. *What have I come to? I would not have dreamed of going into an inn on my own at one time, let alone drink ale.*

Searching the area outside again, in case the child had crept into a nook or cranny, she didn't know what to do next. She couldn't go back without her. Asking several people if they had seen her, including some travellers she would never usually speak to on any terms, she sat on a wall, feeling sick to her stomach.

The mistress had lost her twin. She could not imagine what she would do if Alice couldn't be found.

Chapter 18

"Those in the drama class wishing to audition for the school play in the summer, please assemble in the hall after lessons," announced the headmaster, Lancelot Trout. A murmur went up from the boys as they excitedly discussed which roles they would like to play.

Jamie turned to Oswell to ask him what he thought, but he had already walked away with his prince. They still hadn't made up their quarrel. Although not openly hostile, his friend merely ignored him most of the time. Once or twice, Jamie had tried to have a conversation with him, but without success. None of the other boys acted particularly friendly towards him. They all had their own special chums and didn't want an intruder muscling in so, left to his own devices, he sometimes felt very alone.

"I'll show you all," he mumbled to nobody in particular as he walked out. "I'll audition for the leading role. That'll make you take notice of me."

All day, instead of concentrating on his lessons, he silently, and sometimes not quite so silently, practised snippets of Shakespeare that he knew, and even a few lines he'd remembered from Dickens. By the time the last bell rang, his knuckles were raw where masters had rapped them when he hadn't paid attention. He didn't care. He needed that part.

Pushing his way through the throng of noisy, chattering boys, he hurried to the hall, where he saw a large group had beaten him to it.

Drat. He hadn't expected so many. He hoped it didn't mean he would only be given a small part. He wanted to be the lead. Gradually, more pupils came in, and quite a crowd had assembled by the time the master of drama, Mister Edwards, called them to order.

Jiggling with anticipation, Jamie gritted his teeth. Each boy had to stand on the stage and recite a piece from 'Twelfth Night' by William Shakespeare.

Jamie hadn't read it, so became rather apprehensive, but when his turn came, he marched up, head held high and chest out, and picked up the paper.

"'If music be the food of love, play on. Give me excess of it, that surf...surfting, the appetite may sicken and so die,'" he read loudly and confidently, apart from stumbling over the one word he hadn't encountered before.

That hadn't gone too badly. He heard a faint rumble of giggling echo around the hall. Surely, it couldn't have been aimed at him?

Mister Edwards called for quiet. "Thank you, Dalton. Next, we'll have Alexander Bank."

Jamie knew there would be no wrong words or stumbling phrases in his hero's rendition. Even though he didn't always act in a friendly manner towards him, he still thought of him as the greatest person in the school.

The laughter died down as Bank took his position on the stage. Every syllable could be heard clearly and, when he'd finished, he gave a deep bow, smiling smugly. Everyone applauded as he came down, and Jamie edged towards him, tugging his jacket when he didn't look in his direction.

"Well done, Alexander. That was spiffing."

The older boy looked down his nose at first, but then smiled. "Oh, it's you, Dalton. Thank you for your praise."

"I'd been hoping for the main role, but I think you deserve it."

"Thank you again."

"Do you think I read well?"

"Um..." Bank cleared his throat.

Jamie's face fell. "You don't, do you?"

"Shush, the next boy is about to read. Let us listen to him." Bank turned back to his mate, and Jamie sloped off.

Maybe he had said a word wrong. But he wouldn't give up. He might still be given a part.

When the last boy had finished, the master declared, "I'm going to call out the names of the boys I want in the play. Please move to the left side when you hear your name."

Jamie had been about to leave the hall, convinced that he hadn't done as well as he'd hoped, but decided he might as well stay and hear who had been chosen. When the name of Alexander Bank, one of the most popular pupils in the school, was announced, a cheer went up.

Then he swivelled around, unsure if he had heard correctly. "James Dalton."

"That's me, that's me," he yelled, jumping up and down. Instead of a cheer, a sound like chattering starlings rose up. It didn't bother him. He would show them how good he could be. Edging his way to the group whose names had been called, he pushed through towards Bank. "Told you I done well, didn't I?" In a state of excitement, he almost grabbed the other boy's hand.

"Oo, I wonder which part is mine." He could hardly contain himself in this, the best moment of his life.

"We'll meet here next week at the same time," called the master, although Jamie could barely hear him over the hubbub of voices, "and I'll tell you who will be allocated which role."

He didn't care which one he gave him. That evening, buoyed up with exhilaration, he could barely eat his supper.

Not knowing the play, he went to Bullimore to ask if he had the book so he could learn it all. "Didn't you want to be in the play?" he asked as his housemaster searched his shelves.

"No. I once played the part of Julius Caesar. I enjoyed that, but I've never felt the muse calling me since."

"What does a mouse have to do with it?"

"Not a mouse, you nincompoop, a muse. Haven't you heard of the nine muses?"

Oh, fiddlesticks. "No, I can't say that I have, but thank you." Taking the book that Bullimore handed him, he left. Most of that night he spent rehearsing a line from every major role, to make sure he said it right when rehearsals started.

Bumping into Oswell the following week, he told him which role he had been allocated.

"You didn't really expect a major part, did you?" Pleased Oswell was speaking to him, even if it was in a derogagrotary—or whatever the word was—manner, he determined not to let his former friend curb his enthusiasm.

"Feste is a major part."

"But he's a fool—a bit like you, I suppose."

He wished he hadn't told him after all. But he'd had to tell someone. He turned away. Balderdash and poppycock and…everything else to them all. He'd show them. He would be the best fool they'd ever seen. Did that make sense? Best fool? At least his mother and father would be pleased. He hurried to the study room to write and tell them the good news.

* * * *

Tillie sat rocking baby Daniel, stroking his little round face. His blue eyes, so like his father's, lit up as he smiled. He had definitely taken more milk than usual, some evidence showing on his chin. Gently wiping it off, she hoped he'd turned a corner and would gain weight. He had come this far—surely, it meant he would thrive.

So many babies died before their first birthdays. She prayed daily that he wouldn't be one of them.

"I ought to lie you down now," she whispered, "but it's so good just to sit and cuddle you without Alice vying for my attention."

Thank goodness Nanny seemed to have knuckled down. Hopefully, the episode at the inn earlier in the summer had been a single slip up, and there would be no more such occurrences.

Finding herself dropping off to sleep, she gave the baby another kiss, stood up and laid him in his cot. He stretched, and yawned before settling down. Covering him with his blue blanket, she caressed the wisp of black hair on his little head, then remembered she hadn't put his hat on.

"Where is it?" she asked, searching the nursery. "We can't let you catch cold, can we? It's rather chilly in here."

Spotting it on the arm of the chair, she went across to pick it up, noticing the nanny's embroidery screwed up in the corner. Picking it up and shaking it out, she saw a dirty mark in the middle. "How come that's there?" she murmured. "The poor woman, she spends hours doing this."

Placing it back where she'd found it, she put Daniel's hat on him without waking him. "How lucky I am to have such a good baby," she cooed as he made tiny sucking noises.

Straightening her dress, she thought a coat of paint wouldn't come amiss in the nursery. In fact, the whole room could do with decorating. *I still haven't mentioned it to David. I will do next time I have the chance.*

"That is, when I can catch him in," she murmured. She felt sure something worried him, but would he talk to her about it? If only. She hoped his absences did not have anything to do with a certain woman…

Shaking the invasive thoughts from her mind, she

made her way downstairs, and into the kitchen. The new cook, Missus Lansdowne, came out of the pantry carrying a plate of meat.

"Is that for tonight's dinner?" asked Tillie.

"Yes, ma'am."

"There doesn't look much there. We usually have twice that amount, don't we?"

The red face of the short, chubby cook looked uneasy. "The master said we need to cut down, ma'am."

Tillie gasped. "When did he say that? He's never mentioned anything to me."

"Yesterday, ma'am. Do you think I ought to fetch some more?"

"No, no, if that's what he says, then we must obey his wishes." She found it hard to believe he would do such a thing. Why hadn't he spoken to her about it first?

"Where's Maisie?"

"She's outside, beating the carpets, ma'am. Do you want her?"

"No, no, I just wondered where she was."

"May I say something, ma'am, while we're alone?" The cook put down the plate and wiped her hands down her apron, looking around the kitchen as if she thought demons would appear out of the cracks in the wall.

"Of course, Missus Lansdowne. Do you prefer to be called that, or we could call you by your Christian name if you like? It's Isabelle, isn't it?"

"Um, Missus Lansdowne is fine. No, it isn't anything like that. It's that gamekeeper, Tom Briggs."

"What about him?"

"Well, he..." She hesitated.

Tillie wondered what she could be about to say. All sorts of ideas flitted through her mind. Did she object to his pipe or something?

"He keeps asking me to bake a seed cake."

Tillie's eyebrows shot up. Thank goodness it had

been nothing more serious. "Well, our old cook, Freda, God rest her soul, used to make them, knowing him to be partial to them. He probably misses her, and thinks one would bring back happy memories."

"You don't think he's being familiar then?"

Tillie tried to keep a straight face at the idea of old Tom fancying this little woman with her red nose and small eyes. "No, I'm sure he isn't. Please don't worry yourself on that score."

"That's a relief, I can tell you. One never knows with these country bumpkins. But, the thing is, I don't have a recipe. I've searched through the drawers and cupboards to see if Freda left one, but can't find any at all."

"She'd made so many, the recipe would have been locked in her head. Next time I go to the village I'll look for one, or you could do so on your next day off."

The cook seemed to ponder the idea as she cut up the meat.

"You've always worked in towns, have you?" Tillie tried to remember what she had told them when she'd come for the interview. It had been more of an informal chat, really. She had been recommended by a friend of a friend.

Half an hour later, she had been regaled with Missus Lansdowne's life history. She hadn't planned on staying in the kitchen so long but, as the baby should still be asleep upstairs and Alice had not returned with the nanny, she made herself a drink and sat and listened.

Nellie came in, looking surprised to see her mistress drinking tea with the cook. "Do you know where Nanny is?" she asked.

Tillie put down her mug. "She's taken Alice for a walk."

"Baby Daniel is crying."

She jumped up. "Oh, no. I'll go up to him." Nellie followed her out. At the bottom of the stairs, Tillie turned to the housekeeper. "She has been gone rather a long time. I hope she isn't tiring Alice out too much."

She thought she saw an odd expression flit across Nellie's face but, as she didn't reply, she carried on up the stairs.

Daniel had gone back to sleep by the time she reached the nursery. She checked his chest, to satisfy herself that it still moved up and down in its normal rhythmical fashion—she couldn't be too sure—and went to find David.

* * * *

Frantic, Cecelia scoured the area near the inn, walked up and down the street twice, searched every alleyway and asked everyone she saw, but nobody had seen the child. It would have to be market day, the busiest day of the week, when so much clatter and bustle meant she could barely see a few yards in front of her.

After a fruitless hour or so, barely able to breath, her mouth so dry, she went back into the inn. It had thinned out somewhat, so she easily reached the bar and ordered a drink. The bartender recognised her. "Say, lady, did you find the child?"

What could she say? Lifting the glass to her lips, she shrugged, but he persisted, "You have to look out for them gyppos. They're crafty, you know."

"Thank you, but she's safe and sound." She finished her drink quickly and turned to go.

"Old Henry over there says he saw one of them walking off with a little girl earlier."

She hesitated. Should she acknowledge the fact that she'd heard him, after lying?

"It can't be my charge, as I told you, she's been found." She walked out quickly, without turning around but, once outside, she felt sick once more. What if a traveller had taken her? Taking several deep breaths, she clung to the corner of the wall.

But if old Henry had seen her, she needed to speak to him, to find out which direction they'd taken. Dare she go back in and ask him? She had to do something. She could not go home without her.

Tightening her bonnet ribbons, she took a deep breath and walked back inside. Did any of the men sitting there look like an old Henry? They nearly all did. Going up to the first group just inside the door, she asked, "Please, could you point out old Henry to me?"

"Depends which old Henry you mean," said a youngish man, eyeing her up and down.

"Take no notice of him, me duck," said an old man with long white hair and no teeth. "Old Henry is the bloke in the corner with the red neckerchief."

"Thank you," she murmured, and pushed her way towards the man in question, ignoring the jibes and leers from the others she passed.

A woman with curly black hair and a very low bodice cackled as she passed her. "Supplementing our nanny's income with a bit extra, are we?"

She ignored her.

At last she reached him. Talking animatedly to his friend, he didn't even look up as she stood twiddling her gloves in her hand.

"I think someone wants you." His friend nudged him eventually.

He looked up, his eyes twinkling. "What's a pretty little thing like you doing in a place like this?"

Somewhat taken aback—nobody had ever called her pretty, and little would be the last way she would describe herself—she stammered, "I…um…I…the bartender said you saw a traveller with a little girl."

"Aye, so what?"

"Did you notice if she wore a green coat?"

"The traveller? I can't say that she did."

"No, the little girl." She gritted her teeth with exasperation. Try a different tack. "In which direction were they heading? Please, it's important."

"You're the person who stood up on the bar earlier, aren't you?" his friend asked. "Have you not found the child you sought?"

Looking towards the barman, she hoped he couldn't hear as she whispered, "Well, no, I haven't, so please, I'm desperate."

Old Henry stood up and took her arm. "Come with me, lass, and I'll show you." He took her outside and pointed to a lane some yards behind them. "That's where I saw them, but a while ago, now. You'll be lucky to catch up with them."

"Do you know if there are any travellers encamped up there?"

"Aye, I did hear a farmer complain he had some on his land."

"Thank you so much." Shaking his hand, she lifted her skirts and began to race towards the lane. "Please let me find her," she prayed, "please."

Passing several people on their way home from market, she asked if any of them had seen her charge, but received negative replies. Dodging around carts and chickens and even a donkey, she hurried on. What would she say when she found the camp? 'Excuse me, traveller, have you kidnapped my child?' They had a bad reputation. She had heard they could be violent. *Well, not as violent as Mistress Matilda will be if I go back without her.*

Rounding a bend in the lane, parked in a field, she saw two brightly-coloured caravans, smoke lazily drifting from their chimneys. Hiding behind the hedge, she peeked through the leaves and saw some scruffy children playing in the mud, none of them fair-haired. They all had the swarthy look of a typical Romany.

Perhaps Alice could be a prisoner in one of the caravans. Moving farther along the lane to find another entrance to the field, so she could creep around the back, she found a hole in the hedge. She scrambled through, crept towards the back of the nearest caravan, and peeped through the dingy net curtain at the window. Muted voices came from within.

Stepping back, but staying as close as she could without soiling her coat, she listened hard. Snatches of the conversation floated out to her—'the child' and 'ransom'.

Ransom? *Oh my goodness!* Her hand flew to her face, covering her mouth in case she exclaimed out loud. Sneaking another peek through the window, she screwed up her eyes to see if she could spot Alice. Something green caught her eye on the floor in between two bench seats. The child's coat? Trying to move closer, her foot dislodged a boulder and her ankle turned. Desperately trying not to cry out, she bit her lip and stooped down. Her eyes darting from side to side, expecting to see someone come around the corner, she rubbed her ankle, praying they hadn't heard her. When nobody came out, she heaved a sigh of relief, presuming they were too intent on their prize to notice such a small sound.

"Poor little Alice. I hope they're not mistreating you," she whispered. Hobbling back to the hole in the fence, she gained the safety of the lane once more. "What should I do?" she moaned. "How can I rescue her?"

A swarthy young man, carrying a large bunch of willow branches, came across. "Is anything the matter, lady?"

Should she confide in him and ask for his help? But maybe he had connections to the travellers. He certainly looked like one. "I've hurt my ankle," she replied, playing for time.

Hesitating, he looked down the lane as if weighing

up whether he should offer to help. He shifted the heavy bundle.

"Honestly, I'll be fine." She shook her head. "Thank you for your concern. You carry on."

He seemed about to say something else, but turned and continued on his way, whistling a merry tune.

She went to the gate and had another quick look at the front of the caravans. The children still played, their cheerful voices echoing through her head. *Shut up*, she wanted to scream. *I need to concentrate.*

The door of the rear caravan opened, and two dark-skinned men wearing bright red bandannas came out. She stepped back. The hedge too thick to see through, she had to strain her ears to listen. She heard one of them say, "You lot, keep an eye on my vardo and its precious cargo while your father and me go back to the village. Your mother should soon be back from selling her pegs."

Cecelia thought she had better make herself scarce. Turning, she crossed over to the other side of the lane so they wouldn't be suspicious, and began following the same direction the young man with the willow bundle had taken. He had gone far into the distance, and she could still make out the jolly sound of his whistling. Why hadn't she asked for his help? *Because you're too stubborn*, her mother's voice rang in her ears again. *Always were too independent, too proud to ask for assistance.*

"Stop your lecturing, Mother," she muttered, trying to listen for the men's footsteps to tell her they had left. She caught a glimpse of their backs as they turned the bend.

It looked as if only the children remained, so it should be easy to rescue Alice. Clamouring through the hole once more, she made her way to the window and, peering through it, she could just make out a tiny figure sitting on the floor. She didn't look hurt.

Straining her ears, she thought she could hear a faint

mewing.

"Oh Alice, baby, bear with me, I'll soon have you out of there." She tapped on the window. Maybe they had left it unlocked. The child didn't move, so she tapped again, harder. Alice looked up but remained sitting, her arms wrapped around her bent legs, a look of abject fear on her face.

"Alice," she called as quietly as she could, so as not to alert the children at the front, but hopefully loud enough for her charge to hear. The little girl stood up, gazing at the window.

She repeated it. "Alice." The child came across and lifted the curtain, a smile lighting up her face as she recognised her nanny.

Putting her finger to her lips, so the child would not cry out, she pointed to the latch and made a lifting action.

Alice just grinned, her thumb in her mouth.

She repeated the action, pointing to the latch again and mouthing, "Lift it." Alice's face screwed up. *Oh, please don't cry, you'll alert the children*, she prayed. "Open the window," she whispered, pointing to the latch once more. Alice looked hesitantly at it and then pulled. The window sprang open.

Climbing onto a ledge, Cecelia reached in and yanked her through the small gap. The impetus pushed her backwards onto the grass, winded, with Alice on top of her. Forcing air into her lungs, she lifted up the little girl and hurried towards the hole in the hedge, trying to ignore her throbbing ankle, impatient to be far away.

Which direction should they go, though? If they went towards the village, they could meet the travellers on their way back. *But they've only just left. They won't be coming back yet*, she reasoned. A family came by, giving her peculiar looks as she stood pondering. If they had been going in her direction, she could have camouflaged herself by sticking close, pretending to be part of their group. She looked down at her muddy, ripped dress. No wonder they eyed her in such an odd way.

She could do nothing about that, so started walking in the direction of the village. The opposite way would have taken them to the next town, miles away, and she couldn't waste any more time.

Around the bend she could see a long, clear path, so anyone coming towards them could be spotted well in advance. Also, the travellers' red bandannas would stand out long before she recognised the men. And, anyway, they probably wouldn't recognise the child with her nanny. She didn't want to take that chance, though.

After a while, Alice grew heavy, so she put her down. "Just for a little way," she tried to placate her when she grizzled and held up her arms. "Nanny's leg hurts. Please, I know you've been through an ordeal, but so has Nanny. I've never been so scared in all my life."

As they approached the village, she tried to remember if she knew a short cut. Her mistress would already be anxious, so they needed to find the fastest route.

"We'll go through this field." Though unsure if it would be quicker, it seemed to be in the right direction. Her ankle ached, her legs scratched by the sharp stubble. Alice's little legs soon became red also, so she picked her up again.

Eventually, they came out onto a lane. The Grange could be seen down in the distance. "Thank goodness," she sighed. "I never thought the place would ever look so welcome." She put Alice down again. "We're nearly home, sweetheart. You'll soon be seeing your dear Mama and Papa, but don't tell them where you've been. Please don't. Nanny will give you the other sweetie if you keep your mouth closed."

The little girl looked shattered. She merely nodded, sucking her thumb as if her life depended on it. Her eyes drooped. She looked as if she would fall asleep standing up.

"Come on, let's go." She picked her up once more and trudged the remainder of the way, panting and stumbling with each step.

Chapter 19

Reaching the house as dark clouds began to loom overhead, Cecelia wondered how they could change their muddy clothes without being seen. If anyone accosted her, she could say she'd fallen over, but that would not explain her charge's state of disarray. Nobody would believe they had both fallen in a puddle.

Stopping outside the kitchen door, she could hear voices.

Alice began to whimper. "Shh, my darling, we have to be silent," she whispered. Gathering her to her bosom to muffle any sound, she peeped through the window. Maisie stood at the sink, and she spotted the cook going into the pantry.

Rushing back to the door, she opened it and ran in. Maisie looked up.

"Not a word to anyone," she hissed to her, poking her in the chest, "or you'll be in trouble."

The little maid stepped back, her violet eyes startled. The nanny ran through the kitchen, into the hall, flew up the stairs, and made it to her bedroom. Flinging Alice onto the bed, she quickly poured some water into the bowl and washed her hands and face before changing into her spare uniform. She checked her face in the mirror and saw a large dollop of mud clinging to her black hair, so she yanked it off, and ran a comb through it, tying it back in its usual bun.

Now, how to carry Alice into the nursery without Mistress blooming Matilda seeing her?

Picking off a few twigs and a piece of grass attached to the child's dress, she lifted her up, still fast asleep, and crept towards the nursery. Listening outside the door, it seemed quiet inside, so she opened it, praying her mistress would not be inside.

Undressing Alice, she realised the child had not been wearing her coat. With her dress almost the same colour green, she hadn't noticed, in her haste. What excuse could she give for losing it?

She took off the girl's dress and laid her in her bed, taking a sprig of moss out of her curls. "You have a nice sleep," she said, tucking her in, "and remember, don't say a thing to your mama."

"What about?" came her mistress's voice from behind.

Blooming heck, I didn't hear her come in. Spinning around, she had to think quickly. "Oh, ma'am, is baby Daniel all right? I am sorry to have been out so long, but it is such a nice day…"

Her mistress opened her mouth and then closed it. *Carry on, quickly.* "We had a lovely walk, but poor little Alice was so tired, I put her straight to bed. I'll prepare her tea while she has a sleep."

Spotting another twig in the little girl's hair, she stood in front of the bed so her mistress couldn't see it, but was thwarted when she stepped around her, so she pretended to caress her head, gripping the twig between her closed fingers.

"You were gone rather a long time. I was worried."

"I am so sorry, mistress. I bumped into a friend, and we started to chat. You know how it is. She's a nanny as well. The time just seemed to fly past. Before I knew it, it was…" She blew out her cheeks, hoping she sounded convincing.

Her mistress took another look at Alice and sat down in her chair, preparing to feed the baby, who had started to grizzle.

"I'll go and prepare the lass's tea, unless you need me to do anything else, mistress?" Kicking Alice's soiled dress under the bed, she edged towards the door.

"No, thank you, Cecelia."

After the nanny had gone, Tillie looked around the nursery. Something didn't seem right. She couldn't put her finger on it. The nanny had seemed shifty, guilty even. Her explanation of why she had been out so long didn't ring true, somehow. And why had she told Alice not to say anything? What about?

Pleased at the amount the baby had taken, she put him over her shoulder and stood up, going across to her daughter. She lay curled up, her blonde curls framing her heart-shaped face, her thumb in her mouth. Stroking her forehead, she found a leaf in her fringe.

"What the heck is this?" she exclaimed, making the child stir. Rummaging through her hair, she found another one. "What on earth has the blinking nanny been doing?"

As she bent down, Daniel reached out and grabbed one of his sister's curls. "No, darling, don't wake her." She tried to coax him into releasing it, but his podgy fingers gripped even tighter. Alice opened her blue eyes and began to cry.

"Shh, my darling, everything's fine, Mama's here," she cooed as, sitting on the edge of the bed, she prised the curl from the baby's grasp. His bottom lip began to quiver. "Oh, please, don't you start. I can't be doing with you both crying." He stuck two fingers in his mouth and sucked on them. This pacified him long enough for her to lie him in his cradle while she picked up Alice.

The little girl stopped crying and clung to her mother. The door opened, and the nanny came back in with a tray. "Oh, good, she's awake. I can give her some tea." She put the tray on the table and reached out to take Alice. "She must be starving."

The child looked at her, then shrank back into her mother's embrace, but the nanny took hold of her anyway. "Come on, my sweetheart, your mama is needed downstairs." She turned to Tillie. "The new cook, Missus Whatshername, was asking for you. It seemed pretty urgent."

"It can't be anything important. I need to know why my daughter has leaves in her hair." Tillie stooped down to Alice, sitting on her little chair.

"Leaves?" Wiping the child's hands with a flannel, the nanny presented an innocent face to her.

"Yes." Tillie looked for the leaves she'd found earlier, but they seemed to have vanished. "I found greenery in Alice's hair."

"Surely not?" The nanny gave Alice a sandwich. "Maybe something fell from a tree as we walked underneath. It is Autumn, after all."

Could that be a valid explanation? Tillie looked out of the window at the bare trees.

Daniel began to murmur, so she picked him up as Ruby's voice called from down the landing. "Cooee, anybody there?"

Her sister came in with baby Eleanor. "Nellie told me you were up here." She gave Tillie a hug and sat down on the nursing chair, her baby on her lap. "Phew, I swear those stairs are steeper than last time I came."

Tillie smiled. "You say that every time you come, sis. Are you sure it's not you? You do seem to be putting on a little weight. You're not pregnant, are you?"

"Well…"

"You are? Oh, that's wonderful." Grabbing Ruby in a bear hug, a difficult feat with their babies between them, she gushed, "How far?"

"I haven't had it confirmed yet, but I'm pretty certain. Sam hopes it's a boy. He really wanted this little maid to be a son, and I was scared he'd moan when he found out she was a girl, but he didn't."

"Of course he didn't, you silly goose." Tillie ran her fingers over her niece's downy head. "How could anyone be disappointed in such a gorgeous beauty?"

She'd been concentrating on the baby and had taken her eye off her daughter. Turning back, she saw Alice stuff her sandwich into Eleanor's mouth. "Ellie," she said, looking pleased with herself.

Ruby tried to grab it, but the baby snatched it back and stuffed it in, wiping blackcurrant jam around her face. "Oh Alice, darling, Ellie—I mean Eleanor—isn't old enough to eat sandwiches. They are for big girls like you."

The child's bottom lip stuck out and she stamped her foot, as Ruby managed to retrieve the remainder of the soggy bread from the baby's clutches. Alice took hold of it, threw it on the floor and jumped on it.

The nanny picked her up and slapped her leg. "Bad girl. That's naughty. You know you don't play with food."

Alice screamed and, resisting all the nanny's efforts to hold her, she wriggled and squirmed until she released her and she ran to her mother.

Glaring at the nanny, saying, "You should have been taking more notice of her," Tillie held Daniel out to her and picked up her daughter. "There, there, never mind. Nanny didn't mean to hurt you, darling, did you, Nanny?" She had never seen her smack the child before and didn't know if she approved. She, herself, did not agree with physical punishment, unless under dire circumstances, and jumping on a piece of bread was hardly a mortal sin.

"Of course I didn't, darling," Nanny whined, trying to caress the little girl's head, but Tillie pulled her away. "It was just a momentary aberration, Mistress. Be assured, Mistress, it won't happen again." Lying Daniel in his cot, she added, "I'll go and make the little darling something else to eat. She's evidently not in the mood for sandwiches," and she hurried out before anything more could be said.

Alice's thumb had gone back in. Tillie stroked her leg where a red weal had appeared. Looking more closely, she noticed several other scratches. "Look at these, Ruby." She lifted up Alice's petticoat, covered in muddy patches along the bottom.

"Oh, my goodness, where did they come from?" Ruby shifted her baby to her other knee and took a closer look.

"Well, they weren't there this morning. They must be from her walk with Nanny." Tillie turned her daughter to face her and pulled her thumb out of her mouth. "Sweetheart, tell Mama how you scratched your legs and muddied your clothes."

The little girl made circles with her finger over a large cut that still showed a blob of dried blood. "Blood," she said, pulling a face.

"Yes, darling, how did it happen?"

"Blood," she repeated, trying to wipe it off.

"I don't think we'll gain any sense from her," said Ruby. "You'll have to confront the nanny."

"Yes, I know. I hate confrontations, though. That must be what she meant when I first came in." Tillie explained what she had heard the nanny saying to her daughter.

"You're always telling me to stand up for myself, sis. Now who's being a milksop?

Tillie sighed. She knew Ruby to be right, and needed to find out what had happened.

"You can't let her escape this time." Ruby reinforced her argument. "You told me you had already given her a final warning."

"I know."

Ruby beamed. Usually, Tillie gave her advice.

"You don't need to look so smug." Tillie cuffed her arm. "I must be growing soft in my old age."

"You've always been soft, sis, but firm. You've had a lot to put up with in the last year or so, but you must remain strong." Eleanor pulled her mother's hair to gain her attention. "I'll just feed this little madam—although she might not be hungry now she's eaten that bread—if that is permissible?"

Tillie laughed. "Yes, yes, of course it is. You know you can feel at ease here. After all, it was your home—actually, it's been yours longer than mine."

Ruby unbuttoned her dress and set her baby to suckle. "You're right. I hadn't thought of that. I've lived here nearly three quarters of my life. I thank God every day that...Da...your husband took us in all those years ago."

"I'd have thought you'd be able to call him by his Christian name by now, Ruby. He is your brother-in-law." Tillie set Alice on the floor with some bricks and went to check on Daniel. He had fallen asleep, making little cooing noises. She stroked his face.

"I know, I know," Ruby replied, "but I just can't bring myself to do it after all those years of him being my master."

Breathing in the baby smells and the faint whiff of polish, Tillie walked over to the window. "Oh, it's raining. Thank goodness Cecelia and Alice weren't caught in this downpour. It's teeming down." She stood watching the swathes of rain sweeping across the lawn, as a bedraggled black cat sloped into the bushes. "You believe in all that superstitious claptrap, don't you, Ruby? Does it still count for good luck if a sopping wet black cat crosses your path?"

Ruby laughed. "Yes. I'm sure it doesn't matter what condition it's in."

"Good, maybe..." She shrugged. She still had to work out what to say to the nanny. "That nanny's taking a long time, isn't she? I thought she'd gone to prepare something else for Alice to eat."

"She's probably staying out of your way, hoping things will blow over."

"I'd better put some ointment on Alice's legs. I don't want them festering." She climbed on a stool to reach up to the cupboard that held the medicinal remedies.

Bending down to apply the ointment, she saw something green stuffed under the bed. Pulling it out, she exclaimed, "Just look at this. It's Alice's best dress, and it's absolutely filthy. There's even a tear here on the hem. What on earth has she been exposing my daughter to? Keep an eye on the children for me, please, Ruby. I'm not waiting for the nanny to come back, I'm going to find her and confront her. She won't be able to wriggle out of this."

Ignoring Alice's raised arms, she stormed out, her heart racing. She had never felt so furious.

"Have you seen Cecelia?" she asked Maisie on reaching the kitchen.

"Only when she came to make some sandwiches, ma'am, about half an hour back."

Isabella came out of the pantry looking bleary-eyed. "Do you want me, mistress?"

"No, I'm looking for the nanny, but she's obviously not here. Do you know where she is?"

At the cook's shake of the head, she went out to search the other rooms downstairs. As she began to climb the servants' stairs to check her bedroom, the front door opened, and David rushed in, trying to steady himself as he shook the rain from his cloak.

"Oh, what a day," he exclaimed as Purvis appeared and took his wet cloak and hat.

"Where've you been, David? Surely, you could have returned before the weather became so bad?"

"Good day to you, too, dear wife. It is so nice to be greeted with a smile when one arrives home."

She went across and kissed his cheek. "I'm sorry, darling. I'm just a little fraught. It's that nanny again."

"What has she done this time?" She followed him as he hobbled into the lounge and flopped into a chair. "I am all-in. Pour me a brandy, would you, while you tell me what has happened."

When she'd finished, he looked concerned. "That is serious. I had thought you were going to regale me with some inconsequential matter about the way she combs her hair or picks her teeth when she thinks nobody is watching."

"David! You do malign me sometimes. I never *regale* you with such trivialities. I know you have enough worries of your own."

He had told her the previous evening that Farmer Askew had been having money troubles. Trying to help him out, the farmer being a good friend, he had inadvertently gone overdrawn at the bank. It had all been sorted out eventually, so Tillie had no need to worry…so he'd said. But she felt there he had not given her the full story.

"I know." He held out his hand. "I apologise."

"Anyway, I'm glad you agree this is serious. I was just on my way up to her room when you came in."

David swirled the remainder of the golden liquid in his glass, then drank it down in one gulp, holding the glass out. "Another?" he asked.

Shaking her head, she refilled it. "Anyway, why have you been out so long? You said you had solved the problem with Farmer Askew. You seem to spend more time with him than you do with me."

David sighed. "If you are going to go over that old nutkin, then I shall wish I had not returned. Cannot a man just have a quiet drink without being nagged?"

"I'm not…" Tillie sat beside him and lifted his hand. "I don't mean to nag. I… Oh, never mind." She started to stand up, but he kept hold of her hand and pulled her back. Putting his glass on the side table, he reached over and kissed her. Surprised, she leaned into him, kissing him back with a passion she hadn't felt for a long time. His hand cupped her face, his thumb drawing circles on her cheek. Her whole body felt alive as his mouth left hers and pressed soft kisses down her neck. Arching her head back to give him better access, lost in the moment, she heard someone clear their throat. Looking up, she saw Nellie standing beside them.

"Excuse me, ma'am," the housekeeper wrung her hands, "I wouldn't bother you, but…"

Sitting up and straightening her clothes, Tillie blinked. Fancy being carried away in full view of the servants? David gave a rueful smile as he picked up his glass and finished his drink.

She pushed back a wayward curl that had found its way out of her chignon. "Yes, Nellie, you were saying?"

"It's Nanny, ma'am."

"What about her?" She jumped up. She had been on her way to confront the woman. It must have been her aroused emotions that had made her respond so urgently to David's kisses. It wouldn't do to tell him that, though.

"Betsy saw her running down the drive with a suitcase, and…and some of the silverware has gone missing."

Tillie took a deep breath. "Not again. We shall have no silverware left if any more disgruntled servants make off with it. Have you sent someone after her?"

She looked at David to see if he would back her up, but he sat back in his chair and shrugged. "It has nothing to do with me, dear wife. You keep saying you want more say in running the house. The female servants are your responsibility."

"Well," Nellie continued, "you've seen the weather out. And, anyway, who do we send? Young Maisie offered to go, but she wouldn't stand a chance against that great hulk of a woman, Betsy has a bad leg, and Cook is rather...well, let's say she isn't fit to go chasing anyone. That leaves Purvis, who's too old. It's John's afternoon off, and I...I wouldn't even..."

Tillie followed her out of the room. "No, Nellie, I wouldn't expect you to go haring around the countryside in hot pursuit of a vicious criminal."

"Vicious? Surely she isn't that bad?"

"Who knows? Alice came back from her walk with scratched and bleeding legs, and the woman didn't even tell me about it."

Nellie gasped. "When was this?"

"This afternoon. I'd been on my way to confront her when...well, let's say I became side-tracked."

"And a rare sight it made too, ma'am, if I may say so. I was loath to break it up, but I thought you needed to know urgently."

"Yes, thank you, Nellie. I suppose we had better inform the police."

Chapter 20

A faint dusting of snow covered the ground as Jamie arrived home. Jumping down from the carriage, he remarked to Sam, "Do you think we'll have snow on Easter Sunday? That would be spiffing, wouldn't it?"

Sam laughed as he took down the cases. "Yes, Jamie, it would be spiffing, as you put it."

"Will you help me and Alice build a snowman? Maybe Daniel and baby Eleanor would be big enough to join in?"

"I certainly will, providing it continues to snow. Neither of the babies can walk yet, although Eleanor is trying to crawl, much to your Auntie Ruby's delight."

"Oh, I can't wait to see her. I bet she's grown." Jamie ran to the door, disappointed that it hadn't already opened.

"I hope you mean the baby. I wouldn't want your auntie to grow much more. She's fat already."

Jamie tittered, debating whether to pull the bell rope or just open the door and walk in.

Purvis's surprised face appeared. "Oh, Master Jamie, I was just…"

"Where's Mama? I thought she'd be waiting for me."

"There's been… She's…"

Not waiting to hear the rest of the sentence, he rushed past the butler into the house. What could be so important? He'd been away three months, and they couldn't be bothered to welcome him home again. He searched the downstairs rooms and, on his way to the kitchen, Purvis called, "She's upstairs, Master Jamie."

He stood at the bottom of the stairs, looking up. The faces of his father's ancestors stared down at him. None of them looked particularly happy to see him either. *Maybe I should have stayed at school*, he thought, turning away.

"I'll go and see Maisie," he muttered. "*She'll* be pleased to see me, I know that." He wandered into the kitchen, fully expecting to see Freda standing at the table, kneading dough, or peeling vegetables. He pulled up short when he remembered. He would never see her again, peeling vegetables or doing any other chore. His disappointment at his homecoming turned to sadness. He wiped his hand over the table. It didn't look as clean as when she used to scrub it.

He thought he could hear a murmur from the pantry so, knowing deep down it couldn't be the old cook, he tiptoed across to look inside. A chubby lady with thin, grey hair through which he could see her scalp, bent over the shelf at the back, seemingly in pain.

"Oh." He blew out his breath, "You must be the new cook. Are you unwell?"

Jumping back, she dropped a bottle. It smashed with a loud crash on the tiled floor, shards of glass scattering everywhere.

"Now look what you've made me do," she yelled, bending down to pick up one of the larger pieces.

"I'm sorry. I didn't mean to startle you." Jamie leaned forward to help. "Phwah," he moaned. A strong smell like his father's brandy rose from the floor, as the cook pushed him away.

"No, young sir, don't you be risking cutting your fingers. Leave it to me."

He closed his eyes as her breath reached his nostrils. It smelled as strong. Standing up, he backed out. Should he tell someone the cook had been drinking? Maybe he would later. He didn't want to spoil his homecoming welcome. Not that he'd had one.

Maisie came through the back door carrying a basket of apples. Dropping them as soon as she saw Jamie, she ran and put her arms around him. "Oh, Master Jamie, I'm so glad to see you. It's been murder and mayhem here just lately, I can tell you."

"Murder? Who's been…?"

"Well, maybe that's an exaggeration, but it's felt like it."

Jamie picked up the apples that had fallen out of the basket and put them on the table. "Why, what's been happening?"

Raising her eyebrows, her violet eyes wide, the maid bent her head forwards and nodded towards the pantry, mouthing, "Cook."

Jamie could hear the cook sweeping up the glass.

"Her breath smelled awful," he whispered.

Maisie nodded.

He was prevented from saying anything else for the plump woman staggered out of the pantry, holding up her hand, dripping blood on the floor. "Help me," she yelled. "I'm bleeding."

Maisie grabbed a cloth and wrapped it around the finger as the cook squealed, "Save me, I'm dying, I don't like blood."

"You're not going to die, Cook. Don't be so melodramatic." Maisie lifted the finger up higher. "I think that's what you do, isn't it, Jamie?"

Shaking his head, Jamie puffed out his cheeks. "I don't know."

At that point, Nellie came running in. "What's all the commotion?" Taking one look at the trail of blood on the floor and the cook sitting with her finger in the air, she asked, "What now?"

"Well, I suppose I am to blame," said Jamie, "I made her jump."

Nellie jerked her head towards him. "I hadn't realised you were home, Master Jamie. When did you arrive?"

"Oh, absolutely ages ago." He didn't think it right

that he hadn't received the reception he deserved. "Not that anybody noticed." Maisie raised her eyebrows at him. "Except you, Maisie, you're the only one."

The housekeeper patted his shoulder. "Well, I apologise for everyone else. It's been rather hectic today, what with one thing and another. And now this, to cap it all."

The cook had quietened and sat sniffing into her handkerchief. Nellie took away the cloth to have a look at the wound but blood spurted out again, causing the cook to squeal once more, so she quickly replaced it. "This is all we need—Cook out of action. Have you even started on dinner?" she asked.

Cook shook her head. "No, I was…"

"I can guess what you were up to. If it doesn't stop, I shall have no option but to report it to the mistress."

That'll save me doing it, thought Jamie.

Nellie turned to Maisie. "It looks like you'll have the bulk of the work to do today, my lass. I'll see if Betsy can be spared to help out."

"Shall I go and find her?" asked Jamie.

"That would be grand, if you would."

As he entered the hall, he heard a small voice from above calling "Jamie," saw Alice in her bright red dress, clinging onto the banister rails as she came down the stairs, one at a time. He ran towards her. "Alice, my darling little sister, are you pleased to see me?"

She nodded. He looked up for the nanny or his mother, but the little girl seemed to be alone. "Where's Mama?"

She pointed back up the stairs.

"And Papa?"

She shrugged.

"Nanny?"

She shrugged again.

"Shall we go and find them?"

She put out her hand as Betsy came out of the lounge, carrying a feather duster and a basket full of cleaning materials. "Ah, Betsy, you're needed in the kitchen."

She grinned at him. "Welcome home, sir." Maybe he'd been mistaken that nobody cared. Well, at least Alice and the servants did. He still couldn't imagine why his mother hadn't appeared.

"Come on, sweetie." He tried to lift his sister, but being too heavy to carry up the stairs, he put her back down. "Let's find Mama."

Halfway up, they met their mother, her hair in a mess, and her face as red as a beetroot. "Ah, there you are, Alice. Thank goodness you've found her, Jamie. Welcome home." She hurried down and wrapped her arms around them both. She looked tearful, so he didn't rebuke her for not being there when he'd arrived. "Let's go down to the lounge and have a sit down. I'm sorely in need of a cup of tea, and then you can tell me all about your adventures at school. I hope they haven't been as dramatic this term."

He grimaced as they entered the lounge.

"I'll just ring for Betsy." His mother went across to the bell pull, but Jamie stopped her. "Cook's had a bit of an accident and Betsy needs to help Maisie, so I'll go and fetch you some tea, Mama. Just make yourself comfortable. I won't be long." His mother sat back and closed her eyes. Jamie wondered what had been happening, but decided he could wait to find out until she had rested. He took his sister's hand. "Come on, Alice. Let's leave Mama alone for a minute."

The cook still sat at the table, staring at her finger as if she thought it would fall off, while Maisie and Betsy ran round like maniacs, flapping their hands and bumping into each other. Loath to give them any more work, he hesitated, but his mama wanted a drink.

School for Jamie

"I'm sorry to give you extra work, but please could one of you make Mama a cup of tea," he shouted over the mayhem.

Cook looked up. "Tea, now that sounds like a good idea. Put the kettle on." She looked towards the range.

"I'll do it." Betsy gave the cook an uncharacteristic sneer as she picked up the teapot.

"I could make it myself," Jamie offered. "I used to make drinks for Missus Curtis, do you remember, Maisie, when we lived with her before we come here?"

He edged towards the range, but Maisie stopped him, "Don't let Alice go over there. I remember you being burnt as well."

"Oh, yes." He traced a pattern over the back of his hand where he'd scalded it. He didn't very often think any more about the time they'd lived with the old lady, and the fire that had killed her and Maisie's mother. He shuddered. That had been in the past, as his mother always said whenever he brought up the subject, and best forgotten.

Betsy handed him a tray. "Would you be so good as to take it in, Master Jamie, if you please? We're rather…" She made an arc with her hand to show the state of the kitchen.

"Of course, thank you. Come on, Alice." The little girl had been playing with Susie, the black cat that had been curled up on the chair, asleep until it had been woken by Alice poking its ears. "Leave Susie alone."

"Cat," she said, her eyes lighting up as she gave it another poke.

Having trouble balancing the heavy tray, he couldn't pull her away. "I'll have to come back for her after I've taken this in to Mother," he told the maids. "I'll be back in two ticks."

He found his mother fast asleep in the armchair, so placed the tray on the table beside her and went back for his sister. Hearing a scream, he ran into the kitchen in time to see Alice knock the cat off the chair. Its teeth bared like a lion, its hackles raised, it hissed at her, before running out the back door just as Betsy came through, her arms full of logs. It almost tripped her up.

Maisie looked at the child's hand. "It's only a scratch, but we'd better clean it."

"I'll do it," Jamie intervened. "You have enough on. By the way, where's Nanny? Why isn't she minding Alice?"

"Oh, she disappeared."

"Disappeared?" He could barely contain his excitement. Had the witch vanished into thin air on her broomstick? "Where to?"

The maid shrugged. "I don't know the ins and outs of it, but there was some hoo-hah and she just upped and left."

"So she's gone for good?" He clapped his hands in glee. "Hooray. Oh, I can't believe it." Grabbing both maids, he danced around the kitchen with them, making them giggle as he sang, "The witch has gone, the witch has gone."

"Why didn't you like her?" Maisie asked once he let go.

"It don't matter now. But she really isn't coming back? She's departed, vamoosed?" Maisie nodded, but, at the strange word, she grimaced. "Yes, vamoosed, vamoosed. I'n't that a wonderful word?" he began dancing again. Then he stopped, looking at Alice. "But no wonder Mama is so weary." Despite his elation, Jamie felt guilty about being so upset that she hadn't been there for him. "I'll take Alice up to the nursery and wash her hand. I can check on Daniel as well." He could also make sure the hateful nanny had really left for good, and that he wouldn't have to go through with the half-formed plan he had made to discredit her.

Chapter 21

Back at school for the summer term, preparing for the rehearsal, he studied his part at every break time. So much to learn, much more than he'd expected, and some songs. He wondered if he would have to sing them, but he wouldn't know what tunes to use. There weren't any notes. He decided just to learn the words for the time being.

"I'm glad I don't have the part of Sir Toby Belch," he chuckled. "What a name! And why did Shakespeare use such funny words—'perchance' and 'twelvemonth'?" Sitting on his haunches in a corner of the playground, he realised he had been doing it again—speaking to himself—when he looked up and saw a group of boys grinning at him.

Closing the book, he stood up. Running his finger under his collar, and his head as high as he could hold it, he walked past them. *I'm in the play*, he wanted to say, *and you're not, so who's having the last laugh?* but he went by silently. He did not need to announce his superiority.

The first rehearsal didn't go very well, but not due to any fault on Jamie's part. His character did not appear in the first scene, so he just had to watch. In fact, he didn't come in until scene five. He longed to say his first lines, but didn't have the opportunity that day, for they stopped at the end of scene four, just as he had mentally prepared himself.

"Can't I just show you what I've learnt?" he pestered the master, Mister Edwards, when he told them to leave it for the day.

"No, thank you, Dalton, not until your scene and, at the rate we are going, that won't be for quite a while."

Alexander Bank stood across the room talking to his friend. Jamie sucked in his breath, wondering if he should go and ask him to test him on his words. He moved towards him.

Bank had his back to him, so his friend nudged him when Jamie approached. He turned round. "Yes, Dalton?"

"I bet you're enjoying it now we've started, eh, Bank? You did very well, by the way, pronouncing the words as you did. It wasn't your fault the other boys couldn't say theirs right."

"Thank you." Bank turned back to resume his conversation, but Jamie wouldn't be put off.

"You play the part of the Duke magnificently."

"Thank you again, Dalton, but can't you see I'm having a conversation?"

"Sorry, I just wondered…"

"What?"

"Nothing." Stuffing his hands in his pockets, Jamie turned away. The older boy clearly did not feel in the mood to listen to him. Maybe when they had advanced further into the play, he could ask his opinion.

* * * *

"'I am gone, sir, and anon, sir, I'll be with you again, in a trice…'"

Jamie had just started to enjoy himself when Mister Edwards stopped him. "That will do, Dalton, very good. Just remember that Feste is the spokesperson of the play." He clapped his hands. "Can we have Sebastian on stage ready for the next scene? Come on, men, chop, chop. We only have two weeks left, and we still have a full act to rehearse."

Jamie slouched off the stage. Why did Old Scarface always stop him just as his words began to flow? He stood beside Alexander, due on in the following scene.

The older boy smiled at him and whispered, "It's

School for Jamie

going well, isn't it?"

Jamie looked up with admiration at his hero. "You're the best actor, Alex. You are stupendous."

"Please don't call me 'Alex'. I hate it."

Fiddlesticks. Why couldn't he ever say the right thing to him? "Sorry," he murmured.

Mister Edwards glared in their direction. "Please keep quiet if you are not on the stage. It distracts the other actors."

Jamie moved to the other side of the hall and sat learning the next scene. Some of the words tickled him— 'By my troth, sir.' *What on earth is a 'troth'?* It sounds like something a horse drinks out of. Troth, troth, troth. It rolled round his tongue. His dictionary would have to be investigated once more.

"That's all for today, lads. Well done." Mister Edwards clapped his hands again and dismissed the boys. Jamie looked for Alexander, wondering if he would speak to him, but he caught his back view, already walking out of the door, chatting to his friends.

The rehearsals continued until the day before the actual performance. Jamie's confidence needed a boost, for he still hadn't mastered some of the long, unfamiliar words. Maybe Alexander Bank could help. Skipping down the corridor towards Bank's room, he heard a voice from behind. "Hoy, Quackers, where do you think you're going in such a good mood?"

Grimacing, he slowed down. Silas Brown, the last person he wanted to come across. The bully had given him the nickname when he'd come top of the class in a project they had been given on the topic of birds. His love of his feathered friends had given him plenty to write about, and it hadn't seemed like a task at all, just an enjoyable description of his favourite hobby.

Trying to ignore him, he continued along the corridor, speeding up again.

"Quackers, I'm talking to you."

He rolled his eyes, silently tutting. Just then, the door in front of him opened, and a group of boys, including the prefect who had confiscated his caricatures months before, came towards him. The matter hadn't been taken any further, but he'd never recovered his pictures, so the prefect still had a hold over him.

Oh no, not him as well! He felt he was being hunted down by predators, a sandwich, with him as the filling.

Trying to make himself small and insignificant, he squeezed his body up against the wall to allow the group to pass by. But they stopped on reaching him.

"Our budding artist, if I am not mistaken," jeered one of the boys with goofy teeth.

Brown caught up. "Artist? This is Quackers, our resident bird specialist."

Cowering against the wall, Jamie closed his eyes. He had only wanted to go and see Alexander.

He felt the boys move away as a familiar voice yelled, "What's going on here?" His hero! Alexander Bank had come to his rescue yet again. The group scattered, mumbling obscenities.

"Next time," Silas Brown called after him, but one look from Bank and he scuttled away, his black coat flapping behind him.

"What was all that about?" asked Bank.

Jamie shrugged, biting his lip.

"Never mind, they've gone now." He stood in front of Jamie and reached towards him to adjust his lapels. "You do seem to attract some undesirable attention, don't you?"

Undesirable? "But I thought…" Hadn't he seen Brown coming out of Alexander's room?

"I've had words with Brown. He wouldn't actually admit to pushing you out of the window, but I made him promise nothing like that will ever happen again. Where

School for Jamie

were you off to?"

Jamie beamed. "Oh, thank you. Actually, I was on my way to see you, to ask if you could help me with some of these big words."

He looked down at the book. The front cover had been almost ripped off in the scuffle. More trouble.

His happiness at the knowledge that the bully wouldn't seriously bother him again vanished. Tears pricked at his eyelids, but he brushed them away with the back of his hand. It wouldn't do to let Bank see him cry. He would think him a proper namby-pamby.

"Come on, then. I can spare five or ten minutes. Which particular words are you having trouble with?"

Most of them, Jamie thought. He followed Alexander to his tidy room, decked out in soft colours, pink cushions and purple curtains.

Bank patted him on his shoulder. "Would you like some toast? I had intended to make some, anyway."

Jamie's eyes widened. *Shouldn't that be my job, like with Bullimore and Fenner?* "Th...thank you," he stuttered.

"Sit yourself down."

Jamie sat in the armchair, looking at the miniature statues of goblins and elves on the shelves. A particular one caught his eye. He hadn't noticed it on previous visits. It looked more like a fairy. A fairy? He froze for a moment. Perhaps his hero didn't have the masculinity Jamie had imagined. It hadn't occurred to him before. Maybe he...?

Oh, 'eck! What shall I do? What if he tries to...? Closing his legs with his hands firmly between his knees, he wondered if he should leave. But what excuse could he give?

Bank took the piece of toast off the fork and handed it to him. "Come on, don't be shy. Take it."

Forced to lift his hand, he accepted it, mumbling, "Thanks," and looked for the butter dish.

"You can't beat toast with lashings of butter, can you?" Bank squatted in front of the fire and placed another slice on the fork, holding it out in front of him like a sword.

Jamie tried to answer but a muffled "humph" was all he could manage with his mouth full. *Eat it as quick as you can*, he told himself.

Bank buttered his own slice and sat back in the other chair. "Well, isn't this cosy?" He took a mouthful and started to chew it.

Jamie watched his chin moving up and down.

"Oh, have you finished yours already? You are a fast eater."

Too mesmerised to reply, Jamie stared at the indent in the middle of the older boy's long chin as it shrank and grew again with each chewing action. Pretending to eat, he put his finger to his own chin to see if his did the same. He had never noticed if he had a gap in it. He couldn't feel one. Next time he looked in a mirror, he would examine it.

Realising Bank had asked him a question, he dragged his gaze away from the chin. "Sorry? Oh yes, some of them awkward words." Jamie opened his book to find a hard one. "'Whirligig', although that's a lovely word, isn't it, 'whirligig'?"

"Well, it isn't difficult to say."

"No, of course not, but this one, in Act Four... 'hyper...bolic fiend'."

Alexander leaned forward and turned the book so he could read it. "Have you not learnt about hyperboles in English Language lessons?"

"Um, no, I don't think we have. What are they?"

"Oh, I'm not going into that now. What other words can't you pronounce?"

Jamie began to feel a little foolish. *Ha, that's good. Foolish. I am playing the fool, after all.* He took the book back and stood up. "I think I know the rest, thank you. I'd better be going."

Alexander stood up also. He towered above Jamie. It had never been so evident before, but in the confines of the small room Jamie felt like a dwarf.

"There's no hurry, is there? Why don't you stay a while? We could play a game or something."

An hour before, Jamie would have jumped at the chance to spend time with his hero, but having come to his earlier conclusion, he just wanted to escape. "No, thanks. I...I don't want to take any more of your time." Reaching forward, he opened the door and almost ran out. "Thank you for the toast," he called before scooting off down the corridor, reciting, 'Fly away, fly away, breath'.

* * * *

"Ladies and Gentlemen, we welcome you all to our school this fine evening. We are pleased to perform for your delectation, Shakespeare's 'Twelfth Night'." The headmaster, Mister Lancelot Trout, introduced the play, and the first scene began.

Standing in the wings, Jamie waited for his cue. He had been rehearsing his lines all morning and, although excited, nerves began to overcome him, causing some of the words to jumble up in his head.

Peeping around the edge of the curtain, he saw the hall full of parents and elderly grandparents and even, probably, maiden aunts like Peel's. His father and mother sat on the end of the fifth row. He couldn't let them down.

This is where I come in. Taking a deep breath and puffing out his chest, he strutted onto the stage.

All he had to do was wait for Maria to say her piece, then his moment of glory would begin.

"My lady will hang me for thy absence," declared Bartholomew, the boy playing Maria.

Even with all the makeup, Jamie still found it hard to think of Bartholomew Chivers as a girl. *Oh 'eck. What am I supposed to say?* "Um…"

"Let her hang me!" the prompt in the wings behind him hissed.

Oh yes. "Let her hang me, he that is well hanged in this world needs to fear no colours."

Thank goodness he'd said it right. His nerves began to settle. But then he couldn't remember if he should go to the left or the right the next time he spoke. Panicking, he walked into a chair. Looking up, he saw the drama master, Mister Edwards, gesticulating to him from the other wing, indicating a spot nearer the back. Jamie moved to it, and Mister Edwards nodded. The remainder of the scene went without mishap, and the words soon flowed. The first act ended to rapturous applause.

"Well, done, lads, keep it up," the master encouraged them as the prop men moved the scenery for the next act.

This is good fun. Not appearing in the first two scenes in the second act, he went to seek out Alexander who didn't come in until scene four, and found him in the dressing room sitting very close to one of the prefects. They jumped apart as Jamie went in.

"Have you been watching? Do you think I'm doing well?" he asked, looking from one to the other.

"I'm sure you are, Dalton, very well," Bank replied. "But you had better go back. You're on again soon, aren't you?"

Bank probably hadn't seen any of that act, he'd looked too engrossed, but Jamie appreciated his encouragement.

"Um, yes, quite soon. You'll be by far the best actor in the whole play, though, Alexander. You'll put everyone

School for Jamie

else to shame."

"Thank you, Dalton. Now run along. You don't want to miss your cue."

Jamie had barely reached the door before he saw his—what he now considered to be former—hero lean towards the prefect and whisper something in his ear, to which the other boy giggled.

Not wanting to know if he had been the object of their scorn, he pulled on his jester's cap and hurried back to the wings, just in time for his cue.

When it came to the scene when the duke asked the clown to sing, he felt awkward, but soon forgot his unease as he started to sing the verse, 'Come away, come away, death...'

When he proclaimed the lines, 'I take pleasure in singing, sir,' he meant it. He really did love singing.

In the final scene of the play, he had the stage to himself.

"A great while ago the world begun. With hey, ho, the wind and the rain; but that's all one, our play is done, and we'll strive to please you every day."

He exited and the curtain came down. The audience erupted into applause, many of them standing up as the whole cast came out onto the front of the stage to take their final bow. Through the bright lights, Jamie could just make out his father attempting to stand and clap at the same time. As he lifted his head from the next bow, he could see his mother trying to help him while she also clapped.

Bowing again, his attention on his parents, he didn't realise the other boys had walked off until he heard his name being called. Running after the others, he thought he heard titters of laughter from the opposite wings.

"Who cares if they're making fun of me? I am the clown, after all," he murmured to himself as he caught up.

Mister Edwards congratulated him. "Well done,

Dalton. That was one of the best renditions of Feste's part I have ever seen."

"Oh, fanks, Mister Edwards, fanks so much. D'yer really mean it?" Jamie looked round at the other boys, his face beaming with pleasure, hoping they would agree with the master, but they seemed to be having trouble keeping straight faces. Wondering why, it dawned on him that he'd fallen back into his old way of speaking.

"Oh, blow the lot of you. I don't need your approval," he muttered as he stalked off.

"You may go and find your parents now," Mister Edwards called.

Jamie had already started pushing through the throng of bodies, eager to find their relatives. He found his father sitting in his chair.

"Well done, son. You performed marvellously."

"Thank you, Father. Did I really?"

"Yes, son, superb."

"Where's Mama?"

"She has gone to fetch me a drink. She did not think I would manage to keep my footing in this mêlée."

Jamie craned his neck to see her. "Shall I go and help her carry them?" he asked.

"No, son, sit here next to me for a moment. I want to say how proud I am of you."

Jamie sat down, unable to keep the smug grin from his face. He gave him a hug. "Thank you, Father. That's the best compliment I've ever had. Do you think Mama enjoyed it?"

"Oh, yes, she was in raptures, crying even. Here she is. She can tell you herself."

Jamie jumped up and took one of the drinks from her, handing it to his father. "What did you think, Mama? Father said you were crying."

"Tears of happiness, Jamie. I was absolutely overwhelmed. To think my son is capable of such a performance." She gave him a squeeze. "Did you enjoy acting?"

"Oh, yes. I think I want to be an actor when I grow up."

His father shook his head slightly. "There is plenty of time to consider your future."

That means he doesn't approve of the idea. But it won't put me off. On such a high, nothing could deflate him.

"We don't need to discuss that now, darling." His mother sipped at her drink, looking around the room. "Is that friend of yours...what was his name...um...the one who came to stay with us...?"

"You mean St Clements, I mean, Peel?"

"Yes, such a nice boy. I didn't see him in the play."

"No, he doesn't like standing up in front of people." He didn't like to admit they had fallen out.

"No, I suppose it takes a lot of pluck to do that sort of thing, not to mention the ability to remember all those lines. How on earth do you do it?"

"Oh, quite easily, really." Jamie stuck out his chin, eager to look clever. "It was just a matter of applying one's mind and body wholly to the task in hand."

His mother blinked at him. She looked suitably impressed. He didn't add that he'd used the drama master's words.

"Well, my darling, it certainly worked. I am so proud of you." She hugged him again, and he noticed some of his makeup had rubbed off his face onto her dress. Trying to wipe it off only made it worse.

"Sorry, Mama," he grimaced, twiddling his jester's cap between his fingers. She looked down and stared at the mark for quite a while as if mesmerised, a new word he'd learnt in the English lesson that week.

"It will wash off, fret not." Finishing his drink, his father put down his glass and raised his hand to try to brush off the stain. He only succeeded in making it larger.

He stood up and, balancing on his crutch, put his other arm round Jamie's shoulder. "I am sorry, son, but we have to leave."

"Aw, so soon? I thought you'd stay for a while."

"You know how long the journey is, Jamie," his mother intervened, seemingly recovered from her trance. "It will soon be the end of term, my darling. We are planning an extra special holiday this year."

"Oo, where to?"

"You'll see. Are you coming to see us off?"

He nodded and followed them out. Sad to see them go, but still reeling from his feeling of exhilaration, he ran back inside, bumping into Oswell.

Oswell shook his hand. "Well done, Jamie. You were magnificent."

Jamie looked for his Indian prince, but Oswell appeared to be on his own. "Aw, thanks, Peel. Thanks." True praise, indeed. Feeling more elated than he would have thought possible, he shook his hand again and carried on through the mass of people, grinning until his cheeks ached, but eager to change out of his costume and wipe the greasepaint off his face.

About The Author

Married to Don, Angela has 5 children: Darran, Jane, Catherine, Louise, and Richard and 7 grandchildren: Amy, Brandon, Ryan, Danny, Jessica, Charlotte and Ethan.

Educated at The Convent of Our Lady of Providence, Alton, Hampshire, Angela was part owner of a health shop for 3 years and worked for the Department of Work and Pensions for 16 years until her retirement when she joined the Eastwood Writers' Group and began writing in earnest.

Her hobbies include gardening, singing in her church choir, flower arranging, bingo, scrabble, and eating out.

Her first novel 'Looking for Jamie' was released as an eBook in November 2010 and in print in February 2011. It has been hailed as 'one of those books you can't put down'. Without the help and encouragement from the writer's group, she says her book would never have been finished.

School For Jamie
By: Angela Rigley
ISBN: 978-1-927220-60-3

All rights reserved
Copyright © Nov. 2013, Angela Rigley
Cover Art Copyright © Nov 2013, Brightling Spur

Bluewood Publishing Ltd
Christchurch, 8441, New Zealand
www.bluewoodpublishing.com

Names, characters and incidents depicted in this book are products of the author's imagination or are used fictitiously. Any resemblance to actual events, locales, organizations, or persons, living or dead, is entirely coincidental and beyond the intent of the author or the publisher.

No part of this book may be reproduced or shared by any electronic or mechanical means, including but not limited to printing, file sharing, and email, without prior written permission from Bluewood Publishing Ltd.

To Jack and Pauline
Best regards
Angela Rigley

Also available by Angela Rigley

Looking for Jamie

A Dilemma for Jamie

For news of, or to purchase this or other books please visit:

www.bluewoodpublishing.com